SO FAR AND GOOD

Books by John Straley

THE CECIL YOUNGER INVESTIGATIONS

The Woman Who Married a Bear

The Curious Eat Themselves

The Music of What Happens

Death and the Language of Happiness

The Angels Will Not Care

Cold Water Burning

Baby's First Felony

So Far and Good

THE COLD STORAGE NOVELS

The Big Both Ways

Cold Storage, Alaska

What Is Time to a Pig?

SO FAR AND GOOD

John Straley

Published by
Soho Press, Inc.
227 W 17th Street
New York, NY 10011

Library of Congress Cataloging-in-Publication Data

Names: Straley, John, 1953- author.
Title: So far and good / John Straley.
Description: New York, NY : Soho Crime, [2021]
Series: The Cecil Younger investigations ; 8
Identifiers: LCCN 2021018964

ISBN 978-1-64129-253-5
eISBN 978-1-64129-254-2

Subjects: GSAFD: Mystery fiction. | Suspense fiction.
Classification: LCC PS3569.T687 S6 2021 | DDC 813/.54–dc23
LC record available at https://lccn.loc.gov/2021018964

Printed in the United States

10 9 8 7 6 5 4 3 2 1

In a trailer park or government housing somewhere in America, there is a woman who was born with the body of a man. When she gets in an argument with her neighbor, she rushes outside in her robe with her makeup badly applied. The other neighbors call her a "freak," or worse, an "animal," and they film her. She carries a pistol in her underwear because she feels forsaken. She carries a razor in the pages of her Bible because she is hungry for salvation.

This book is dedicated to her, because I am her brother.

We live in an occupied country, misunderstood;
justice will take us millions of intricate moves.
Sirens will hunt down Berky, you survivors in your beds
listening through the night, so far and good.

—WILLIAM STAFFORD, "THINKING FOR BERKY"

SO FAR AND GOOD

1
THE TEST

It's not hard remembering how long you have been in prison. Days pass and your daughter's birthdays, holidays without the usual food, then seasons go by: a fall where you need a wool cap but don't have one, a winter where slush wets your socks in the exercise yard, and your feet may stay wet all day depending how many pairs of socks you have, and a spring where unseen songbirds titter from the rocky field beyond the coils of razor wire. I can remember how long I have been in. What bothers me is that as time goes on, I begin to forget when, if ever, I will be getting out.

There is a single time-accounting sergeant who is in charge of keeping the book on time. He or she keeps track of your time, down to the minute you were logged into jail when you were first booked in on your charges. The TA sergeant also calculates your "good time." In Alaska, for every three days of time in prison that you don't cause any trouble, you earn one day off your sentence; but not always. If you participate in certain rehabilitative services, that time within the program does not earn good time. It can be tricky to know how much time you have officially lost for certain infractions. Inmates are supposed to be informed of loss of good time, but often that information slips through the cracks. Infractions can be written up or not, and inmates are never sure if the report makes it into the hands of the probation officer and then to the TA sergeant. An inmate can ask for a TAA or a "time accounting audit," but it's a pretty big deal, and it's generally believed that unless your attorney requests the audit with some justification by the court, the TA sergeant will simply add days or weeks, just for making them go through the extra work. The truth of it is no one ever likes the answer the TA sergeant gives, so most of us don't ask. We wait.

I was originally sentenced to twenty-five years, but my lawyers and I went before the three-judge panel, and I gave the longest allocution in the history of Alaska, and they lowered my sentence to seven years. On the day I'm writing this, I have served four years. I'm close to what should have been my release date, but the events I am writing about occurred six months ago. It wasn't too long after the decision of the three-judge panel, and I was still feeling the weight of the twenty-five lift off my back. I was floating. Sad still, and sick of being inside . . . but floating. Perhaps it was the floating that made me do some of the stupid things that resulted in my losing a chunk of good time, and set this whole horrific shitstorm roaring through every part of my life—my caged life and my free life too.

So I wait and I spend the time writing. I know I lost some good time, but I'm not sure how much and what for. It could be months or a year. My lawyer doesn't want me writing anything down, of course, but I have to. I want to write it all down, not because I'm trapped inside prison but because I'm frightened of prison being trapped inside of me. During the years I have spent here, I have seen human beings so overwhelmed by rules, walls and changing protocols that they become pale with something I once thought was the result of insanity or inconsolable grief. They take in everything they ever used to enjoy as if it were now an insult to the very idea of pleasure. The food, the sex, the work, the books they read, the art they make—it is all meaningless without the freedom to enjoy it.

Just two weeks ago, a story made the rounds about a guy who made it out after being in prison for twelve and a half years. He had dreamed of rebuilding his motorcycle and riding it to the Arctic Circle with a big-breasted girl riding bitch on the back. Well, the "girl," who was almost forty years old, bailed somewhere outside of Tok Junction not far up the highway because the bike's hard suspension hurt her back so much she decided she would rather work in a roadhouse serving wildland firefighters than rattle her way up that bumpy road.

Once alone, our man became more and more obsessed with limitations—speed limits and traffic signs. He was in violation of his parole and screaming across the northern tundra, trying to eat up the horizon before his arms turned numb or the bugs and road dust sealed his eyes shut. But eventually even a straight road to the horizon seemed too limiting, too narrow.

Word came back to us that the RCMP found him wrapped around a bridge abutment somewhere in the Northwest Territories, his bike in pieces and his body having been consumed by scavengers.

A majority of the inmates, even the short-timers, envied him.

This is all a long way of saying that I am writing this story about my daughter to remind myself of a certain kind of freedom that I want to carry in my mind throughout this entire experience inside. It's a freedom that I associate with my daughter's goodness, and maybe, more broadly, with just the possibility of human goodness.

There were several investigations concerning the events that caused me to lose good time and will keep me in here until . . . I don't know when. One was conducted by the Alaska State Troopers and the Department of Corrections; another by the office of Child Protective Services, which got involved, as you will soon learn. Obviously I wasn't present to see anything that happened outside Lemon Creek Correctional Center, so in writing this, I wanted to double-check the facts from those investigations. My attorney was given those reports. I've also had the advantage of being able to talk with my daughter, Blossom Younger. She gave me her written reports, letters and diary, which you might think is a rare display of openness between a teenage girl and her incarcerated father. In truth, she gave me all her written materials in order to hide them from the other investigations, which turned out to be a well-reasoned ploy because my lawyer and the Department of Corrections threw up quite a few walls against the discovery of my personal possessions. No adult investigator thought there would be much of Blossom's stuff in my possession.

Blossom spoke with me during her visits about what happened in the basement, and she cried like a baby, long after her bruises had healed and the cuts had sealed together and the stitches had come out. She wept without control, but she hadn't cried when it first happened. Then she was a tough and smart-mouthed teenager who could handle all the troubles of the adult world, thank you very much. She thought she was a freedom fighter, and she thought she was fighting for my freedom, bless her soul, but once she learned I had that more or less covered, she started opening up to me and her mother, and her rage all spilled out "like the insides of a gutted fish." Those were her words. She made me promise not to paint her as a wimp in this account, and as you will see, there is nothing wimpy about our daughter. But you might judge me harshly and miss my love for her if I didn't clue you in to her tender nature.

I write now in pencil on a yellow pad—several yellow pads, actually. I usually work while I'm at my job in the library or when I'm alone in my bunk. I make two copies of everything I write, and I hide both copies: one in a safe place and the other with a person I trust. I write to keep from beating my head against the wall for whatever time I have left in here, and I write to remember how much I love my daughter; that love is the most civilizing force that remains in my life. Loving her and respecting her, eventually learning to let her go, will make me a valuable human being . . . at least that is the belief I cling to.

I'll tell this story as if I were on the outside with Blossom. She is only seventeen, but she thinks of herself as my partner in our investigative business, which is not true, but there is nothing much I can do about that now. I enjoy writing as if I know what she is thinking and what happened to her. I also believe this account is accurate. For all the harm and what ultimately happened to her, I am deeply sorry, but again, there is nothing to be done about it now.

Blossom's mother is Jane Marie DeAngelo. We were married in a small ceremony in Sitka on the beach out near the ferry dock. Blossom is our only child. Jane Marie was born and raised in Juneau; her sister and her family still live in the family home there. Jane Marie lives on her boat, *The Winning Hand.* Our friend and the man I'm supposed to take care of, Todd, now lives in Jane Marie's sister's house. Todd did not like living on the boat—Jane Marie takes it out at unexpected times—and he is now working at a nursing home downtown and takes his schedule very seriously. Even though there is a lot of noise in the house with people coming and going, it is near the nursing home, close to the capitol building, and Todd has a tiny room where he is comfortable. Blossom sees him every day and she takes him shopping whenever he needs anything. They also enjoy going to the movies in Juneau, where there are more choices than in Sitka, where we used to live.

Jane Marie is a research scientist and professor at the University of Alaska. She moors her boat, which doubles as a research vessel, in Aurora Harbor, which is close to Juneau-Douglas High School, where Blossom goes to school. I'm incarcerated at Lemon Creek Correctional Center, some eight miles down the road from the high school. Jane Marie also works out of a small office near St. Ann's Rest Home downtown, where Todd is a custodian, and from there she can see the tourists walking up the hill from the cruise ships on summer days and the legislators trudging back toward the capitol in the rain during winter. I think of her stooped over her computer there, with her old-fashioned milk crates filled with notebooks and reports. I imagine framed pictures of Blossom as a child hanging on the white wall: smiling on the deck of a boat, her life jacket on and sun filling her eyes and dazzling her hair.

Blossom got her driver's license in Juneau the day after her sixteenth birthday. Her uncle had a 1993 Renault Le Car that he dearly loved and preserved. It had only a few hundred miles on it, and it was kept dry and salt-free in his garage. He allowed Blossom free use of it under two strict conditions: one, she had to park it in the garage every night and lock the door; and two, she had to pressure wash every inch of the car, top to bottom, at a setting selected by Uncle Pete, and then she had to adequately dry it before putting it away. While most teenage girls would consider these rules draconian, Blossom was eager to follow them because she loved the car with the kind of devotion usually reserved for religious artifacts.

The Le Car was blue and had a nearly full-length sunroof. It was French, zippy, unique and yet somehow "uncool" among people who knew cars. It had a unibody construction, which meant that it would probably have the life span of James Dean out on the highway in the rainy climate of Juneau, Alaska, and was more than likely to crack in half on the few miles of freeway than it was to get into an accident. It had two small seats in front and two in the back. With the roof open it felt like a convertible on a sunny day. It had a stick shift, and learning to operate it made Blossom feel like a race-car driver. She doted on this car and would fight almost anyone who didn't wholeheartedly admire it in a parking lot.

On the day that her adventure started, she drove to Lemon Creek at visiting hours, and the guard who checked her in kept making offers on the Le Car.

"I'm telling you, Stanley, it's my uncle's car and besides, I would never, ever in this world let him sell it. That car is my baby. I'm telling you, man."

"Girl, you need yourself something bigger for all your boyfriends," Stanley said, "and something safer. That little tin can is gonna crush up on you. You just better give that little go-cart to old Stanley to take care of."

"Nice try. No way." She smiled at him as the thick door buzzed, and he showed her through.

After months of trips and paperwork, we had been allowed "contact visits" in which we could sit in the same room. Despite this designation, though, we were careful not to touch each other because if we were seen touching, Blossom could be subject to a body search on the way out—anything from a light pat-down to a complete cavity search. Though the search would be conducted by a female officer, it could be traumatizing and sometimes punitive—that is, done in a way to discourage a visitor from ever coming back. Visitors had been known to be stripped and kept waiting in a cold holding room for hours while appropriate personnel was found to perform the search. There was no indication that the prison staff had anything against Blossom or me, but it was difficult to know what was going on in my jacket (or file) . . . or in hers, so it was best to be careful.

There were several cheap sofas, three vending machines for sodas and snacks and three tables with chairs. I sat at the table farthest from the door. A Black inmate and his wife and baby girl sat on the couch by the oldest candy machine. The baby girl sat on her daddy's lap. She had a red bow in her hair and smiled like a crescent moon. The mom had tears in her eyes. As Blossom passed the small family, she cupped the baby's head in her hand and stopped a moment to kiss her.

"Heya, Kiya, baby . . . you look so sweet today."

"How you, darlin'?" the mom asked.

"You know . . . how 'bout you, Alicia?"

"Same. Thanks for asking, girl."

"You take care. Promise to call me for babysitting?"

"Hell, yes."

"Good."

Then my daughter walked to our table and sat across from me.

Blossom was well into her junior year. She had missed more than a whole school year after the mess with her being kidnapped and then me and my friends kind of blowing up the hotel where she was being held. Blossom needed a break after that. Her mother was great about it and did not push her. Blossom spent a lot of time rowing a dory around the Sound and hiking the mountains with some friends and sometimes with her mom. Blossom worked in her mom's lab and eventually got all of her science and English credits from the college. She became an expert shot with a pneumatic rifle and a crossbow and took DNA samples from orca, sperm and humpback whales for her mom's lab. The sperm whales were offshore when the black cod season opened. Blossom often got rides on fishing boats out near the shelf edge, and when the fishermen pulled in their gear, sperm whales would pick the oily codfish off their lines, and Blossom would put her dory in the ocean from the fishing boat, then row up next to the large males to shoot a small dart into their back, which would bounce out with a plug of skin and blubber the size of a pencil eraser. She would preserve and mark the sample, which would be used to identify the animal and could also be tested for diet, contamination and biological health. Perhaps this is just a freedom fantasy of mine, but I have spent a lot of time in my iron bunk on the thin mattress imagining her in her wooden dory beyond the sight of land, riding the swells with nothing but the albatross squawking around her as the oars rattle in their locks. Out where there are no highway lines, but a few friendly faces keeping a hopeful eye out as they ride the swells that hug the curve of the earth.

Blossom's face is more relaxed and mature than it was a few years ago. She is smarter and maybe wiser, but she is still impulsive, and I worry about her. Anger comes quick, and this hunger to set the world right—while I understand it and am in no position to offer counsel—runs hot. Soon she will have a lot of important decisions to make, and I grieve every day that I'm in here and that the fucker who hurt her so badly will always play some role in all those decisions.

"So . . ." Blossom said, "how's the convict?"

"I'm good."

"Shank anybody lately?"

"Not lately. How is school?"

"School is good. You will be happy to know that I too have not killed anyone lately."

"This is progress. How are your friends, your car?"

"The Le Car is fantastic. Dad, I can't wait to drive you around in it."

"You following your uncle's rules?"

"Rust is my mortal enemy."

"How is your boyfriend?"

"Ned is NOT my boyfriend. He just likes me. We're friends. He has a cool motorcycle."

"You know you're not allowed on the back of that thing if any . . . and I mean *any* . . . alcohol has been consumed. Have I mentioned that?"

"One million times."

"Any . . . alcohol. That means one drop of beer. Don't talk to me about blood alcohol levels or legal limits. The limit is zero."

"Says the convict. In PRISON."

She looked at me and smiled, and I knew she understood me. I wouldn't have known a few years ago. Now I do.

She is tall now. Her hair has grown out, and the clothes she wears don't take on the aspect of a costume as much as they used to. Where she once dressed like a girl from a horror movie, she now seems to make an effort to complement her features and coloring, and she has incorporated some sense of practicality and takes the weather into account. But again she might be doing all of this for my benefit in the visiting room, so that I take the least amount of anxiety back inside as possible. I don't really know why, but it makes me cry sometimes back in my cell when I consider how much she has grown and how sweet she has become.

"How is Todd, B?"

"He doesn't like living in Juneau." She made a sour face, like she didn't really want to talk about it.

"What, he doesn't like staying at Priscilla's house?"

"He's okay with . . . well, you know Aunt P. She yells a lot, and Todd doesn't like that. He pretty much hides in his room most of the time. He listens to his podcasts about the law and about church stuff."

"Is he becoming a Christian?"

"No. He just likes to pray a lot. Somebody at the place he works got ahold of him and got him into praying. It's not bad. Don't worry. I keep talking to him. It's good."

"Well, honey, what does he pray for?"

"Dad . . . let's talk about something else."

"Blossom, now you've got me worried. What does Todd pray for?"

"He prays for you to get out of jail and for us to go home to Sitka."

I sat there not speaking. Of course he would, I thought.

Todd is my age and is a functioning adult man with autism who was screwed up by trauma and a kind of indifferent abuse when he was a kid. Tweezing all his issues apart would be impossible now. What really helps him is unchanging routine and pretty constant reassurance that he is doing the right thing to keep the chaos of his childhood at bay: the fists and the belts, the tears and the wild, frightening death of his parents. Todd is not sure how it works, but it seems as if the chaos stays away if he acts in a certain way, in a way that he can only guess at every day. Todd is a fine and gentle man, and most of my life I have tried to provide him with nothing but unconditional love. Of course, when I swerved off course and landed in jail to save my daughter, I abandoned him. Blossom knows this and she tries to protect me from it.

"Just try to help him, Blossom."

"I will, Pop. It would be better if I could give him a date to look forward to. You know him. He can almost hold his breath waiting for any date. He is amazing."

"I know, sweetie, but first, I don't know a date, and second, I would hate to give him a date and not be able to keep the promise. I might lose some time, or something might happen."

"Nothing bad will happen, Pop. We will keep it together. You will get out pretty soon."

"Okay. What else is going on?" I asked.

She bit her lip. "George is planning a surprise for her mom." George is a girl at Blossom's new school, and Blossom adores her. They drive around and have their own little study group. George's mom is a Democratic legislator in the Alaska House of Representatives, and they live out in the Mendenhall Valley in a classic suburban house with a tire swing in the yard and a view of a glacier.

"Can you tell me about the surprise?"

"Well, George is getting her DNA tested from one of those places, and she snuck a sample from her mom."

"What do you mean 'snuck'?"

"I don't know. I guess while her mom was sleeping she swabbed her mouth."

"Why in God's name would she do that?"

"George loves her mom sooooo much, Pop, it's crazy. She has this plan to figure out their ancestry, and George is going to plan trips to all the countries they're from. George has saved up all of her summer job money since like forever, and she got people to donate airline miles into her account. She doesn't even know where they're going because she hasn't gotten the tests back yet."

"She should have asked her mom before she took her swab, don't you think?"

"It's a birthday surprise, Pop."

"Yeah . . . I suppose," was all I said at the time. There were no real alarm bells going off other than I just don't like secrets, and this had the feel of something that could backfire. Ida Paul was married to Richard Paul. It turned out that Ida was of Irish/Welsh/German heritage, but her family and neighbors thought of her as "white." Richard was Tlingit. George, their only daughter, had black hair, but other than that, everyone joked that she didn't appear to have picked up any of her dad's heritage. But he took it in stride, joking that Tlingit was a matrilineal society and that everything always came from the mother's side anyway, so it didn't surprise him in the least. George's real name was Georgianna, but she loved calling herself George Paul and had done so since junior high school. She liked to joke that she was half of the greatest band in the world and swore that if she ever married, it would be to someone named John, and their child would have to be named Ringo.

After Blossom left that afternoon, I had other things on my mind than George's DNA test or the fact that she may have breached Ida Paul's trust by sneaking a swab into her cheek. I was going to have to go to my unofficial tutoring job in the prison, and I was starting a new section on poetry, which I was worried about, and which, in fact, could get me killed if things went badly.

That the two subjects—the DNA and my particular teaching curriculum—would eventually become inextricably related would not become clear to me until much later, when everything had blown up like half a stick of dynamite in a prison toilet that no one stops using no matter how plugged it gets.

2

FOURTH STREET, AUNT JENNIFER AND HER TIGERS

Friends write me letters wanting to know how I survive in jail. I don't know why they don't come right out and ask if I have become someone's bitch, which is what they both do and don't want to know.

The fact is, I have become someone's bitch, in a strange sort of way. And it is for this reason that on the day Blossom first told me about George and the DNA test, I was sweating bullets over how I was going to talk to my man, Albert Munro, otherwise known as "Fourth Street," about the poetry of Adrienne Rich.

Among people who have served hard time in other states, Alaska prisons, particularly Lemon Creek, are considered easy places to do time. This is partly because Alaska has few really hardened criminals. Alaska ranks very high in domestic violence, and while painkillers and heroin abuse are on the rise, alcohol abuse is by far the most prevalent. Sex abuse draws long sentences, and most sex abuse cases are cross related with alcohol.

Alaska also has a disproportionate number of Alaska Natives behind bars and under the supervision of the

DOC. Not because they are any more prone to criminality, but because they often suffer from a type of cultural dislocation, a failing economy and crowded housing problems, which leads to rapid reporting of all disputes. According to the Department of Corrections, Alaska Native men are not prone to violence and are very mellow in jail. They find safety in numbers and serve time quietly.

Pacific Islanders and African Americans are overrepresented compared to their percentage of the population in Alaska, but here too, few of them are actual gangbangers. The most dangerous men in Alaska were the early pioneers of the drug trade in the eighties and nineties. They came from New York City when Rudy Giuliani lowered the murder rate by driving out the Black crack dealers and allowing the Dominicans to take over the heroin business. For a time, the Dominicans came to Alaska to expand their drug trade and buy their guns, because it was so damn cheap and easy.

The Lamplighter Hotel shootings happened more than thirty years ago but had quite an effect on the culture. A set of Dominican drug dealers came in and shot another gang and left them all for dead; but one guy got up, flushed the drugs and, even though he was shot through the jaw, called the cops on the rival gang. He became a street legend and all the youngsters bought big whopping handguns of their own and started shooting each other for stupid drunk reasons since they didn't have business reasons to act on. These became the most dangerous men in Alaska: the wannabes.

Real money-making gangsters of that era were swept up pretty quickly by state and federal law enforcement. State prisons had some stupid kids. But in each lock up in Alaska there was at least one genuine hard-ass, a real gangbanger from California or Nevada who did a nice quiet and violent business in Anchorage or Fairbanks, and who, while in state custody would enlist genuine dead-eyed killers to enforce order among the children to teach them manners. There were very few dead-eyed killers. But there were those who were vacant enough that a good leader could train them to become a decent prison protection outfit.

Our boy from Sitka who murdered his family was psychotic but was not dangerous as long as he took his medication. But the old man from Anchorage who had hunted prostitutes with a bow was a celebrity and was eager to maintain his status. He knew he was never going to get out—he was a different story. The Native hunter, who had done unspeakable things to several corpses in his hunting camp when he was black-out drunk, was a sweet and wise elder when sober and a peacemaker in jail. But the white sexual assault perp from the suburbs wanted nothing more than to earn his stripes as a genuine American badass by killing a Black man in jail.

When I first came to Lemon Creek, I had some friends and former clients who helped me, but they had short sentences and they also got caught up in the circumstances of my case, so the prison officials tried their best to keep us separated. Plus, it was written into the terms of our probation that we were not to have contact with one another in any "material way, written or telephonic," a wording that would let the Department of Corrections off the hook in the event that they had to house us together due to overcrowding.

Until I came to prison, I enjoyed the privilege of being white and old. I'm almost sixty now, and I've been told by more-experienced convicts that I have "worried eyes" that make me an easy mark. I had been an investigator for the Public Defender Agency, which made me unpopular to a large portion of the population and a popular object of ridicule for some of the weakest minds inside the walls.

Within Lemon Creek, there are activity centers, classrooms, admin offices and visiting areas, as well as kitchen, laundry, library and sick bay facilities. All areas are joined by gated hallways and stairwells that allow for travel from the tiers or dorms for different inmates with different clearances at different times. When the facility is locked down, nothing can move at all. Doors are locked and there is a hard body count—done by personnel, not by camera—because there are still a few blind spots for cameras. These lockdowns happen almost five times a day, but again, protocol changes.

Early on if I got trapped in a blind spot with the wrong person during lockdown, I could expect a beating. The first day I got caught out, I took a beating from a former client with a grudge. He broke my nose and opened up an old cut in my right eyebrow. The kid cut his knuckles on my teeth, so I'm tempted to say that I gave as good as I got, but . . . not really. I got a lot worse.

I made it to a bathroom I had never been in before. I didn't know that it was off-limits to anyone who didn't have business with Mr. Munro. I walked in and grabbed towels from the dispenser and a very large and very feminine African American man, who was well-muscled and well over six feet tall, looked at me and said, "Sweetheart, you very lost. You can't come in here to fix your boo-boo and get that juice all over Street's office. I just spent the morning scrubbing it. Shoo now, go on, girl, shoo." Later, I would find out that this person preferred the pronouns "she/her." Her "dead name" was Sean Night, and she had been an All-State end for a large Gary, Indiana, military academy. She then went to two years of college on a football scholarship at Grinnell, where she found the Black football players not as friendly as the members of the LGBTQ student union. So she left Iowa, became her true self, and began using the name Shawn Day. She had stepped into the light.

But all that information didn't come until much later. That first day a very commanding voice said, "Shawn Day, please give us the room." And that was the day I became one of the Street's bitches.

Albert Munro had come from Hayward, California, to Fairbanks in 1971. He had learned welding and worked for a time on the pipeline, then saw there was an opportunity to make much more money selling cocaine and being a pimp. After the pipeline was built, Fairbanks longed for some more civilization, so Mr. Munro moved to Anchorage, the main oil town in the state, where there had always been an appetite for cocaine and pussy. Mr. Munro began with strip clubs and prostitution, card games and drugs along Fourth Avenue, hence his nickname. Eventually his clubs moved out toward the smaller suburb of Spenard.

Fourth Street was an old-school post-pipeline gangster; he was of mixed race—African, Hispanic and Irish—and there was no one he couldn't charm. He was charged with murdering a man from Las Vegas who was said to be trying to move in on his business in Anchorage. The evidence against him was weak and several snitches were used by the FBI. The snitches never served time in Alaska. One of the snitches was a man named Johnny Clark who ran a card room in Spenard at his own house. Johnny Clark died of an apparent suicide in a transport cell in Seattle before the jury came in. The other snitch was unavailable to testify at trial, but the prosecutor was allowed to read the snitch's grand jury testimony to the jury as well as tell the jury about Clark's death, which was the subject of several appeals.

The crazy boys who came into jail may not have known Street's reputation in the real world, but they were made aware of it as soon as they cleared the "observation tank" when they first booked in. Someone from Street's set would give them an orientation to Lemon Creek. Mine was gentle and much like a Welcome Wagon visit. I was old and educated. I was not violent, and Street seemed to like people with genuine legal knowledge. I had, in fact, been invited to have a sit-down with the man, an invitation I had declined, because it had been my plan to do my time unaffiliated with any criminal organization and as easily as possible, which was harder than you might think. I had already been stabbed once, but the homicide I was convicted for was the killing of a man who had trifled with my daughter. Even the hard guys in prison had some respect for that. But because I was charged for the killing, and because it was quite graphic with a lot of blood, and because it happened right in the shower room of my own dorm, and it appeared that I had some protection from a high-ranking police detective, inmates in this relatively mellow correctional institution gave me a grace period for a few weeks.

Until my former client cornered me in the hall and broke my nose.

"You are the famous Mr. Younger," Street said as he cradled my head in his large hands before the mirrors. Then he snapped the cartilage in my nose back in place. He reached under the sink and pulled out two small vials and uncorked them. Tilting my torso back as if we were dipping in a tango, he supported the small of my back with one hand while he packed one nostril at a time, pouring the powder and then using the blunt end of the vial to compress it. "Don't sniff," he said. "Just let it absorb." At first it hurt, but after he stood me up, my face began to numb and I understood what was happening.

"You should have come see me sooner, Cecil."

"I like just doing my time."

"How's that working out for you?"

I didn't answer him but looked at my face where the shadows under my eyes were starting to darken. "What do I say when I start looking like a raccoon?" I asked him.

"Tell the officers you didn't see who hit you. They will believe that. You are a grandpa, and not particularly popular. These boys would all love to break your nose just to tell their punk friends they hit their fucking lawyer."

"I'm not a lawyer."

"I know that, but they don't. I was friends with a few of your colleagues in Anchorage." He mentioned a few names, two men I knew well—big names in the field, respected names—and one woman who had been highly regarded until she got too involved with the cocaine industry. We didn't discuss details.

"I want you to work for me, Mr. Younger."

"As I said, Street, I simply want to do my time."

"Don't call me Street. Let's be professional. You can call me Mr. Munro."

"I'm sorry. I meant no disrespect."

"I'm certain of that."

"I am willing to listen respectfully to your proposal, Mr. Munro," I said, realizing as I spoke that my diction was becoming somewhat stilted, "if you will respect my ability to make my own decision about whether or not to accept."

"Huh?" He looked at me and smiled. "You know, I could just break all your teeth and fuck your mouth until you walk out of here in"—and then he listed a very specific number of months, weeks and days, which made me wonder if he had seen my official time accounting. It worried me so much I didn't even remember the amount of time I had left to serve.

"Yes," I said, "I know you could do that, but I have a feeling you would have done that already if that was all you wanted from me, and I'm betting what you actually want would be better done if I were more willing . . . and if I had teeth."

"I suppose that is true."

"So, what do you really want from me?"

"I have a parole hearing coming up in twenty-four months. There are four white women sitting on the parole board. I want you to teach me how to speak respectfully to these bitches."

"To the white women on the board?"

"To all of them . . . my lawyer's a woman. It didn't used to be this way, but everywhere I go now there are white bitches as lawyers. I don't want them fucking up my chances in twenty-four months. I got some things cooking so that I may have a shot. But I'm old like you now, and I don't want to come back inside. I don't understand shit on the outside anymore. Money doesn't take care of everything for a Black man. You got to understand white women now. You have to be correct, you know what I'm saying? I have got to know how to talk to them. The world is different from when I came in here. Plenty of them are judges. They're the ones writing the laws and even if they aren't the judges, they are the clerks. I feel like even if they aren't running things directly, the white men like you are so fucking afraid of the bitches they are in effect running everything. I *got* to know how to talk to those bitches. I know you do. You fucking slit a man's throat and your white woman lawyer got your full bid down to seven years . . . and you the most fucking hated white man I know. That's some deep skill. You talked for hours to those judges. Two of them on the three-judge panel were white bitches."

My allocution to the judges had become legendary in the prison system since I had spoken to them for the longest time on record, almost eight hours, and had walked away with a greatly reduced sentence.

"Well . . . not referring to them as 'bitches' would be a place to start," I muttered.

"I don't need you to tell me what to say to you," he said. "I need you to tell me how to talk to the white women on the fucking parole board. You understand that?"

I stared at him for a moment. "You know it's not that easy, right? I mean, I don't know any magic words to get along with women. You are the greatest pimp of all time. You are the man who can talk with women."

"Those were *my* bitches. I'm talking lawyers and shit. I want to talk all that smart stuff so that they will want to respect me, want to see me as a real person and worth keeping out of jail. They did that for you."

"For me? Really?"

"Fuck, yes. They did amazing shit for you. That was skill. The motherfucking judges hated you. They wanted to make an example of your ass to show the press how 'we don't just throw brown people in jail.' I could not *believe* the sentence you got."

"There are women teachers who visit the prison who could help you, aren't there?"

"Fuck that. I don't want to sit and listen to a bunch of lectures about *Plessy versus Ferguson* and shit. I don't want to hear about how Reconstruction was the most pivotal time in our country's history for race relations. I want to know the current language of fucking power, Goddamn it."

"Why don't you study finance?"

"Shit. I know finance. Buy low, sell high. Give people what they want, lower wages as much as you can, dilute the product as much as the customer can stand, crush your competition until the cops come after you, buy off the regulators. Avoid all the taxes you can, but don't draw attention to yourself. Bury the bodies deep. That stuff is easy. What I want is to be accepted as a human being and not to be put in a cage by language again. You know these things. I want to talk with you. I want you to teach me new words, new ideas—ideas that white people respect and that will help an old Black man make money and stay out of jail."

"Are you going to break my teeth?"

"I have to let people think that I'm doing that, because that is the only way things get done in this place: fear, sex and broken bones. I will give you a pass . . . it's bad for me, you know, so you don't get a free pass. But because of your special gift, I will give you a choice. You understand that if I don't break your teeth, every con out there will think that I am doing you and you like it."

"I will take that risk. But I have to tell you, I'm not into smoking your pole."

"Don't dismiss it out of hand, Professor. I might grow on you."

The other large person in the room shook her shoulders

suddenly as if she had been stung by a bee, and turned her back to us.

"Listen," I said, drawing the word out, trying to think of the next thing to say, wondering if it was going to catch me another broken bone. "How about we study this problem together? The best we can. I'll get some books, you choose some books, we'll talk about them, we'll talk about our own experience. We will have to practice which words to use when you go before the parole board, and we'll work on getting your mind right before you talk to these women—*women*, okay?—who have so much power over your future. That's what I can do. But I can't guarantee anything, Mr. Munro. I can't promise a result, you understand?"

"You already talking like a fucking bitch." Then he smiled and held his hand out to me. "Okay then, it's a deal. Now, take those pants off."

"Wait . . . that's not . . ."

"I'm fucking with you."

"Okay." I looked at him skeptically. "Deal then," I said. And that's how I became Mr. Albert Munro's private tutor and bitch.

That was months ago. It had been a struggle. We started with a book called *You Just Don't Understand* by Deborah Tannen, which provoked a lot of vigorous debate in our entire section of the prison. The concept Dr. Tannen tries to make clear is that the conversational style of men is shaped by the desire to gain status or power, while women focus more on intimacy or finding consensus. This prompted a lot of arguments and anecdotal evidence and storytelling. I had to keep going back to the prime directive of Street's original request and reminding him, "Listen, if you really want to get into the heads of white women and understand your female lawyer, you've got to stop using the word 'bitch' in the way that you are, and start examining your feelings about women."

This resulted in my first black eye, for which he later apologized, and I used it as a reason to cancel classes for a week. We then relaxed while studying Richard Wright's *Native Son*, which Mr. Munro had already read. We read about Wright's life in France, read his book of haikus, and arranged to work in the prison garden for a few days, which we both enjoyed. Mr. Munro had already read James Baldwin's *The Fire Next Time* and *I Am Not Your Negro*, but when I read *Giovanni's Room* aloud to him, he became angry with me again. Shawn Day was applying some cream to Mr. Munro's face as I finished the novel, which is very sad. She was tearful as she was placing the lid back on the container and wiping her hands clean with a very nice blue non-prison washcloth, when Mr. Munro stood up and backhanded me across the face hard enough to sting my cheek red, but not hard enough to open up my nose again.

"Goddamn it, Younger, I told you to teach me something about white women, and you reading to me about some old Black faggot."

I held my face to my hand. "If I were a free white woman, you know what I would say to you right now, Mr. Munro?"

"What, bitch?"

"I'd say, 'You can't hit me anymore, Mr. Munro.'"

I let that sit between us and Shawn Day for some moments. Then I added, "I'd rather you kill me and get it over with, but I'm not going to take your abuse. Then if I were a free white woman, someone with money and power . . . someone like your lawyer . . . I'd say, 'What is it about that story that threatens you, that makes you want to hit me?' Until you figure that shit out, I'm doing you no good and you are going to keep going to jail. In fact, you are already in forever jail."

Shawn Day was weeping openly now as she sat on the top of the toilet wiping her eyes and fussing with her nails.

"That is your homework. Let me know when it's done, and we will proceed with the next discussion." Then I left his bathroom office and walked out into the relative danger of life without the certainty of his protection.

The next day as I was working at the library, I was accosted by an unpleasant jailhouse lawyer asking about a missing rules of evidence book. I told him it was on a special checkout.

"That's bullshit. That's not supposed to leave the library."

"I'm sorry. It's not here."

"I could have your ass, you know that." He was thin and white, an older white-supremacist type with a shamrock tattoo on his neck and 14/88 tattooed on his forearm. "I have a brief due in the next week and I need that book. You better get me that book or it will be your ass, Jew boy."

"Listen, I'm sorry. Let me see who has it," I said with as much patience as I could muster. I looked in the card catalogue next to my notepad—they didn't trust us with computer files for this stuff. "Sure, you can ask Mr. Munro in Golf Dorm for that. He might understand your emergency and give it back." I smiled at him.

"Yeah . . . Okay . . . Yeah . . . I will." He walked back into the stacks. I didn't feel bad about not getting anything for him. There were plenty of other resources in the library, and besides, I had read some of this guy's work. He was most fond of citing obscure terms that often had Latinate spellings from the US Constitution, which asserted that only "landed men" had rights to be jurors and citizens. He also always submitted a deed to property in Wrangell, Alaska, with all his filings and a subpoena for the birth records of the jurors who served on his trial. His court filings were just a way to pass time, but never took up much of the court's attention.

That day I wrote another assignment for Mr. Munro. One of his minions was back in the stacks hiding his drug stash in an obscure reference book on real estate and taxation law from 1974 (many volumes were donated from other state agencies or law offices). When this man came walking out, I signaled him over and gave him the folded paper. He didn't want to make eye contact with me, which I couldn't read much into because I knew he had seen my black eye when he came in and probably thought he knew my relationship with Street and was embarrassed by being so close to any kind of emotional intimacy, which in prison is what a black eye is.

"Take this to Mr. Munro, please."

"Yeah . . ." the tall young man said as he walked away.

On the paper I had written the lines of a poem by Adrienne Rich.

Aunt Jennifer's tigers prance across a screen,
Bright topaz denizens of a world of green.
They do not fear the men beneath the tree;
They pace in sleek chivalric certainty.

Aunt Jennifer's fingers fluttering through her wool
Find even the ivory needle hard to pull.
The massive weight of Uncle's wedding band
Sits heavily upon Aunt Jennifer's hand.

When Aunt is dead, her terrified hands will lie
Still ringed with ordeals she was mastered by.
The tigers in the panel that she made
Will go on prancing, proud and unafraid.

Below the last line, I wrote:

Mr. Munro, I am not afraid to go on teaching you. These white women you want to learn about are not afraid. Are you afraid of them?

CY

3

THE CASE OF THE BAD RESULTS

On her next visit, Blossom walked straight into the visiting room. There was no joking around with the guard and there were no smiles for me.

"Hey, Pop," she said. She sat at the table and looked down at her hands in her lap, which was unusual for her.

"Hey, doll, how are you? What's wrong?"

"Nothing."

"Come on."

"You're in jail, Papa. You got enough trouble."

"I know I'm in jail, B. But now I've got your sad face to worry about, so spill."

She looked around at the others in the room. She looked at the sullen guard and the woman in uniform who had patted her down. She looked at the family playing a card game and the baby crawling on the floor with the mother ignoring her while she was kissing her inmate boyfriend. Blossom is a good person, strong and resilient, but just then, she looked tired and like she wanted to cry, as if she wanted out of jail and all it implied as much as I did.

"Come on, sweetie . . . maybe there's something I can

do," I said, knowing there probably wasn't much truth in that.

She looked at me with impossibly sad eyes and started crying. "What are you going to do, Cecil?" She gave great heaving sobs.

I put my arm around her. The little baby looked up at us with her big moon eyes and gurgled. Blossom smiled at her and wiped her own snot on her sleeve.

"It's George . . . she got the DNA test results back. You won't believe it, Pop. Her parents aren't her real parents. That's what it looks like. She is freaking out. She doesn't know what to do."

"Maybe the test results are wrong," I offered.

"We talked about that. I could believe that one test, maybe the one she snuck from her mom, could be a bad sample or something. But two tests? George's own test? No way."

"No connection at all?"

"Completely different. Her mom's test shows Welsh and English, and some South Pacific Island-Australian ancestry. George's test shows French, Native Alaskan, Irish, English, Eastern European, Slavic and some Greek heritage. The tests are guaranteed. They have her picture stapled to the report and talk about her features."

"They could still be wrong, sweetie."

"She talked to her mom and her mom acted all weird and got angry."

"Well . . . that could be explained by the surprise . . . or the deception . . . of having the sample taken without her knowing. Did she offer any explanation?"

"We thought maybe she was adopted, but Mrs. Paul got so angry at first and then so sad. She locked herself in her room and cried. She wouldn't talk to George. Everybody is so upset. I don't know what to do."

"Honey, maybe you should let them work this out for a while. Just support George in whatever she decides she wants to do. Be a good friend to her. But don't push her."

We watched the baby on the floor for a while. The clock on the wall moved its needle-thin second hand slowly around its face. A skinny boy got up and bought a soda. We listened to the clattering of his quarters rolling into the guts of the machine and then the rumble of the can as it came thumping out.

"Yeah . . . maybe," Blossom said. She wiped her eyes.

I had a notebook—which I was allowed to carry because of my work in the library—and the stub of a number two pencil in the front pocket of my jumpsuit. I wrote down the name of the investigator at the Juneau office of the public defender, and added her inside line number. "Call this woman and ask her for the name of the expert who worked on the last blood spatter case I did with her. He lived in Portland. Tell her who you are first. It's Doctor somebody . . . I can't remember his name. Dr. Kelly or something. He knew a ton about DNA testing and he also knew about these companies that do ancestry tests, because he had been hired by the guy caught by the cops using the public records of one of those outfits. Anyway, call him. He will remember me. He's a good guy. Don't talk his ear off, or he'll get pissed. Just ask him what the chances are of two of those tests being wrong and whether it's worth getting tested again. He'll give you a good quick answer."

My own dear daughter looked at me with a baby's wide eyes. "Jesus, Pop. Really?"

"Sure. Call him. He knows about my trouble. He offered to help me when I got arrested. He's a stand-up guy."

"I can't believe it," she said.

"What?" I looked at her lovingly but still concerned.

"You actually did do something for me."

"I'm here, where you can always find me," I said, smiling at my daughter.

Later that day I got word that Street wanted to meet me in the greenhouse. After my shift was over in the law library, I was able to walk through the dorms and out into the garden area. One of Street's set was leaning against the perimeter fence. A small radio was sitting in his lap and he was smoking a cigarette. The radio was playing an old pop song at top volume as the sun spread down over his shoulders like buttery rain: "A Change Would Do You Good."

Inside the greenhouse in the far corner was a block of herbs. Street was brushing his hands across a row of chives, lightly picking out small imperfections and tiny weeds from the dark soil. He glanced up and saw me walking toward him.

"I got your note. I looked her up—the lady with the poem about the tigers. The white lady. She was a lesbian. What are you trying to tell me?"

"It doesn't matter that she was a lesbian."

"She hates men."

"She doesn't hate men, Mr. Munro. She doesn't want to be afraid."

He picked a slender spike of chive and bit into it. "But she is talking about being afraid of tigers: jungle cats. Come on, man, is she talking about Black men? Is she talking about just being afraid of me?"

"I'm not sure, Street. What do you think?"

"Listen, man, I know white girls are afraid of Black men."

"So where does that put you?"

"Fuck you, man. You want me to plead, you want me to

forget Emmett Till and Black men being killed for whistling at a white woman? To me white women are a threat."

"Okay so where does that leave you? We are just two men in jail talking about how to act. You asked me how to act around white women on your parole board who may or may not be afraid of you. Let me ask, how would you act if you had to get past a tiger for your freedom?"

Street looked at me and he didn't speak for a good while. He picked at a scar on his knuckle. Finally he spoke. "You saying white women sometimes feel like Black folks?"

"I'm saying that I think they also don't like to be bullied."

"They don't know what it's like to be like Black folks."

"No, they don't."

"What that man mean when he wrote that little poem?"

"Which one?"

"The one about the black boy holding out his hands to the falling snow."

"I don't know. I think it just means what it says. It's just a snapshot of his life. What do you think it means?"

"I think it means it's a white man's world, no matter what anybody does, no matter if you go to Paris an' shit."

"Maybe so."

He ate another spike of chive, then picked a piece of basil and handed it to me. We didn't speak for several long moments. The herb tasted fine, fragrant in my mouth, and took me back to long meals on summer days, sitting under a tree.

Street wiped his hands together, looked at his palms and said, "Okay then, you still going to be my teacher, and I'm going to try not to hit you anymore, and I'm going to say this: I wouldn't try to bully no tiger to get out of here."

I nodded, then walked out of the greenhouse, where his

man was now listening to Talking Heads' "Burning Down the House" on the classic rock station. A raven was hopping on the ground outside the chain-link fence where he had thrown a half slice of bread over the razor wire, which could have landed him in a ton of trouble, but no one seemed to be watching.

Though I wasn't there, here is what I imagined happening next, from everything I know and from what I have put together from everything I did hear and see. Blossom and George were upset about the test results, and they went to their science teacher to ask about the accuracy of the results. He told them they were almost certainly accurate down to any reasonable sliver of a doubt. Blossom called my old expert, who talked with her a lot longer and gave her many details about lab protocols and statistical analysis and areas of inquiry if you wanted to challenge the results. He talked about how mistakes can happen and how samples can be tainted. He suggested retesting, but said it essentially all came down to whether the testing and sampling had been done correctly. George was adamant that she had not screwed up the swabbing and had handled the sample correctly.

The one thing the girls didn't know was that the science teacher had written a short heads-up email to the school counselor about George's situation and that the school counselor's husband was a retired police detective. This was a pivotal detail in all the events that would come to pass.

The next day when Blossom pulled up to George's house in the blue Renault Le Car with the roof down, there was a police car there. George and her mom were out in the yard near the tire swing crying and arguing.

George was pulling on her mom's sleeve, trying to get

her to walk away from the two officers, and Ida Paul was yelling at the police. Tears were streaming down her face. Ida was still in her morning robe. She had set a cup of coffee on the concrete steps. The female officer was standing still trying to take notes in her small spiral notebook, and the male officer was shifting his weight from foot to foot with his right hand on the grip of his service weapon. Blossom got out of her car and went to her friend.

"Go to school!" Her mother spoke to both of them. "Now. Your father and I will handle this." Ida looked at Blossom and then glanced around the yard sadly as if she were taking an inventory of her life.

"Please, honey . . . Go."

Blossom took her best friend by the hand and led her to the car where the radio was still playing. Blossom loved driving so much that every day she walked from the harbor near the high school, up the hill near the capitol building to pick up the car from her uncle's garage. From there she drove the twelve miles to George's house, then *back* to the high school for the early morning study hall where they could drink coffee and get ready for their day before classes started. It was their favorite time together. But this day, there was a cascade of tears. George had no idea what the cops wanted. She only knew that her mother was upset with her and that her idea for the perfect gift of a travel vacation to their homelands had somehow gone horribly wrong.

When they arrived at school, the vice-principal met them at their study area and asked them to come to the counselor's office. Now, here is where George could have saved herself some grief. She didn't have to talk with the counselor. The counselor had screwed up by talking to her husband, and the husband may have screwed up by talking to the duty cop. All that would be the subject of a later argument. What wasn't in dispute is that once the victim of a crime talks with a school counselor, that counselor is a mandatory reporter and has to go to the police.

The counselor sat behind her desk as if she had been waiting there all night. She had three files lying open. Two of them were student files. One was Blossom's, which was thin as she was a new transfer, and the other was George's, which was somewhat larger. Of course, most of the student information was kept on the school's confidential computer system, but these were the hard copies the counselor had clearly studied and had used when she conferred with teachers prior to the meeting. There was another, much older file that appeared to Blossom to be full of old newspaper clippings.

The counselor's name was Nan Fishman. She had a round face and short blond hair that accentuated her roundness, and the sweater hanging on her shoulders was a halo above her desk framing her torso. She was a bland angel with an uninspiring voice.

"Now, girls, we should start off together, but, Georgianna, if at any point you feel uncomfortable having your friend Blossom here with you, we can ask her to leave. Do you understand? Normally we would ask your parents to be here with you in a meeting of this nature, but because of the specifics of this set of circumstances we think it would be best if you have your friend here for moral support. Unless you would like someone else, honey?"

"Circumstances?" George asked.

Ms. Fishman was looking down at the blue file. "I see here that you don't have a therapist or clergyperson listed in your file as an alternate support person, is that accurate?"

"Blossom is fine, Ms. Fishman."

"That's good, honey. Now, I understand there is something going on at home that is troubling you. What's going on, George?"

And George told her. She described taking the DNA test and sneaking the swab from her mom, and how careful she had been handling the procedure and the shipping. She told Ms. Fishman about the results and about Ida Paul's reaction and even about the police showing up at her house this morning. Tears came to George's eyes, and Blossom took her friend's left hand and squeezed it firmly as George ended her short soliloquy with: "Please tell me what is going on, Ms. Fishman. I'm so worried about my mom."

There was a pause as Ms. Fishman leaned forward, then backward, and forward again in her office chair, the hard flesh putty of her well-made-up, professionally concerned face unchanging the entire time.

"Honey, I cannot imagine how confusing this must be for you. I think the first thing we need to do is bring some clarity to the situation. That's why I have already gone ahead and asked Detective Mallard to come on down to discuss your options in getting a retest to confirm or disprove the results of these tests you had done. Now, dear, if it's okay with you, she is going to take another swab and have it tested by the crime lab up in Anchorage, and we will see what we can find out."

As if by magic, a smiling woman from the Juneau Police Department was already standing in the door with surgical gloves and an evidence-collection kit.

"And she will get a new sample from Mrs. Paul?" Blossom asked.

"Yes, she will get a sample from Georgianna's mother," Ms. Fishman said. "After that, we will meet again in the next few days and talk about the next steps to take. Okay, hon?" And here I imagine Ms. Fishman standing up at her desk to quickly end the meeting.

Later, in science class, the teacher could not look either of the girls in the eye, and after school there was a woman with curly brown hair and thick glasses waiting for them. She introduced herself as Shannon Lakeside, a reporter for the one print newspaper in Juneau. She asked one question before Blossom slammed the door of the Le Car, with George crying in the front seat, then jumped in the driver's seat and squealed the tires for the very first time as she drove away.

"What does it feel like to know the woman who raised you is a kidnapper?" Shannon Lakeside yelled after the car, her voice landing like mist on the back window.

When they arrived at George's house, her parents were barricaded inside. Three strange cars were parked out front, as well as a police car with two officers inside. A news crew was setting up lights and cameras. Blossom called the house, dialing Mrs. Paul's cell number so that she would see who was calling her.

"Yes . . . Blossom. Where are you, dear? Is George with you?" Mrs. Paul said without preliminaries.

"We're outside. What do you want us to do?" Blossom asked.

"Circle around and park on the next street. Cut through the backyard and come to the back door. We will let you in." She hung up.

George was not crying when she got out of the car, or when her father came to the door. Richard Paul is Tlingit and in his forties. His family was very traditional, from Angoon Village. He was of the Killer Whale clan. Mrs. Paul was white for all intents and purposes in the community. They had met at the Native Health hospital in Sitka years ago, when Mr. Paul had come in for treatment for sepsis after his appendix burst on the ferry ride to the doctor's office. Even when most critically ill, Richard did not show his emotions much, unless it was through laughter. He loved puns and jokes, but today his eyes were rimmed red from crying.

He put his arms around his daughter and hugged her long and hard. Then he hugged Blossom, which worried her all the more because Richard Paul was usually not very physically demonstrative. He showed them to the small living room. Two lawyers, a young man and a young woman, sat on the sofa near the television. They had legal pads on their knees. They stood up and shook hands with the girls. At first they asked Blossom to leave the room, but George insisted that she stay. They gave her a warning that she might be called as a witness to anything that was said, and Blossom said that she understood. The lawyers didn't like it; one of them was not going to go forward if Blossom stayed in the room. Blossom stood up and started to walk out, but George started crying, asking for someone to tell her what in the hell was going on, and Mrs. Paul got up and pulled Blossom down onto the dowdy old couch and said, "It's over. It's all over. This is never going to trial."

Then Ida Paul went to the kitchen, poured everyone coffee and juice, brought out a package of cookies, and then began telling her story.

The story was essentially this: Ida Paul and Richard were unable to conceive children. They were told this eighteen years ago. It may have had something to do with the sepsis that brought them together. Ida became a midwife and loved being with pregnant women and their babies. About seventeen years ago she was working with a couple, a Tlingit woman and a white man, who were expecting a baby. Here, Ida paused, looking down into her coffee cup as if the mysteries of the past could be answered there. "They were going to have a mixed-race baby just like we would have had, and I decided I was going to"—she took a deep breath—"do something that I felt would help us both."

The lawyers leaned forward, about to say something, but Ida Paul held up her hand to stop them. "I don't want to tell you why . . . I just want to say that I believed in my heart that Richard and I could be better parents than anybody on earth for this child. We could love this baby"—she looked at George and tried to smile, but only grimaced with self-directed disgust—"more than anyone ever would or could. I believed that then, and I still believe it today. So I did it. I did it. Richard didn't want to, but I did it."

Richard cleared his throat and was about to speak.

"No . . ." she said. "I did it. It was wrong, but I did it, and I don't really regret it."

There was silence for a moment and the little living room was filled with the sound of a family clock ticking and the sniffling of all the people sitting there.

"I faked my pregnancy with the use of training tools and pillows: a big inflatable prosthetic belly in public. We did our birth training together. Richard and I told everyone we had a home birth a day before George was born. We didn't announce the sex. When their baby was born, I went for a visit. Kristy was weak and not feeling well after the birth. I had always played the robust mother to be. I was up and around early after my home birth, which of course was a fraud. Sometimes I think I should have been an actress. I faked my weakness and made so much of my birth pains to anyone who would listen. I even faked my postpartum depression; when I went into the hospital, I acted like a war veteran and used makeup to look like a ghost. I wore one of my old maternity dresses with a deflated belly underneath. When I saw they had a girl, I told them I had a girl as well. I held her and walked her around when she cried. I returned her to her mom and watched the mother go to sleep. Then I slipped the baby's bracelet off —they weren't fancy with lock alarms the way they are now. I put George under my dress while I was in the bathroom; she was a bit wiggly at first but soon enough she slept soundly. Then I just walked out. I had to take care of my own birth records for the home birth. I went to the nurses' station and stole the birth mother's records of the footprints and destroyed them before they were copied and registered. Then I was good. I was known and trusted in the hospital. Yes, they questioned me after the baby disappeared. But I gave testimony about a suspicious homeless woman hanging out around the hospital—and there actually were a few of those, and they made better suspects than I did—so soon enough the uproar faded. Except for the birth family, of course. They suffered terribly, especially the mother."

One of the lawyers cleared his throat. "Knowing that they suffered and would continue to suffer, why did you go through with stealing the child? Help me understand that."

Ida Paul smiled thinly and only said, "I just felt that Richard would be a much better father."

George finally spoke up. "Mom, who are my parents?"

"We are your parents, George," Ida said.

"My biological parents, Mom."

"Their names are Kristy and Thomas Thompson. She is Tlingit from Carcross, Canada, and he came to Alaska from Detroit, Michigan."

"Do they have other kids now?"

"Yes. They have a little girl. They live down near the federal building. He used to work as a part-time teacher and a writer. I think he works for the legislature now. She works for the fire department as a dispatcher, or she did. I believe she is retired now."

It was George's turn to look down into her cup. More silence . . . more ticking of the clock. "Are they . . . are they nice people?"

Ida looked at both the lawyers. "If I go to prison, will the Thompsons have custody of George?"

The lawyers looked at each other. "Well . . . probably . . . up until she turns eighteen anyway. The state of Alaska and the Department of Child Protective Services have been given direct orders under this governor to keep children with their biological parents whenever possible. This administration is very firm on children being raised by their biological parents."

"That must never, ever, happen," Ida Paul said, with more volume and force than she had used so far.

The lawyers wanted a word in private and the girls left. They slipped through the fence and then through the neighbor's backyard to the street. There by the blue Le Car was Ned the boyfriend, leaning against the passenger's side door with his death machine parked nearby.

"I heard, George. Jeepers. I'm sorry," Ned said. Ned's father was a cop, and Ned was the kind of kid who said "jeepers" even when he was breaking the rules by picking up his girlfriend on his motorcycle.

"Thanks, Neddy," George replied.

"Let's get out of here," Blossom blurted, "before that reporter babe gets hold of us. Meet at the boat?" And without a thought for his own safety, Neddy jumped on his motorcycle and turned over the grossly overpowered German-designed engine.

The Winning Hand is a retired seine boat, once used for commercial fishing, that Jane Marie had refitted for research. The boat originally had a boom and a powerful winch to deploy a large fishing net and a heavy skiff to pull the net in a circle and draw the bottom of the net closed. Now the large back deck carried two inflatable skiffs and had several workstations for sampling and monitoring hydrophone arrays, which could be towed behind the boat. There was a crow's nest at the top of the mast for observation and remote steering, as well as a flying bridge—a warm, protected bridge area with full navigation and scientific gear for monitoring the bottom and reading the feed layer, as well as the density and temperature of the seawater beneath the boat. Blossom considered her group on the boat to be the youth auxiliary of the C. Younger Investigative Agency, or Free Younger Investigations, FYI, as she liked to think of it. They convened in the flying bridge.

"What are we gonna do, Georgie?" Ned began.

"Well . . ." George bit down on a stale gingersnap, which had become the official snack food of the FYIers. "This cannot stand. I mean, I'm not going to live with those other people, no matter who they are or how nice anybody says they are. That's not happening. Ida's my mom. I don't care what she did."

"Okay . . ." Blossom said.

"So . . ." Ned said, and there was a long pause.

"So, if they arrest Mom, then we have to get her off at trial. We get her a badass lawyer and we win. My mom is not going to prison. Isn't that what your dad would do,

B?" She looked at Blossom with arched eyebrows and an expression of desperate hope.

"My dad? My dad, who is currently *in* prison?"

The three of them laughed. Then Ned said, "I know . . . that is so badass. But really, that was his job, right? Helping people with their legal problems?"

"Like a policeman?" George said.

"Not exactly," Ned added. "My dad investigates for the district attorney with the objective of proving the elements of a crime; a defense investigator puts that evidence to the test to see if it holds up to the standards of proof and reasonable doubt."

"That's very good, Ned," Blossom said, genuine admiration mixed with the usual sarcasm in her voice. "I will talk with my dad about this case, and I'm sure he will help us."

"Who will help you? What's going on?" A voice came from the ladder leading up from the main deck below. Jane Marie, Blossom's mom, poked her head up through the opening to the flying bridge. "Oh, Georgianna, hi. I heard about what's going on. How are you? God, it must be so hard."

"Yes, Ms. DeAngelo, it's hard."

"We were just talking, Jane," Blossom said, as if to cut off a longer conversation.

"Who were you talking about getting to help you?"

"We thought your husband could give George some advice, Ms. D.," Ned piped up, and just as he finished his sentence, Blossom kicked him hard in the foot.

"Oh my God. No." Jane Marie looked around at all three teenagers. "Blossom, may I speak with you in the cabin below for a moment?"

"No, *Jane.* I'm not going to go below and have another one of those whispery lectures about my *father*, about how he is such a bad man and how he cannot be trusted because he got drunk when I was in trouble, and about how you're so gosh-darn perfect."

"Young lady . . ." Jane Marie's face was red. Blossom was staring straight into her mother's eyes while her two friends were staring down at their own feet. "Young lady . . . I know how you romanticize him. I know that you love him. But this is a serious problem for George. She needs serious help."

"And we are going to listen to George, Jane. We are going to listen to George, and we are going to try to help her get what she wants. How about that?"

"It's all so hard and complicated. All so new. George . . . take some time before you make any rash decisions. Please, darling . . ." Jane knew her daughter well enough to know that to try to convince her now would be futile. She just looked at George hoping she could sense her own goodwill.

"I will, Ms. D.," George said, still looking at the deck. "Don't worry about me too much. And don't be mad at B. She really is a good friend to me. She was with me all day and she gives me rides and she . . . she really is a good friend and she helps me so much . . . don't ground her or anything . . . please."

Jane Marie climbed all the way up into the flying bridge and hugged George. "I won't, darling girl. I won't take your best friend away now. I promise." They both cried.

Then they all ate stale gingersnaps, sealing, I suppose, for the time being, Jane Marie's position in FYI.

The next day in the visiting room at Lemon Creek Correctional Center, Blossom was not very sassy. She had brought

Todd with her and bought them both Snickers bars from the vending machine—which I had never seen her do before—and they chomped into them like gangsters into Havana cigars. It was raining hard outside even though it was a warm spring day. I had been in the greenhouse earlier with Street, and we had been discussing Adrienne Rich and the development of feminist literature as we followed the flight of several ravens and gulls back up the valley into the snowfields behind the prison. We could hear the cold creek running beside the buildings and the hum of the steam laundry that took care of the cleaning for the ferry system, government buildings and the halfway house as well as the prison compound. My mind was drifting as Blossom explained her situation.

"How long will it take the crime lab to get the test results back, Pop?" she asked through a mouthful of candy, seeming more like a child than I had seen in years.

"Depends on how hard the investigators push and what kind of priority the lab gives the case. You said there was a camera truck at the house?"

"Mmm yeah . . ." she was able to say as she swallowed.

"Then I suspect they will get it back in a couple of days. If it was on the news and if a reporter is bird-dogging George, then there is pressure on the police and their bosses. Ida Paul is in the legislature and it will be news. They will be out for blood. Her opponent tagged her as soft on crime, didn't he?"

Blossom looked at me as if I were high on crack. "I have no idea."

"Well, she is a liberal Democrat, so I think he probably did, which means they will come after her hard. They will get the results back soon. What about George's dad? Has he spoken to the police?"

"Not yet. She said it was all her. She told the police that he knew nothing, and he's not talking to the cops."

"That won't last long. They will build a case against him, but they will have to find direct evidence he knew his wife wasn't pregnant. They won't want to take a purely circumstantial case against a lone Native man."

"But they didn't come and get a fresh swab from her." Blossom was picking a nut out of her back teeth.

"Her lawyers probably wouldn't let her, and the DAs didn't want to go through the fuss of a warrant. I imagine they just got a swab from the woman they suspect is the biological mother, who would be more than happy to provide one. They get a match there, that's all they need. It's more convincing that George actually belongs with her."

Blossom snapped an ugly look at me.

"Uh, I mean in theory, it would support the DA's claim that George belongs with the biological parent . . . not that she actually does. It just helps to establish the . . . the biological connection . . . not the important family connection," I backtracked.

Todd was looking down at the table. He had finished his candy bar and sat with his hands relaxed out in front of him, some chocolate rimming his lips. Blossom looked up at him and suddenly smiled. She hugged him with her left arm and pulled a bandana from her back pocket and handed it to him and pantomimed wiping her own face. He sat up straight, took the bandana and vigorously wiped his mouth.

"How is the job, Todd?" I asked him.

"Oh, good," he said, and he handed the kerchief back to Blossom.

"Cecil, did Blossom tell you that I have a friend there?"

"Yes, she did. What's her name?"

"Mrs. Feero. She is very nice. She and I pray every day that you get out of jail really soon."

"That's great, Todd. I think it's working. I really do."

"Really?" He looked at me and smiled as if his prayer had already been answered.

Blossom tapped her fingertips on the surface of the table, then she took Todd's hands in her own. "What can I do, Pop?" she asked me. Her eyes were welling up, and she let go of Todd's hands and rapped her knuckles on the table. "I mean, about George . . ." I was beginning to worry that she would bruise her hand hitting the table so hard, and I could tell Todd was worried too. "I mean, I have to do something," she said.

"Be a good friend to George. Listen to her. Cook for her and her dad. Don't judge. Don't panic." I was spitting things out.

"Pray," Todd said softly.

"Cripes" was all she said for a long series of raps and taps, rocking back and forth in her chair. "I want to sue somebody. Or blow up someone's house."

"Yeah . . . I did that, remember? See how that worked out for me?" I took her hand in both of mine. "Look. Mrs. Paul is going to need a good lawyer." I took a fine-tipped marker that they let me use at the library out of my pocket, and I wrote a name and number on the back of my daughter's hand. It was not the name of my lawyer because that would be a conflict of interest. I wrote Harrison Teller's name.

"Listen," I said, "this guy is not a good person, and he is a very hard person to like, but he is the lawyer she needs right now. Everyone in the system—judges, cops, clerks, other lawyers—they all hate him. But once you hire him, he will chew through reinforced concrete to get you out of jail. This guy doesn't fucking quit, B. He is expensive. Have them call Harrison. Don't mention me or that I'm in jail. Just have them hire Harrison Teller. Mrs. Paul should cash out her retirement. She won't want to, but she won't need retirement money if she is in prison, and she will be in prison if she doesn't get a lawyer like Harrison Teller."

The truth was that Harrison Teller was picky about which cases he took. He liked cases with maximum impact in what he called "righteous justice." Harrison Teller would have liked to represent John Brown at Harpers Ferry, but his last big win had been three years ago. Now, he mostly spent his time in a trespass cabin built inside Denali National Park, with a current wife, two ex-wives and six children. He had an underground bunker for his weapons and ammunition. In the summer, his children ran naked along the ridgelines where the bugs were blown out by the wind, and the kids could pick berries, and his wives would work down by the stream processing fish and growing a garden. In the fall, the tribe would harvest and can up cases of meat as well as spawned out fish for dog food, and in the winter, they ran dog teams and spent long nights under blankets studying particle physics and reading metaphysics, religious poetry, law books, comic books and Western gunslinger novels. In the worst of the spring mud season, the entire family went to town for haircuts, and every other year they would go to Paris or Laos to stay in the finest hotels and eat only from room service.

Teller's long-suffering assistant paid all his accounts long-distance. When he was in civilization, Teller was famous for never having cash, and rarely having a credit card. He now had a long white beard that he rarely trimmed, and his piercing blue eyes had never dimmed. He wore a long wool coat in Paris, and the pockets often held only a few bus tokens, a wad of francs—which were long discontinued, hotel keys from places he had stayed years ago, and the occasional walnut or fishing lure without the hook. Yet he was on a first-name basis with the manager and most of the staff at the George V, where he was running up a considerable tab.

Blossom looked at the name I had written above her wrist. Even though she had heard of him, she did not gain the same satisfaction in getting the name as I had in giving it. Getting an "in" to becoming one of Harrison Teller's clients was like being given a box of hand grenades to take to a knife fight, but my poor daughter did not know that yet. She just stared at the letters that were inked above her wrist.

"Wow . . . thanks, Pop. Another expensive lawyer. That's cool." She started with the tapping again. I didn't blame her particularly.

"How is your mom?" I asked, trying to change the subject.

"She's a bitch."

"Hey, hey . . . be nice."

"She is! She is still so snotty about you being in jail."

"It's not easy for her. Give her time. That's between us. How is she to you? Does she beat you?"

"No," she sulked.

"Does she starve or neglect you?"

"No." Slight trace of a smile.

"Chain you in any dungeons where rats nibble your toes?"

"Only on Friday and Saturday nights, when Ned comes over."

"Okay then." I smiled at her, and she finally looked up into my eyes and smiled in a way that made my chest ache.

"Okay, Pop. I will tell Mr. Paul to hire this guy." She pointed to the lettering on the back of her hand, then she got up to go, in a somewhat better mood.

But the mood didn't last long, for when Blossom pulled the Le Car up to George's house, the police were there leading Mrs. Paul away in handcuffs.

4
THE CASE OF THE DELICATE FLOWER

A buzz went around the jail the night Ida Paul was brought in. There was a nice cockeyed morality to the prison gossip. She was a high-profile white woman accused of stealing a Native girl from her Native mother. That she was married to a Native man and that the Native woman was married to a white man was left out of the news story as well as the gossip in jail. It was just so juicy to have a white Democratic legislator linked to a famous unsolved mystery—the kidnapping a Native baby some sixteen years ago—that it was like a celebration for the shitbirds when she was brought in. Guilty or not, it was great to have her in jail.

Before her trial, Ida Paul would be held at Lemon Creek Correctional in the general population. A serious charge meant that she might be held for up to a year before her case would be resolved. Still, she wouldn't get a job or be able to do many programs. She could get some medical care and continue whatever medication she was on when she came in, but there would be no classes or self-improvement while awaiting trial, other than doing pushups in her cell, chin-ups on her doorframe or shuffling through her legal file.

The perp walk does not take place near Lemon Creek but in downtown Juneau, in the hallway from the courtroom to the elevator in the Diamond Courthouse. The arrangement had been made between the judge and the local press. During Ida's trial, she would be taken in and out of the courtroom by the troopers through a back elevator to the downstairs holding facility. But for this one occasion after her arraignment, the judge, a Republican appointee, allowed the press sixty seconds to photograph the Democratic lawmaker in cuffs, leg irons and an orange jumpsuit, standing between two massive guards at the closed metal doors of the elevator. Her head was down. Even her public defender at the time stood aside so the photographers could get their shots of the mysterious kidnapper.

Sixteen years before, the stolen child had been known as "Baby Jane Doe" out of respect for the family's privacy, but even after the Thompsons were identified, "Baby Jane" stuck and was circulated all over the country, and even the world. Kristy Thompson's stricken face appeared on television in tearful interviews; her husband kept out of the spotlight but wrote letters to the media and to politicians. In many of the early publicity photographs, Ida Paul stood by the Thompsons offering her full support.

A stolen baby outraged the community of Juneau. At first, suspicion was cast on the staff at the hospital, particularly the Native health aides and Filipina nurses and technicians, for purely racist reasons. When a backlash to the racism kicked in, a story circulated about a homeless woman seen in the hospital the night of the disappearance. Police visited the soup kitchens and the usual gathering places around the city. Neighbors checked yard sales for suspicious people buying infant clothes. Investigators received calls from the Salvation Army thrift store about suspicious sales of baby books. Grocery stores reported unusually high sales of formula. Suddenly infant accessories were as criminalized as the makings of methamphetamine. Everyone seemed to want to bring that baby and her kidnapper in dead or alive.

Shannon Lakeside had been a young reporter just up from Seattle when the kidnapping happened, and it was fair to say that it made her career. One day she was reporting on DUIs and assembly meetings, and the next day she was fielding calls from national news organizations and acting as a stringer for several major outlets on this story. She even had an offer for a film deal . . . if the case came to a satisfactory conclusion. Something that satisfied the three elements of a potboiler: romance, swordplay and moral rectitude. Lakeside was determined to make the facts of the missing baby fit this formula and give her a golden ticket to Hollywood.

Shannon was smart and thought of herself as fair, but she didn't realize just how much she wanted to catch and convict whoever had taken this baby. She would deny it if asked, but she wanted to see the person in cuffs not only to satisfy the community's sense of justice and the family's need for closure, but also to restore the hospital employees' reputation. (Shannon never subscribed to the employee conspiracy theory.) She also wanted the case to be solved so she could write the book about it and be famous. She didn't like this about herself . . . but there it was. She was driven, and she wasn't going to give up. Her fat file had never been put away; it sat under her desk, and every month she continued to make calls, even after the family wanted to move on, and after the next scandal moved the story off the back pages.

But now it had come back into prominence again, and no one—no one—was going to take this story away from her. Shannon Lakeside was finally going to write the ending of the child kidnapping. She had called the agent who had come to her with the film deal and was waiting for her to call back, but in the meantime, Shannon was snapping pictures of the elevator doors closing on Ida Paul and the two immense troopers taking her downstairs in the courthouse. Shannon had already put in a request for an interview with Ida's lawyers and they had told her that Ida was "considering it."

Ida spent the first day in jail in the pressure lock, or transfer cell, being observed. She cried a great deal. She was alone. She was told she could not have any visitors or phone calls until she was cleared. The shrink told her she had to stop crying and she did. The second day, she spoke to her lawyers and told them she wanted to talk with the reporter from the paper. They heartily advised against it. They gave her their quick and dirty test to see if they could get her a full psych evaluation against her will on short notice. They decided it would probably not happen, and knew the prison authorities would let the reporter talk with her on the phone or in person, and they would record the whole thing. Her attorneys told her not to talk with anyone under any circumstance about anything to do with her case if she ever wanted to live with her daughter or husband again.

Ida said solemnly, "I understand everything you are telling me, and I thank you for your counsel. Really. Thank you." Her cellmate reported that Ida cried most of the night and that she said the Lord's Prayer several times at breakfast.

Rumors float around the joint like pollen in spring. Here is what went around after Ida Paul turned up dead: on the third day of her incarceration, Ida Paul took a piece of braided fabric made from her second pair of prison-issued coveralls, looped one end over a shower fixture and the other end around her throat, and slowly lowered her body toward the shower room floor so as not to break off the showerhead. According to the autopsy, it took at least fifteen minutes for her heart to stop beating and for her to finally expire. Several inmates were reported to have seen her hang herself, but none stepped in to stop her or call prison authorities for help.

After she was found, the entire institution was on immediate lockdown. I was stuck in Street's office for an hour right before dinner. Street and I spent the time talking about the music of John Coltrane. Street was making connections between the poetry we had been talking about and the music he had loved on the outside.

"Trane expressed all that in music, you see?" he said. "He was very big-picture. I went to New York to see him once. I heard him play numbers from *A Love Supreme* live, you know what I'm saying? I cried, I'm telling you. I cried. It was powerful."

"How?"

"What are you saying to me?"

"I'm just curious how it was powerful."

"Man . . . you don't understand a Black man at all. What I'm telling you about crying . . . that's change . . . That's revolutionary shit right there."

"Wait, are we talking about music, or are we talking about you crying?" I asked him. I didn't know.

His illegal cell phone rang and Shawn Day handed it to him. Street only said "yes" three times into the phone and then handed it back to her.

"Your client was found dead," he said.

"Who?"

"White lady who stole that baby. She choked herself out."

"Shit! No."

"Oh, yes."

"Why? It was too soon to lose hope. Were people on her in here?"

"Naw . . . not bad."

Then Street looked down at me for several long moments, and for the first time he seemed genuinely sympathetic, almost kind. "You want my opinion, Cecil?"

"Of course."

"She was hard. I know she called that reporter. Told that lady she wanted to talk to her."

"So . . ."

"That was a mistake. I don't know, but maybe, just maybe, she kilt herself just to piss that reporter off. Keep her from getting the neat ending to the story she wanted. Sounds crazy, I know . . . but, shit, it's all crazy, right?" And he smiled at me, sad, with his eyes wide. "I'm sorry for your child, brother. I am. I know she was invested in all this."

My heart sank away and tears came to my own eyes because, once again, I realized that I was into something deeper and more dangerous than I'd recognized. I was going to be involved in this case because of Blossom, and getting involved was something I didn't want to do. But now I was, and one thing I knew was that Ida didn't take her own life as vengeance against a reporter. The world is crazy, but Ida Paul was not, and there was something Street was not saying.

The next day, newspaper headlines screamed, KIDNAPPER ESCAPES JUSTICE THROUGH SUICIDE, with an unhinged story by Shannon Lakeside that claimed to be a recitation of the history of the case and what little was known about Ida Paul's death, but really it was a personal screed in favor of some sort of revenge, some sort of rough justice for the kidnapping of Baby Jane written in the form of an indictment of Ida's husband, Richard, as her co-conspirator. Suicide would not do. Someone had to be convicted and go to jail, according to Ms. Lakeside. I later found out that readers actually bought copies of this edition from newsstands downtown and from delivery children making their rounds to houses, which is rare for the local paper.

That afternoon Blossom came to see me. She was dressed in black sweatpants and a baggy Mountain Goats T-shirt from an old tour that happened long before I was arrested. Her hair made her look like she had just gotten up from a nap.

"Hey, Pop," she said.

"I'm so sorry about George's mom, baby. Where is Georgie now?"

"I don't know. Holed up with her dad somewhere. They are avoiding everybody."

"I'm sorry, B."

"What can I do to help her, Daddy?"

"Be good to her, honey. Don't push her. Listen. Make sure she eats and gets out a bit, and doesn't fall too far behind in school. That kind of thing . . . I guess."

"Yeah . . . but . . . what else? I mean about the whole mess? They want to take her dad away. Jeepers." She was swearing like her boyfriend now, which I couldn't help think was adorable, even though at the time I didn't much like the guy.

"Have they sent anyone around to talk with Richard, or mentioned arresting him?"

"I don't know. They are holed up. I don't know. I think that lawyer you recommended came down from up north. I think Richard talked to him. I think one of the last things Mrs. Paul did was cash out her retirement and hire that lawyer . . . hired him for Richard. That's what George told me before she and her dad disappeared. Cecil . . . I'm worried about her dad. He's really sensitive, and he is super scared about going to jail. He's not like you. He won't do well in here."

"Why do you say that?"

"He has never been in trouble his whole life. Ida handled a lot of the business, you know? Richard took care of food and family and the house and . . . the spiritual stuff . . . He's not a badass like you."

"Aw, thanks, sweetie."

"Shut up. You know what I mean."

"But are you sure Harrison Teller is in town and is going to take Richard Paul's case?"

"That's what I think that reporter lady said when she called me this morning."

"Okay . . . that's one thing you can do. Don't talk to the press."

Blossom stared at me as if I were an idiot child. "I didn't tell her anything, Cecil. I just got information out of her and told her old boring stuff."

"Don't . . ."

"I got this, don't worry."

"Really, don't talk, B."

"Cecil, I found out about Mr. Teller, didn't I?"

"Or she was just testing you to see what you knew."

"Okay . . . is he really as good as you say?"

"Good is a relative term, sweetie. Let's just say he is the lawyer that Richard and George need right now."

"Is he a friend of yours?"

"No, I wouldn't say a friend. But don't worry. He can be counted on to help them with their legal troubles. That I can promise you."

I didn't want to explain to my daughter about the complexities of friendships between lawyers and investigators. For one thing, there are class and educational distinctions that will always persist between attorneys and investigators, no matter how many drinks or how many bad nights in side-by-side beds at crappy hotels they share. No matter how much admiration there may be between a lawyer and an investigator, there is always the feeling that the lawyer will inevitably be most comfortable scratching the investigator between the eyes in front of the fire like a faithful hound.

Weeks later, Mr. Paul told me about his first serious meeting with his new lawyer and the investigator who would be working on his case. We were sitting in the dining hall at LCCC and Mr. Paul described the meeting in his very soft voice as he stared down into his coffee cup. Paul spoke English with a deep Tlingit accent that I don't hear so much today. It made me feel good, as if I were outside of jail, somewhere in a fish camp talking with him, except that he was not telling the usual jokes or teasing me in the way that he would have if we had been comfortably gathering food. He described his legal team as if he were describing a talking bear or some kind of mythical creature, so strange did they seem to Richard Paul. What details he didn't know about Harrison Teller and his investigator, I already knew from my past experience working with them and the lore that surrounded them.

So, that very afternoon, while Blossom and I were talking in the visiting room in prison, Harrison Teller had just finished up his meeting with Richard Paul and his daughter, Georgianna, at the Catholic shrine past Amalga Harbor, to work out the details of Mr. Paul's turning himself in. Teller left his investigator to unpack his suitcase containing two broken-down shotguns and six nine-millimeter Heckler Koch handguns with a full complement of ammunition. Otis Betts, the investigator, had once been a Navy Seal, and was the only African American to ride with the Fairbanks branch of the Banditos. He had very little legal training other than knowing never to talk with the police if it wasn't cleared by his boss. Mr. Betts had once been detained for two hours on a faulty-taillight stop. Mr. Teller could not be reached by phone, and Mr. Betts refused to give his name or any identification or exit his four-wheel-drive truck. If asked, Harrison Teller would swear an oath of devotion to Otis Betts, but Teller was not going to be there in that cabin if the police came to take in Richard Paul before the agreed time. Otis Betts would have to deal with the violent fallout that was expected of him if anyone—the press, the police, or anyone being particularly nosy—bothered Mr. Paul or his daughter. Such was the nature of Teller and Betts's relationship.

George and her father had retreated to a cabin to mourn. George mostly slept and walked on the beach with her pop, who mostly prayed for the tormented soul of his dead wife. When they finally had to deal with their legal situation, they went down the road and stayed at the Shrine of Saint Therese, where Harrison Teller was holed up, and tried to make plans. That afternoon both George and Mr. Paul sat near the big plate glass window staring out as the wind blew up from the south along Lynn Canal, mounding white crested waves forward like small prairie hills. George had her fingers entwined in her father's while he prayed. Periodically she kissed his wrists.

"Promise me, Dad. Promise me you won't follow Mom," she said softly.

"I don't know . . . I will try," was all he said.

Mr. Paul looked at me as we sat in the jail's chow hall. I think it was the first time he'd ever looked me in the eyes.

"I tried to promise my girl, Mr. Younger. I tried. But"—he rolled his cup around on the painted top of the metal table—"God will just have to help me through this." He looked back down past the rim of his mug.

"Yes," I said, "but God will have lots of help."

5

THE CASE OF MY FIRST KISS

Two days later, the police arrived at the Shrine of Saint Therese. There were two police officers in a black Suburban with darkened windows. Harrison Teller was riding with them. He walked to the house by himself and knocked on the door with the coded knock that all had agreed upon.

Harrison Teller's long prophet's beard had grown bushy white, and he had trimmed it back some. He wore a wide-brimmed hat and a duster-style wool coat with pockets filled with mostly gold coins, forgotten hotel keys and pocketknives—at least, that is, assuming he had not been on a commercial plane recently. He seemed to enjoy making TSA agents take the knives away from him. Most often now, though, he flew in a private prop plane rather than on commercial flights because he still liked to travel with the cremated remains of his father and one of his ex-wives.

Otis Betts opened the door holding a shotgun. He spoke to Teller for a moment and then Mr. Betts went back to his room and locked the shotgun away. Harrison

Teller returned to the Suburban and brought the police officers into the house, where they cuffed Mr. Paul. They read him his full Miranda rights as Mr. Teller looked on. Then Mr. Teller told the officers in his formal baritone voice, the voice usually reserved for courtrooms or press conferences, "Officers, as I have told the district attorney, Mr. Paul is my client, and my name is Harrison Teller. I am a member in good standing of the bar of the state of Alaska. Are your tape recorders running now?"

The two police officers stood silent, not used to lawyers asking them questions about whether they were surreptitiously recording a lawyer and a client after the client had been read their Miranda rights. The cops just shifted from foot to foot like little kids.

"It's a simple question, gentlemen, with a simple answer. I actually prefer that you are recording this. Just answer the question, please. Are your recorders activated and recording our voices now?"

The taller of the two cops cleared his throat and spoke up. "Yes, sir. I am recording this."

"Good. See, not so hard. Then let's be clear. Mr. Paul is my client. He is represented by counsel. He understands his rights, don't you, Mr. Paul?"

"Yes, sir, I do," Richard Paul said, just as he had practiced. Just as he had been told. Georgianna patted him between his shoulder blades and Mr. Betts smiled broadly at him.

"Fine then," Harrison said. "Mr. Paul will be exercising his right to remain silent and his full right to counsel. We will be riding along with you up to the jail."

The short cop looked at the taller one with alarm and was about to speak.

"This has all been worked out ahead of time and is not

negotiable. If either of you are not comfortable with these arrangements, you are to uncuff Mr. Paul and leave."

"Steve, this isn't some ride-along . . ." the short one said.

"Shhh. This is different, Ted."

"Do we have a problem, gentlemen?" Harrison said in a much sterner voice. Otis Betts was now standing directly behind Mr. Paul. Georgianna had been sent outside as planned.

"No, sir," Steve said. "As you said, this has all been worked out."

"Good," Harrison said. "As I was telling you, we will all be riding together. You will not ask Mr. Paul any questions. None. There will be no friendly chats, no open-ended musings, no condolences offered to him about the death of his wife. Absolutely no conversation openers, nothing. If . . . God forbid . . . we crash and the car is engulfed in flames, your only job is to jerk him out of the car but not . . . do you understand, *not* to ask him which way he wants to get out or how he feels about getting out. Is that understood?"

Then Harrison Teller looked at his client. "Mr. Paul, on this drive, which will last a little more than forty minutes, you may pray with Georgianna, you may talk with her about her future as long as it has nothing to do with the outcome of the trial or any evidence that may come up at trial. Actually, I prefer that you just pray." Here he took a deep breath, and he acted like he was going to launch into a lengthy lecture about the rules of evidence and about how this was a bad idea all around and he regretted this whole arrangement, but instead he let out the long breath and said, "Okay . . . let's go."

They all piled into the Suburban. The tall cop drove with Mr. Betts in front. Mr. Paul sat in the middle bench seat. Harrison prevailed upon the cops to have him cuffed in front, but they insisted on chaining his feet. There was a brief argument, but when George started crying, Harrison relented and they chained him up and she sat next to him. The short cop and Teller sat behind them, Harrison behind George, and the cop directly behind Mr. Paul. Harrison tried to lighten the mood by talking about guns with the short cop, but the little guy was not having much of it and kept shifting his eyes from side to side as if he were trying to spot an ambush. While Harrison Teller prattled on about hand loading and stopping power versus speed and accuracy, the big boat of a Suburban floated along the glaciated coastal forest floor of southeastern Alaska.

Rain had fallen the night before, and as the sun burned through the clouds, steam rose off the blacktop and rays filtered down through the spruce and hemlock trees. The light was milky white and almost juicy as Mr. Paul prayed and George held onto his shaking hands. George noticed the form of a waddling porcupine across the road easing down into the brush on the ocean side, and just as the fat pig of a car they were in scooted by, she caught a glimpse of a baby porcupine tottering next to its mother. She inadvertently jerked her head around to see if she could see more.

"How sharp were the baby's spines?" she thought to herself. "When do they grow in?"

The prison is on a dead-end road. At night it lights up the little canyon, but during the day it's a gray rain-filled cavity in a stream bed, like a gravel pit, surrounded by chain-link fencing and razor wire.

The black Suburban drove into the visitor parking lot. The road to the intake area went up and around to the back gate. The officer stopped the car.

"This is where I was told to drop you."

"My truck was dropped off here earlier," Harrison Teller called up to the front seat. "It is parked two hundred yards over there in the lot. Can you just drop us over there?" It was raining now, like lead pellets falling into a well, like a cow pissing on a flat rock. Drenching rain.

"No. The agreement says here."

"Jesus Christ." Mr. Betts spoke his first words of the entire trip.

"I don't appreciate your taking my Lord's name in vain," the short cop spit out.

"I don't think he was taking the Lord's name in vain, officer. I think he was invoking his name in order to help us get to the truck."

They opened the doors. Betts jumped out, while Teller helped George out. She kissed her father several times. Her tears were lost in the rain coursing down her hair and onto her cheeks. The small cop got out and ran around to the front seat. Teller held the door open as the cop climbed in, then kept the door open to speak with his client.

"You did great today, Mr. Paul. Really great. I will be working on your case full-time. No one else. Both Otis and I will be in Juneau for the duration. My wife and some of my kids will come down to be with me. We are renting a house. You are my client. Nothing else matters to me. In exchange, I want you to not talk about your case to anyone. You got that? Things seem bad, I know, but they could get worse if some jailhouse snitch comes forward and says you talked with them. Okay? Anyone wants to talk with you, what do you say?"

"You talk to my lawyer." Mr. Paul mustered a smile.

"And I am your lawyer. You got that?"

"Yes, sir. Thank you."

"This place isn't that bad. You will be okay."

"Yes, sir."

The rain was soaking down on them. Mr. Betts was leading George to the big four-wheel-drive truck Harrison Teller had parked in the visitor lot.

"Good. I'm going to do some work. I've got to pester the DA's office for all their files and recordings. I'm going to review all that, and I'm going to start looking for motions to file, and I'll be in to see you just as soon as I can. Don't expect me for at least ten days, okay?"

"Okay."

"Good." Teller banged on the roof of the car and grabbed his huge leather shoulder bag and started sloshing through the mud around the black Suburban. He left the door open, letting the rain pour in on the little cop, and as he passed the tailgate he opened that, and as he rounded the very back passenger's door he opened that too. He didn't open the door where his client sat, for that might have been considered aiding an escape rather than juvenile assholery, which is what he intended by making the little cop get out in the rain and go around and close all the doors.

Teller shook off his coat and threw it in the back seat where Otis was already spread out. George was buckled up in the front seat. She was trying to dry her hair off with her hands. Teller squeezed water out of his beard and twisted it so it looked like a little wet string under his chin.

"Otis, give us one of those towels from under the seat there . . . the ones from last night from the sweat."

"You guys took a sweat?" George asked.

"Yeah. We built it down by the beach. Heated up rocks. Used plastic sheeting and alder for the structure. It was great. I would have asked you and your dad, but, you know, we were naked and we got high . . . not good for his conditions of release."

Otis tossed the towels up front. They were still damp and sandy.

"Jesus, that little Ted cop was something, wasn't he? That guy needs to pray to a different god, don't you think?" Teller looked up into the rearview mirror at Otis, who looked like he wanted to go to sleep just then.

"Jesus," was all Otis said.

"I think you say that a little too much, Otis. I mean, I don't think you are saying what you mean to be saying . . . Anyway, we have work to do. Listen, George, you want to go to school today? I want to get breakfast. Shall we do that first? Let's go eat."

"I really want to see my friends," George said.

"Good. Let's go get them and take them out for breakfast."

George looked at her watch, blew her nose from all the crying and said in a sniffly voice, "But they are in school. It's third period already."

"Oh, Jesus Christ. This is important. Breakfast is the most important meal of the day. I'll talk to somebody. It's an important meeting. We'll have breakfast."

And so they did.

Donna's Restaurant in Juneau is mostly an old man's greasy spoon between five-thirty in the morning and about ten o'clock: it attracts fishermen, cab drivers, cops, prison guards between shifts and retired gentlemen of all stripes. Later in the morning, travelers and families start coming in. It's an easy walk from the airport and from a fairly depressing mall out near the Mendenhall Valley. The large group—Harrison Teller, Otis Betts, George Paul, Ned

Hume and Blossom Younger—wandered in, after shaking off their wet coats outside under the eaves. They took the largest booth in the corner. Ned looked uncomfortable not knowing where to sit after the two big men squeezed in on one side and the two girls on the other. Harrison Teller jumped up and grabbed him a wooden chair from across the room and set it up for him on the end, seeing that the poor kid was embarrassed about squeezing in too tight against Blossom when her blouse was so wet.

"Please," Teller said, gesturing for him to sit down. "Remember, everyone"—he looked around the table—"anything you want. It's on me. Business expense. Really."

Teller's hair had gone gray since I'd seen him last, and his face was lined with wrinkles, but his eyes were still piercingly blue, and he still trained them on everyone he talked with. When he was younger, women had found him attractive and disarming. Now he simply seemed intense, like a circuit-riding preacher struck by lightning, perhaps.

Harrison Teller insisted that they get nine orders of eggs, toast, waffles, biscuits, pancakes and hash browns, as well as full pitchers of syrup, orange juice, milk and water, so that they could all eat family style. There was so much food that the flinty old waitress had to bring over a second small table to serve as a sideboard. Teller acted the father and kept passing food and pitchers and making additional orders as he ate and told wild stories about cases he had won, flicking food off his beard, throwing his elbows and almost spilling Mr. Betts's juice. Mr. Betts had an uncanny ability to move his glass just in time to avoid the swinging elbow of the lawyer. The young people smiled, even the distraught George. She ate and laughed with her friends and wiped her plate with pork sausage and syrup, then wiped her greasy chin with her napkin.

George looked at Mr. Betts and said, "Blossom's dad is a famous private investigator."

The big man nodded and smiled, showing his gold-capped bridge. "Yeah?" he said.

"Not really famous," Blossom muttered, wanting to avoid the discussion.

"His name is Cecil Younger," George said, quite proud of her friend.

Both Otis Betts and Harrison Teller pushed themselves back from the table, their eyes wide.

"Not really famous??" Teller bellowed. "He's a fucking legend!!" Then he put his hand over his mouth and looked at the girls sheepishly. "Excuse me, ladies. Excuse my language."

Apparently, Teller and Betts went on for about forty-five minutes telling the teenagers stories that ranged from ninety percent truthful to complete fabrications having to do with other people, with my name pasted into the narrative. All of the stories were inappropriate for the ears of a minor child of mine. Most of the stories started, "There was this guy . . . a real dirtbag . . . guilty as hell . . . but your dad . . ." Most involved ethical breaches, as well as drug and alcohol abuse. "But you know, with a heart of gold." Jesus. From Blossom's telling, Harrison made me sound like a thug out of a Mickey Spillane novel.

But the kids laughed so hard, I guess Ned sprayed orange juice out of his nose. They settled down and Teller ordered pots of tea and coffee with a pitcher of whole milk and a bowl of sugar to settle their stomachs. School was out by the time they finished their business brunch. The rain had stopped. Teller craned his neck around and saw the sun.

"I'm not going to get much out of the DA today. Mr. Betts will take my truck and I will go down to the district attorney's office and harass them for discovery. Any of you got a car and can give me a ride?"

Blossom raised her hand.

"Good. Otis, will you take these other two to that Western Auto place and pick up enough ear and eye protection for everyone, and we will all meet at the private range out the road at . . . what . . . four-thirty?"

Otis nodded. Harrison Teller put on his wet coat and asked Mr. Betts to pay. Then Otis Betts fished out a silver money clip holding a thick wedge of damp bills from his pocket and counted out the tab for the wide-eyed waitress. He left her a $120 tip on a $180 tab.

"You want to make those old girls happy when you make them work that hard, Blossom. That way they like to see you come back. Also, those old girls not only show up on juries, they feed a lot of jurors. You know what I'm saying? Trying these ugly cases is like an ugly person running for office," Harrison Teller whispered to Blossom.

So, the operations staff of Free Younger Investigations spent the rest of the day getting their gear together and meeting up again on the north end of Douglas Island, in the woods off the highway where a hundred-yard swath was cut back into the mountain. Mr. Betts met them with several padlocked plastic cases, which he opened up on a shooting bench downrange from a series of circular targets.

He quizzed them on their skills. Ned had some experience, but only with long guns. So Mr. Betts took them slowly, one at a time, through all the precautions with the handguns first. He was a patient and kind teacher. His voice was calm and steady. There was nothing threatening or ominous in his tone. When Teller arrived, he was a little crazy. He just wanted to shoot. It was clear that Harrison Teller shot large-bore guns to burn off anxiety and aggression. He started in with a .308 semi-automatic, firing the long gun at the center circle as fast as he could. After six shots there was only one hole about an inch wide made by the six rounds.

The kids wore their safety glasses, earplugs and earmuffs. They did not put a round in the chamber until they approached the firing line. They each took six shots alone. They understood the rules. And then they shot the bejesus out of the targets for an hour and a half.

At first the nine-millimeter handgun frightened George. It seemed to want to leap out of her hand when she pulled the trigger. Mr. Betts leaned over her and pulled one of her earmuffs away from her head. He spoke into her ear with a loud voice so she could hear him through the earplug.

"Grip it tighter. Don't be afraid of it. You are in control. Lean into it with your weight and your muscle." He wrapped his big hands around hers and leaned forward a bit. She felt his hard arms and his weight on hers. "Squeeze," he said, and she did. The gun barely moved. She tightened her own grip, leaned in and went from spraying slugs in the dirt to slashing them across the target, then putting them into a grouping.

They finished their allotted ammunition and took off their gear. Each of them thanked the two adults politely, as if they had been to a tea party.

"You like that, George?" Harrison asked her.

"I was surprised, Mr. Teller, but I did. Very much." She smiled at him.

"You are an American, young lady. What's more, you are an Alaskan, and you have been visited by injustice. Of course you liked it." He smiled back at her, and they all started breaking the guns down after making sure there were no rounds in any of the chambers or magazines. Then Mr. Betts opened a beer and passed it around.

On the day my child was introduced to the Alaskan ritual of firearms and alcohol, I was out in the prison greenhouse getting a lesson in Black music and repression.

"I understand what you are saying, Cecil," Mr. Munro said, as we both worked down row after row of wisteria and rhododendron plants that were to be shipped out for state office building gardens in Juneau within the week. We were cleaning and watering them one last time as they sat in the greenhouse. Somehow Street had gotten me assigned to work with him for the last two days. Shawn Day was running errands back and forth, bringing Street messages and snacks as he asked for them. Prison culture is generally racist, misogynistic and transphobic. Yet it surprised me every day how little trouble Shawn Day had navigating the world of the joint. I'm sure that her intimidating muscle mass had something to do with her quality of life, but I also wondered if Street's reputation wasn't part of the magic shield around Shawn Day.

"I understand what you are saying about the repression of women, Cecil," Street said, "but you understand that when a rich white woman holds her baby child for the first time in a hospital, that woman knows, must know, that that child has every opportunity to grow up to be educated and free of the stigma of criminality. That child will be seen as fully human by the world." He lightly touched the red flower of the rhododendron with the pale bulb of his fingertip, scarred with the undefined smoothness of old cuts. "But that is not true for Black mothers in this country."

Over the months, Fourth Street had learned to control his temper around me. We had been working together on not using curse words, each of us paying attention to the words we chose, talking about how word selection would be important in front of the parole board. We also started enjoying simple moments of silence when we were together, just thinking about things we had read and working on our thoughts, which was something neither of us had done much of while on the inside.

I let my white fingers dig into the wet black soil in the pots. I pulled out sticks and impurities. I poured water from a plastic can and wetted the top two inches of soil.

"I understand," was all I said. I was not trying to argue with him. Our lessons had been derailed for a few days by his teaching me after I had started with feminist literature. Street was not defensive, and I could tell he was thinking things over, for he kept reading the things I was reading, and we discussed Adrienne Rich and Nikki Giovanni. He had read a lot of Maya Angelou and was quite familiar with her and with *Caged Bird,* but I got the impression there were things in all of the work he didn't really like to talk about. There were several occasions when I could tell he was holding his temper back while talking with me, and at least twice he had to keep himself from hitting me. I constantly worried that I was whitesplaining, but he would become angry with me when I showed insecurity or weakness.

But no one had attacked me in months. I had seen the young man, the former client who had attacked me, and he did not even make eye contact. Others in the law library were unusually respectful toward me. The gangbangers showed their manners, while the Shamrock boys and the white supremacists, who liked to demand law books for their endless motions, held their tongues when told their requested books were in use. When I got word to report to Street's office or to the greenhouse, I never had any trouble with the guards or the admin guys running the gates. I was serving relatively easy time, and I had to think it was because of the protection from Fourth Street.

Street looked up at the ceiling of the greenhouse. He saw that one of the glass panes in the metal structure of the roof was missing. Rain was falling in, but more importantly, heat had been escaping. He went directly under the broken pane and found a good-sized stone. Tied to the stone was a small bundle of white powder.

"Oh . . . f—, . . . uh, darn it," he said. He bent down and picked up the stone. Quickly he took the bundle off the stone and put the packet in his pocket. "Some dummy hit the greenhouse. You got to fix that pane."

"Me?" I said. "I'm not involved in this."

"Exactly. You got to fix it. Quickly. It's going to be found out if we don't do it now. We get it fixed before I get out of here and before some Nutty Buddy comes back in. Then they got to write this shit up."

"Nutty Buddy" or "Nutty Buddies" is what Street liked to call the operational staff, or the guards who patrolled the inside of the institution.

"But they will see me from the tower." I pointed over toward the guard tower, which rises up out of the admin building. There are no other towers at LCCC. Just one, looking over the institution and the one fenced-in area surrounded by razor wire.

"The Tower Buddies only care about things going over, under or through the wire or the doors. In and out. That's all they care about. Who is going in and out. As long as you are not escaping, they don't give a shit. Usually they are too busy looking at their video cameras and their sensing devices to even look out the fucking windows anyway. They barely fricking talk to the operational Buddies, negro."

"Did you just call me 'negro'?"

He smiled broadly at me and took my hand, and we started walking toward the toolshed on the opposite corner of the greenhouse. "You have just become my negro, negro."

He got to the shed and found a ladder that was painted bright orange, and a bucket of tools that contained putty, a putty knife, a small scraper and a pre-cut pane of glass. The ladder was just the right height to get to the top of the side wall of the greenhouse: approximately six feet, about a third of the height of the prison fence, and not really any use for an escape.

There was no instruction, no preparation. We set the ladder up outside the greenhouse, on the opposite side of the structure from the tower. Then Street tied one end of a rope to a belt loop on my waistband and the other end to a bucket. It wasn't until I had my right foot on the first rung of the ladder that I asked, "Wait, wouldn't the guys in the tower have seen who threw the rock with the drugs into the compound?"

"They better fricking not have," was all he said.

"Wait . . . wait . . ." I said.

"Go, go, go," he said.

The roof was made of a light metal frame held rigid by panes of glass. As soon as I put my full weight on top of the structure, I could feel the flat plane of the roof bow. The farther I climbed toward the middle, the more deeply it bent. Edges of glass panes ground against the metal and I heard a slight cracking sound.

"Quick," his voice came up from behind me.

Beneath me the colors of the flowers were smeared through the glass, blending with the reflection of the gray clouds. I noticed the gray-green mountains, and for the first time I caught sight of the perennial ice field in the valley above me. It too was reflected on the glass. Now my breath was gone. I was stuck for a moment, suspended above the blur of red and purple, the blue of the wisteria. The glass was warm to the touch, yet so was the sky, the stone, the ice, and I could not breathe as the glass was about to crack into dagger shards.

"Cecil . . ." His rich voice was calm. "The roof is more stable on the ridgeline. Just a little bit more. Try to spread your weight out like a polar bear on the ice, hands, feet, stomach. Slither up. You will be fine, man."

I looked down at the garish pom-poms of the rhododendrons and sucked my way up to the ridgeline with the rope sliding along behind me. I then pulled the bucket onto the roof without breaking any more windows. I prepared the frame, spread the putty, and gently replaced the pane, like the last puzzle piece, and puttied the top. Sure enough, the ridgeline of the structure was more secure. I noticed that there were larger lateral ribs of plastic roof bracing the metal, and I was able to position myself over one of those. As I lay flat, I lowered the bucket to Street, then prepared to start crawling down, but on this more rigid section, the surface was slick. I distributed my weight; I took in the view one more time. I saw the wind push a green puff of pollen up on the forest hillside, and then a large hackle-throated raven landed on the greenhouse roof to scold me for my foolishness. I lifted my head and neck to look at him, and as I did, I started to slide, bumping quickly down the entire length of the roof until I landed on the rocky apron around the side of the greenhouse.

I was out of breath, and my head hurt. A few little sparkles danced in my eyes before Fourth Street stood over me, smiling.

"Nicely done, Cecil." He bent over to help me up with very little effort. I don't think I had any of my own weight on my feet as he lifted my face to his and kissed me on the lips for a full ten seconds, biting down gently with his teeth where my lip was bleeding from the fall.

6
NON-CONTACT VISIT

I didn't discuss the kiss with Street as we walked back to the unit. He just talked about what a good job I had done on the greenhouse. We went different directions when we approached the central control area. I indicated I was headed to my unit, and he simply rubbed my back and said, "Tomorrow then, my man. Tomorrow we will talk more," and they buzzed him through to his section.

I did my best to avoid him the next day. Shawn Day shot me hard eyes at the library and tried to slip me a note. I gave it back to her.

"He wants to see your ass," was all she said.

"I'm working," I said.

Shawn Day made a turn like a runway model and walked away with a great deal of style, so much so that the pedophile at the nearest table stared for a moment with wide eyes of sexless curiosity.

Late in the afternoon, my heart sank when I got notification from a guard that I had a request for a non-contact visit in one of the new bigger legal cells. Visits from lawyers were rarely good. I made my way down the stairs and through the gates. Near the central staircase by the admin tower was a row of visiting rooms. The newest one, a combination of two rooms, had been created for a spate of cases involving multiple defendants with their various lawyers. Some of them were gang-related, but the prison system didn't build the room until a large group of legislators and a governor were arrested on conspiracy charges.

When I got to the room I looked through the pane and saw my entire family inside. My chest felt like shattered glass. Jane Marie was flipping through papers she had taken out of a large manila envelope. Blossom and George sat looking at their hands, and Todd, poor Todd, was sitting uncomfortably. He clearly didn't want to be there. His hands were clasped together and his eyes were closed. I only hoped that he wasn't praying for me. There was a slot on the counter just large enough to pass legal papers through. We would be allowed to shake hands, though I could allow them to touch the top of my hand "in a comforting gesture" through the slot with my palms down so as not to take any tiny packages from a visitor. Still, I would be given a cavity search after the visit. The visitors had all been given a thorough pat-down screening and a very sensitive metal scan. Pens may have been unscrewed, books and paperwork may have been gone over—but not read, simply looked at—to see if any stains from hallucinogenic drugs could be detected, which was doubtful because currently it appeared that drugs were being slingshotted into the grounds attached to stones. There was one chair on the prison side for me, and the four of them sat on the other side of the barrier. We could speak through the metal grate and the slot.

I walked into this formal legal visiting room, and Jane Marie laid the papers out on the bench. I put my hands through the slot hoping to be allowed to at least touch her hands.

"Please Janie . . . those aren't divorce papers . . ."

"Jesus, no." Blossom grabbed my hand at once. "I wouldn't have come along for that, Pops. Come on!" She kissed my hand. Sweet child.

Georgie looked up at me and she was biting her lip. She waved at me like a shy little girl. Todd then took my hand. "Hello, Cecil. You really wear an orange jumpsuit every day?"

"Yep . . ." I said. "It's easy to pick out my clothes. It is good to see you all." I felt suddenly emotional. The dread I had been carrying around in my heart since the fall off the greenhouse roof was melting now, and I was worried that I was going to start crying.

"Hi," Jane Marie mumbled. "It looks like you've lost weight. You have a bruise on your lip and forearm. You okay in here?" Her eyes were sad. I could tell she didn't like seeing me in here.

"I'm fine."

She cleared her throat. "I . . . we all wanted to talk with you about something."

I interrupted Jane Marie. "I'm sorry, Jane." I stuck my right hand through the document slot to George. "We've never actually met. I'm Cecil, Blossom's dad. I bet you're Georgianna."

She shook my hand and could see the tears welling up in my eyes, and I could see the sadness in hers. "It's nice to meet you, Mr. Younger. I've heard a lot about you."

I tried to chuckle. "I suppose you have. I'm so sorry for your suffering right now, George. Call me whatever you like now. You can guess we aren't all that formal." I gestured around the room. Here, she smiled.

"I have a lot of good jokes to tell you, Cecil," Todd blurted out. Jane Marie let out a long breath. Blossom looped her arm through Todd's and squeezed him close, cutting him off before he launched into one.

"Oh, Pops. You won't believe some of them. They are sooo good. I promised Todd we could come visit and have nothing but joke time."

"And I want to hear them, Todd . . . I do. But I think Jane Marie has something important she needs me to take care of, and I think we don't have much time."

Todd had his tight-lipped "I will keep quiet" face on as Blossom kept squeezing him.

Tears were falling down my cheeks now; my heart was full of love for these people.

"Cecil," Jane Marie began again, "we need to talk with you about George, and you are correct, time is kind of short"—here she looked at her wristwatch—"because they told me they are going to need this room in a few minutes. I understand that Blossom has told you about George's situation?"

I nodded and looked around at the group.

"Well, the Division of Family and Youth Services has gotten involved. Mr. Teller has helped her get a good public attorney, and the court has appointed a guardian ad litem already. Things are moving right along."

"Okay . . ." I said, looking at George this time. "How do you feel about that, George?"

"It's confusing . . . I guess. They tell me I get some time to think about it and they will listen to what I want, but . . . but you know . . . I don't know." And there she stopped, looking up at the ceiling. Her eyes were sparkling with tears similar to mine. "They really, really want me to live with these new people, the Thompsons, who are, apparently, my biological parents."

"I understand. It's really hard." I looked back at Jane Marie. "What can we do?"

"Well"—she took a deep breath—"I have asked to be a foster parent to George during this interim while she is thinking about things." Jane Marie was carefully choosing her words.

"Poppa, now don't get mad," Blossom said softly.

"Mad?" I looked around.

"The problem came up that you and I are still married, and, Cecil, you are a convicted felon."

There was silence for a good long moment. A metal door slammed shut in the background, and a couple of wise guys made faces at my family behind my shoulders. Todd was smiling at them.

"Okay . . ." I said. "What do you want me to do?"

"This form says that you won't have any more contact with George and will not be in our home for four years, or for the period that George is in foster care. Everyone is sure it won't take that long, but I have to be approved for the length of time that she might possibly need care. All it really means is that if you sign these papers, there is a good chance they will approve my application."

"I might get out of here in less than three years. I mean, I should."

"We know . . ." Blossom said, "but everything is going to all be worked out way before that. Mr. Teller is going to get her dad off and they will be living together again. Don't worry about that, Pops."

A buzzer sounded loudly on the freedom side of the room. Jane Marie turned around and yelled, "One second!" Then I motioned with my fingers to have her slide the papers under. I saw that they needed to be notarized and pointed that out to Jane Marie, who stood up and opened the door. A short woman from the administrative staff walked in with a book and a notary stamp. She also had a laptop in which she could look up my booking picture to confirm my identification. I signed the affidavit. Jane Marie did not touch my fingers as I gave the papers back to her. I was crying loudly as they filed out. Todd was confused, for he thought I wanted to hear a joke. Blossom lingered and put her hands flat on the glass above the iron grating.

"Poppa, I love you so much. I will still be able to come visit you in the other visiting room during the regular times. Don't worry about this. You are my hero. Poppa, I couldn't love you any more than I do right now. Forever. Forever."

Then the little notary public touched her elbow and said only, "Please, miss," and they left.

If it was true that someone else needed the room, they were screwed, because head count started just then, and I got caught on my side of the visiting room for forty-five minutes. I made good use of the time, sitting on the floor crying my guts out. There are moments in prison when your emotional barriers are up and it feels somehow correct to be behind doors of steel and away from the squishy sensitivity of the world. This was not one of those moments. This was a moment when somehow the world found a way to squeeze between the bars and slide a ragged sliver of ice into my heart and leave it there.

Later that same day a woman from the Division of Family and Youth Services came by *The Winning Hand* and took George to meet her biological parents. George had not wanted to meet with them, and had either forgotten to tell anyone that a meeting had been prearranged, or was trying to blow it off. But when the large white woman in open-toed sandals and a Mexican-style dress showed up at the boat with her wet wool coat over her shoulder, George did not act all that surprised, and she went with her quickly so as not to draw attention from Blossom or Jane Marie.

The social worker was tired and it was clear that she had been browbeaten into coming down to the boat to get George, for as they walked up the ramp to the harbor parking lot, her chipper-sounding voice was cracking, and the irritation was beginning to show.

"It's really fine, but it's just that I have a very full afternoon and the Thompsons are so, so anxious to meet you. I think you are really, really going to enjoy meeting them," she said as she dug around in her shoulder bag for a notebook and pen to document the time of day and her location.

"Do you have big animals?" George asked.

"Why do you ask that?" the social worker asked with a frown.

"Your bag . . . it smells funny, like a wet goat or something."

"It's from Mexico . . . and very old." The tired woman fished out her car keys, then beeped open the car locks on the little compact, which did indeed have dog hair all over the inside.

"Just get in," she said, "and let's remember our manners when we meet the Thompsons. First impressions are *critical.*"

By the time they arrived at the old refurbished apartment building that now housed a state agency, they were not speaking at all. On the way over, George had listened to more of the social worker's backstory about how hard her job was and how this "unexpected trip" had thrown a "hiccup into things" and that it was still okay, but "we can't make a habit of this because unfortunately we are really very busy and not everything can come to a standstill for one person's mistake, even though it's perfectly understandable and okay."

When the social worker opened the door to what had surely been a child's bedroom long ago, there was a metal desk piled with papers, a row of filing cabinets, and a stair-stepping machine in the corner. Some gray metal chairs along the windows led to an interior alley space, where Mr. and Mrs. Thompson were sitting. Mrs. Thompson was a small Tlingit woman wearing a blue suit with a stiff skirt and white blouse. She held a bundle of flowers in her hand. Mr. Thompson was a thin white man with khaki pants and an expensive synthetic pullover sweater. He held a very large teddy bear in his hands. He seemed to be hugging it himself. They looked up at George with wide eyes and impossible expectations.

"Okay . . . we don't have as much time as I thought we did but . . . here we are." The social worker kept looking at her files and gestured over to the frightened adults. "Georgianna, these are the Thompsons."

Mrs. Thompson had tears in her eyes as she stood up. Mr. Thompson had an awkward smile as he appraised the young woman. They both held out their gifts at the same time, their arms hitting, the flowers getting caught under the bear's arm.

"Hello," George said, smiling, trying to be polite.

"Hello," Kristy Thompson said in a very soft voice and much the same way as George had spoken.

"Come here . . ." Thomas said, and he grabbed George, then hugged her while still holding the big bear. When he patted George's back in the embrace, he was actually patting the toy.

"Thank you, God," he said. Then a strange sort of groan came from his lungs. He clung to George for a long moment until the social worker came forward and touched his arm and George's shoulder.

"Okay . . . okay . . . good, but we don't want to go too quickly with physical contact, remember? We discussed this. We all are going to need some time."

Thomas Thompson backed up. His jaws were tight, and he wiped his eyes. George could see he was angry at the social worker, angry at her tone.

Mrs. Thompson asked in a meek voice, "But could I give her a small hug?"

"You heard what the woman said, Kristy." It wasn't a snap or a bite at his wife, but the way Mr. Thompson said it so quickly and then tried to turn it into a joke with an awkward, toothy smile, made George wonder what was going on.

"Yes, I understand," Mrs. Thompson said, and handed the flowers to George. George took them and then gave Mrs. Thompson a hug and a kiss on the cheek. She later wondered why she had done that, but there was something about the woman that made George want to make her happy.

"Oh, for pity sakes, don't listen to me then," the social worker said, and plopped herself behind the desk. "Go ahead. You three should sit down and talk. We have about twenty minutes left for this meeting. I will just be here trying to catch up on my reports. If you have any questions, feel free to interrupt me." She gave the three of them her best overworked public servant smile and made a show of picking up a huge pile of files from her desk and putting it back down in the same place. Taking the top file, she opened it and began to read.

George pulled her chair up so they were all sitting knee to knee.

"They tell me that you are my biological parents," she said softly, not wanting to involve the social worker.

"We are," Thomas said. "Absolutely, scientifically, your parents. We took the swabs."

Kristy touched the top of George's hand with the tips of her fingers. "That's what they tell us too—that we are your parents." She smiled. "What do you think?"

"It's hard to understand right now," George said after a moment.

"I know," Kristy Thompson said. "I knew Ida Paul, you know. I wish she were here now."

"Boy, so do I," Thomas said angrily.

Kristy gave him a hard glance, and he stared down at the glass eyes of the teddy bear.

"I wish she were here to tell me about your growing up. I wish she could tell me everything about you, about what you like to eat and what they got you for Christmas and where you have been on vacation. That kind of stuff. Ida Paul could have been such a help to me now."

"When she died, at first it felt like I was going to die too. I miss her so much," said George.

Thomas let out a breath and shifted in his chair, impatient.

"I know you do," was all Kristy Thompson said. Then for a long time George sat and squeezed the teddy bear, crying onto the petals of the grocery-store roses that had been cut in Mexico and had pricked the hands of a dozen or more brown-skinned women before they made it all the way to Alaska to collect the tears of these broken-hearted women, all while Thomas sat in an uncomfortable chair flexing his hands into fists.

Kristy cleared her throat and spoke. "Did you know you have a little sister as well? Her name is Lilly."

"Yes," George said, "I read that about you guys. She sounds nice."

"She is very nice," said Thomas. "Very well-behaved and very sweet. I think there is no reason that you two won't get along perfectly."

"No," George said.

After some time, the social worker got a call on her phone, then told the group that her next appointment was in the outer office. She wearily showed them to the door, where she introduced them to the office's temporary secretary, who had been called in from home to drive George back to *The Winning Hand.* The secretary and George had barely made it out of the office building before Shannon Lakeside found them, and a photographer was in wait to snap George and Kristy's tentative goodbye hug. The photograph appeared on the front page of the next day's paper with the headline: FAMILY RESTORED; AWAITS JUSTICE.

7

A CASE OF BAD FACTS

Final exams were the next day at Juneau-Douglas High School. Blossom and George sat out on the back deck of *The Winning Hand* early in the morning studying for their tests. Blossom was sprawled out on an overturned inflatable skiff in the sunshine reading through the notes she had written in the margins of her chemistry textbook, and George was in a hammock in the rigging with her laptop working on a take-home test her Alaska history teacher had given her. Blossom looked down at a file of old homework papers she had kept and riffled through them to check on a formula that she was memorizing.

"Jeepers, I can't wait for school to be over . . . just a couple of days," Blossom said.

"B?" George asked.

"Yeah?"

"I really don't want to move in with my biological parents."

"Okay . . ." Blossom said, not looking away from her formula, "but I thought you kind of liked the mom?"

"Yeah . . . I just don't want to move in with them. Something about the guy gives me the creeps."

"Okay."

"I think they're gonna make me move in with them . . . will you help me?"

"Sure, of course I'll help. I know my mom is working on it so you can just stay here with us." Blossom stretched and looked at the old Timex on her wrist. "Jeepers, I gotta go take this freaking test."

Then Blossom was up off the inflatable skiff with her books and her backpack, over the gunwales, and off to school across the highway. Such was their absolute confidence in each other's friendship that they never discussed the problem of George living with her biological parents again.

That afternoon, the staff of Free Younger Investigations had an impromptu meeting in the open activities room at school. The spring energy was high among the underclass students. Seniors were all gone on the senior sneak and the juniors were sowing their oats as the new rulers of the school: boys were running and jumping to see how high they could reach toward the ceiling, and they were pulling down old spring dance posters. Smaller students hid in storage spaces and jumped out at girls walking past talking seriously about summer plans. Everyone wanted to be out of the building.

Blossom had found Ned astraddle his BMW motorcycle in the parking lot, helmet on, wanting nothing more than to ride out into the sunshine on Douglas Island, maybe up the winding road to the ski hill just for the fun of it. But Blossom took his helmet off and convinced him that she would go with him later if he would come in for the meeting first.

Ned, George and Blossom sat in the nearly empty activities room. They were all feeling good about their tests, for they were all decent students, and even though George was sad and distracted, the teachers were cutting her quite a bit of slack.

"Now," Blossom began, "George doesn't want to move in with her bio parents. I think the best thing is that we help make sure her father is not convicted, and that she remains with him. Agreed?"

George looked at Ned and then back at Blossom. Ned cleared his throat. "I have something that I wanted to tell you two."

"What?" George asked, a little worried.

"Mr. Teller offered me a job this summer. He knows that my dad is a cop. He also somehow knew that I have a good driving record. I dunno how he knew that, but he and Mr. Betts want to live out at the Shrine as much as they can. Teller wants me to run messages on my bike back and forth from his house to the courthouse and the office. He wants me to file things and deliver the copies first to the office and then to him. Sometimes I will drive his truck. I will maintain his office in town. There is another thing, B . . ."

"What?"

"He wants to talk to you. He says that Mr. Betts is going to have to interview you first to see how much you know about the case. If you are a witness, then you can't work for him, but if you aren't a witness, then he wants to give you a job too."

The meeting of FYI was adjourned and quickly reconvened an hour later at the new temporary office site in the flats near the federal building. When they arrived, there was a stunning blond woman in a tight blood-red dress with perfect black fingernails typing very fast from a dictation machine. Blossom could hear Mr. Teller's voice rattling off case names as fast as automatic gunfire on the dictation machine. The woman's eyes were closed as she typed. The room was full of taped-together banker's boxes and odd pieces of furniture: a black captain's chair, what looked like an old chaise longue, a beach chair, a rough-hewn coffin with rope handles, an iron bed frame and a very large oak rolltop desk. The typist was sitting on a large blue plastic ball. The three young people stood in front of her, and eventually she opened her eyes. At first she didn't focus, but when she did, she slowly reached down into her desk and lifted a small blue piece of gum and started chewing it.

Then, as if the gum had magically woken her from a trance, she looked at them. "Hello," she said flatly, "I was just typing this bullshit motion for Harrison. He likes to file at least two or three bullshit motions when he first gets assigned a case to lull everyone into a false sense of security and then WHAM!" she slapped her hand down on the desk, causing the three of them to jump. "Then the substantial motions start rolling in one after another and everyone starts freaking the fuck out."

Her voice was soothing and a little oily, almost as if she were a bit drunk, but the most startling thing about her was that her eyes were two different colors. One eye was deep blue like a prized marble and the other was sea-glass green and a bit hazy, as if it had been damaged.

"My name is Darcy. I'm his girl Friday. His invaluable, irreplaceable girl Friday." She looked at the three of them standing there like unpacked Russian dolls. "I bet you are Ned, Blossom Younger and George Paul, come to rescue me."

They shook hands all around and without much preliminary discussion of work or wages, they started putting together shelving and moving filing cabinets, opening banker's boxes and putting books on shelves. Harrison Teller was old-school. He did not like to read legal cases online. He preferred books. Prosecutors and police now shared evidence electronically, but Teller had Darcy print everything out and put it all in notebooks, just as it had been done thirty years ago.

Teller still approached witnesses on the stand and handed them papers, even if it was possible to zap a document onto a monitor. No matter how much a judge objected, Teller had a very compelling motion to be filed allowing for a physical chain of evidence to start with the attorney of record. Teller loved the drama of the click of the three-ring notebook, the removal of the paper and the walk to the stand, just to refresh the memory of a recalcitrant witness, particularly if it was a police officer. He was not giving that up for the sake of the court or the prosecution's convenience. "The Constitution does not protect the state's convenience, Your Honor, but it does protect the hard-won recognition of my client's rights to keep the evidence well out of the clutches of any *virtual* reality!" he had said on more than one occasion.

After setting up the sparse suite of offices, Darcy brought in a large bag of popcorn and a case of cold bottles of apple juice of a brand that the young people did not recognize.

"Harrison buys these in bulk and has them flown in. Try it; it's organic and unfiltered. The bathroom is down the hall, if you get my drift," she smirked. She put the treats on the floor along with a big pile of police reports and grand jury transcripts.

The members of FYI sprawled out on the floor like Great Dane puppies and started reading the evidence against Richard Paul. They propped their heads on their backpacks and shoveled popcorn into their mouths as they traded the files around.

After a couple of hours and several trips to the bathroom for the entire investigative team, Harrison Teller blew into the office like a storm squall.

“Hey, looks good in here. Nice job with the shelves and the furniture. How is the bullshit motion coming, Darce?” he asked, while digging through his leather shoulder bag.

“Draft is on your desk, needs some punching up. Sign it and file it.”

“Sweet . . . I can’t wait to hear the howling begin.” He found what he was looking for and fished out the newspaper with the headline concerning the restored family awaiting justice, and he threw the paper down into the pile of puppies.

“Do not talk to the press. Do not get photographed . . . unless we talk about it first.”

The group of them looked up at him. Each one of them had dozens of questions and concerns, and none of them had seen the paper. George saw it first, then Blossom, who pulled it from her friend’s hands.

“Jesus H. Criminy,” Blossom said under her breath. “You got used, George.”

“Exactly,” the attorney said. He slipped out of his heavy coat as if he were a bear removing his skin and threw it on the floor, then slumped into the old captain’s chair. “Now, I’ve read enough of the evidence to know that I can’t hire you, Blossom; it could be viewed as tampering with a witness. I can talk with you, but I cannot advise you in any official capacity. I cannot pay you, but I can pay Ned here, and what he does with his money is his business. Blossom, you can speak to the prosecution or the cops if you want to, but you do not have to if you do not want to. It is perfectly okay to tell them that you will obey the orders of the court and you will obey the subpoenas they give you. I am telling you that you should always, always, listen to the questions and tell the truth when you testify. Do you understand? If asked, that is what I am telling you. And you too, George. Are we all clear?"

Both George and Blossom nodded.

"Okay . . . and clearly, George, I can't pay you. If you want to talk with me or Mr. Betts, I have to get permission from your guardian ad litem, as well as your foster parent, which I understand is soon going to be Blossom's mom, right?"

"Yes, Mr. Teller," she nodded again.

"Okay, and as far as reading any of this material," he motioned to the police reports and grand jury testimony, "it is my position that you have a right under the Victim Rights statute to have access to this material as long as I don't discuss this with you or ask you your opinion about it. Which I have not, have I?" He paused and looked at her. "You need to answer, sweetie."

"No . . . ah . . . no sir, you haven't asked me about anything, Mr. Teller," George stuttered slightly.

"But we want to help Mr. Paul. George doesn't want to live with the Thompsons," Blossom blurted out.

"Where George ends up living is none of my concern, Blossom. My job is to represent Mr. Paul in his criminal charges of child stealing . . . I'm sorry. I can't use you two girls." Here he gestured limply with his hand to the door.

Blossom got up off the floor and grabbed her backpack. "Lawyers! Well, you are not in charge of me, anyway. I can do what I want to do, right?"

"That's right."

"Come on, George." She looked at her pal. "And I'll talk to whomever I want to talk to, and I don't care what you say." Then she kicked the newspaper on the floor.

"Yes . . . I imagine you will . . . but, Blossom, be careful around the Thompsons. Who they are and why Ida Paul got involved with them is key to our case. I won't have you mucking it up. You understand?"

"Oh yeah?" Now Blossom looked hard at the lawyer. She wasn't sure what she was going to say next. "Well . . . you . . . you . . . just stay out of my way too!" she said. Then she grabbed George's arm and walked out.

They were halfway down the stairwell when George giggled and said, " 'You stay out of my way too'? That was some nice badass comeback, girl! I liked it better when you swore like a logger."

"Fuck you . . . I know it was lame . . . Jeepers. Ned says cursing is violent. He says it's the precursor to assaultive behavior, anyway." She looked back down the street. "Do you think I should go and tell off that arrogant fuck again? What should I have said?"

"You could have just added that he was a big poo-poo head. That would have sealed it pretty well." They both laughed and stepped out onto the street.

Soon enough Ned caught up to them on his motorcycle. He pulled up ahead of them and got off, removing his helmet at the same time.

"Mr. Bond," Blossom said in her best fake Scottish accent. "Delightful party. Pity I wasn't invited."

"Jeepers, B. I don't make the rules. I only took the job because I thought I was going to see you more. I thought you would . . . you know . . . I thought you would dig it."

"Dig it? Jeepers. When did you get all sixties all of a sudden?"

"Cram it, Moneypenny," Ned sulked.

"I am not Moneypenny!" She slugged him on the side of his arm, denting the sleeve of his leather driving jacket.

"Fine, pick your own Bond babe name."

"Alotta Fagina," George whispered.

"Gross," Blossom said.

"Crimson Crotchsylvania," she said a little louder.

"Will you stop it, please. I'm not going with a Bond babe name."

"Plateface Poopsie?"

"I am going to become violent, I promise."

"I'm sorry . . . I'm losing it." George looked at her. Tears were running down her face, and she was both laughing and crying. "I forgot"—here she looked at her watch—"I promised my dad I would try to visit him today."

Blossom looked at her own watch and then hugged her friend. "You have time. Maybe our errand boy can run you out there right now. Ned?"

Ned nodded and started to put his helmet on, but Blossom stopped him. She walked over to him, then kissed him on the cheek. "You are sweet. I think it's great you took that job with Teller. It's good. We will be together more. I think he wants me poking around on my own. I think he wants me and you to work together. He as much as said so." And she kissed him again. Ned looked shocked, happy and a little sleepy all at once, as if she had made him drink a shot of mescal.

"Wake up now, lover boy. You got to get my girl to the jail on time." Then Blossom patted him on the cheek.

"What are you going to do, B?" he asked as he gave George his helmet to wear.

"I'm going to look into some stuff. I'll talk to you both later, okay?"

They both gave a thumbs-up from the bike and were off.

Blossom drove the blue Le Car to the middle school, arriving just as the girls' track team was getting out of the showers. The track season went past the end of school in southeastern Alaska to make use of the good weather in this part of the world. The sunniest months of the year are April, May and June, so track had its final meets in the middle of June, when school had already been out for ten days.

Blossom was sitting in her car with the large fabric sun roof pulled back, scrolling through her phone, looking at the track-and-field roster and trying to enlarge the team photo so she could recognize the face of Lilly Thompson.

The girls were spilling out onto the sidewalk. Some were tying their hair back; others were combing their hair out with their fingers in the sun. Almost all of them wore sweats and T-shirts and had bags slung over their shoulders. They walked in twos or threes, talking or joking. Most walked slowly, clearly tired from their workout. Two or three walked directly to cars or vans with adults behind the wheel. Others stood around waiting. Then Blossom noticed a mousy girl shuffling by herself, head down, big glasses steamed up, brown hair tangled and wet over her ears. Blossom bolted from the car.

"Hey, Lilly . . . hey . . ." she blurted.

"Hey?" Lilly stopped and stepped back.

"I'm Blossom Younger from Juneau-Douglas. I'm friends with your new sister, Georgianna Paul. She is too shy to come talk with you herself, but she really wants to meet you."

"Really?" Lilly picked at her wet hair with the tips of her fingers. "How'd you find me?"

"I read in the paper that you were in middle school and then I looked you up online and saw you were on the track team. That's pretty cool, that you are a runner."

"Yeah . . . I don't like it. My dad says I'm fat."

"That's crazy. You look great. You can probably eat whatever you want after all that running."

Lilly hunched her shoulders, looked down, and kept pulling at her hair.

"How do you feel about getting a brand-new sister?" Blossom spoke out in a big happy voice.

"Good . . . I guess," Lilly whispered.

Blossom noticed that Lilly hugged her gym bag in front of her as if she were naked.

"How are you getting home?" Blossom asked. "Because you could call your folks, and I could talk with them if you want, and I could give you a ride after you clear it with them. You know, they could check me out and everything. They would probably want to meet me because I'm a really good friend of George's and all. How about that?"

Still looking down at her feet, Lilly said, "My dad will be here in a second. You probably shouldn't be here when he comes. He doesn't like me talking to people."

"Really? I'm cool. I can show him my school ID. I go to school with George. I'm like her best friend. I really want to meet him. I really want to get to know you too."

Lilly's hands started to shake as a black VW van with oversized tires pulled up. Her voice cracked. "I . . . I got to go. Don't come over, please. Don't look at me." As the door on the passenger's side opened suddenly, the girl clambered in. Blossom took a step toward the van, which had tinted windows all around, but the hidden driver jammed the transmission into reverse and squealed the tires out of the parking lot.

"What the heck?" Blossom said to herself, as she stood in a cloud of burnt-tire smoke. Then she looked around at a couple of the other track girls who were watching the van drive away. "What's that about?" Blossom asked them vaguely.

The girls shrugged, then one finally said, "Her dad is weird. Very over-protective."

"No kidding," another chimed in.

"I feel sorry for her," said another.

"She used to be, you know, a little plump, kinda, but now she only brings celery and raisins in her lunch."

"Bummer," the first one wrapped it up.

"Yeah . . . bummer," Blossom said, getting back into her own car and starting the engine.

That same day, the newspaper made the rounds of Lemon Creek Correctional Center, and Richard Paul was let out into general population. He was assigned to my dorm, and once he was dressed out and had his bedding, he came into the unit and made his bunk. He would be here for a while, until, and if, he got a two-person cell. He ate lunch and sat with other Native inmates.

I didn't speak with him because I was with Street's crew, and I had not been given permission to talk with the new fish. Street had no policy on Mr. Paul as of yet. He was unprotected as far as I knew. But there was a lot of loose talk about someone who would allow his white wife to steal a Native baby. There was no good reason for anyone to beat down Mr. Paul, but reason has very little to do with prison violence. Deep in prison there is always someone who believes that there is something good to be gained from being the most violent man around.

So, after lunch, when Richard Paul went back to his

bunk, a group of young men of mixed ethnicity grabbed him, put his pillowcase over his head, took him into the shower room and beat him with bars of soap in gym socks until he stopped moving. Afterwards, they carried him to his bunk and replaced the pillowcase with a clean one. When Mr. Paul regained consciousness, it was explained to him that he had fallen down the stairs and that if he reported anything different, he could expect to continue falling down the stairs every other day.

Mr. Paul did not report the incident to prison authorities. When a guard noticed his injuries, he told the guard that he had indeed fallen down the stairs and that he would be more careful. The guard took him in and offered him protective segregation, which Mr. Paul declined. He did call Mr. Teller and told him of the attack. Which was when I received my first visit from the illustrious attorney.

"You are looking well," Harrison Teller said as he leaned back in his metal chair behind the glass.

"As are you, sir," I said.

"Yeah. You know who is not looking well, Cecil, is my fucking client, Richard Paul. What did you shitbirds do to him in here?"

"Hold on now. I didn't do anything to your client."

"But you know who did."

"Some troubled youth. What the fuck you want me to do about it?"

"I want you to make fucking sure it doesn't happen again. That's what I want." Teller lurched forward and tapped on the glass with his large index finger.

"Who do you think I am, Pablo Escobar?"

"Cecil . . . I know you. I also notice you are not cut up. I know you are not in protective segregation. I know other people in here. I know who you are hooked up with."

"You don't know what you know. Nobody does."

"What, are you a philosopher now?"

"Prison makes a philosopher out of everyone." I stood up and banged on the prison side of the glass for a guard.

"Wait . . . wait . . . calm down," Teller said more softly now. "I have seen your daughter. You know she helped put my office together. You know, kind of off the books. We had brunch. I took her to the range. Blossom is a really great girl."

It was my turn to bring my face close to the glass. "Harrison, you are NOT threatening my child. Do you remember what I am serving time for? You must remember that I too have friends on the outside, friends who would do me favors."

"What are you talking about, Cecil?"

"You endanger yourself and your family by bringing my daughter into this discussion."

"Prison really has changed you."

"I haven't changed that much. It's just that you have no idea how condescending you have always been and how much I have hated you for that."

Harrison Teller sat up straight and squinted through the thick glass at me. He was studying me as if for the first time. Back on the prison side, iron doors slammed shut and buzzers blared, guards keyed their mics. Bars slid and rattled on their tracks while prisoners, with their soft-soled shoes, squeaked down the painted concrete floors.

"Fair enough," he said finally. "I can see that, but I can't change the past." He held his palms up, empty-handed, on the ledge in front of the document slot. "You see, Cecil, right now, my client is in this jail with you and he is in grave danger. I'm asking you to help him if you can. I would never do anything to jeopardize your daughter. I swear on my own children's lives."

He looked at me and his eyes didn't sparkle as they did when he was meeting women or fighting with a judge. Instead, he seemed deflated, out of energy.

"You know prisoners," I told him. "They have their own self-serving code. They feed on the weak in repudiation of their crimes against the weak."

He smiled at me. "But aren't you in with a strong man?"

"No. Not really. I am like a mouse a cat plays with before eating. At least that is how it seems to me now. How influential I am all depends on how hungry he is at the moment and how much kick I have left in my legs to get away."

He drummed his fingers on the shelf. I could tell he was running through arguments in his head to convince me, probably conjuring dollar amounts and methods of payment to bribe me to help his client. But I interrupted him before he could start working me over with his charm.

"I will do what I can for Mr. Paul. I will do it for Blossom, because she loves Georgianna, and because George loves her pop. I will work for you on this so that I will officially be under attorney-client protection. At least that's what I will tell any court that tries to get me to testify against him for statements made to me here in jail. I am working for you. I will remind him not to talk to anyone else. No jailhouse lawyers. No snitches. No more beatings, if I can work it, but I cannot promise that. He might have to live in protective seg."

"I will tell him that," Teller said. "We will talk about payment later."

"You should pay Blossom. Help her figure out the paperwork, the taxes and any permits she might need in Juneau. I don't want her to get in any trouble with the law.

She will be in enough trouble already when her mother finds out. Leave my name out of this if her mother comes after you, okay? And if Blossom doesn't want to do any work, she doesn't have to. Understood?"

"Understood." Harrison Teller stuck his hand through the narrow slot, and I shook it.

"You will vouch for her safety, and I will do my best for your clients. That's the best I can do."

"Yes . . . I understand, and I acknowledge your trust in me, Cecil."

With that, he stood up and rang his buzzer. I slapped the glass on my door and waved to get a guard's attention. We stared at each other for a few seconds in the silence of locked metal doors. His door buzzed, then clicked. He nodded and walked free. I stood in place another twenty-five minutes before someone came by to let me out into the main body of the noisy prison, and with that, the Free Younger Investigations had taken on its first official case, with me as an auxiliary staff member.

Mr. Paul looked rough by the time I got to him the next day. He was hiding in his bunk. The bruising had darkened to a deep black around his swollen eyes. His forearms were swollen where he had tried to shield himself, and I could tell it hurt him to laugh or sit up. I let him lie flat as I introduced myself again, because I wasn't sure he could see me or recognize me at all. Someone was treating him good, because he had a paper towel wrapped around some slivers of ice covering his cheeks to help reduce the swelling. I went through the basics: That I had been contacted by his lawyer to watch out for him. That I was Blossom's dad. He nodded and indicated he knew my story, that he knew and liked B.

I told him that I didn't want to talk about the case right then, because the first rule that he had to understand was not to talk about the case. He needed to talk with Teller about me before he told me anything. He understood. At least he nodded that he understood, and he did not give any indication that he was going to talk in detail about anything. I told him not to talk with the prison authorities about his beating. Just say that he didn't see or know anything about who did it. But it was okay to tell me if he knew anything, any small detail, that might give me a clue to help figure out who had been involved in the beating or had wanted it done. He could tell me, and I could try to find out who did it. He said "Irish Spring soap" with great difficulty. I asked if they said anything at all and he shook his head.

I looked around his dorm for any other Native guys. Two guys sat watching me with cold stares from their card game. I walked over to them and sat down.

"You know me?" I asked.

"You the public defender guy who killed that cracker in the showers," the biggest of the two said.

"That's right. I'm worried about Mr. Paul over there. Can he get to meals?"

"Yeah . . . we help him. He doesn't want to go to the infirmary. He is afraid someone might get to him there."

"What do you think? You know who did this to him?"

The little one perked up. "Why you asking us? White guys probably done it to him. They the ones all mad about his wife stealing the baby."

"Listen, you write your names down. You make sure he gets fed and is safe getting his meals. I'll put fifty bucks in your commissary accounts every two weeks."

"A hundred," they both said in unison.

"Fifty. And let's see how you do. Goes good your first two weeks, you get a bump. I make the call tomorrow. Check goes out tomorrow. Gets to your account by the end of the week. But your protection starts now. Good?"

The little one tore off the flap of the pack that the cards came in and wrote both their names and their prisoner numbers in tiny writing using a pencil he kept in his jumpsuit. Then he handed the small slip of paper to me.

"No snitching. I just want him healthy, okay? I know his family."

"Fine. If the money doesn't come by the weekend, we will let you know."

"Okay, but you bring it up with me. Don't lay a hand on him. He is not involved in my business, got it? You deal with me. He gets hurt, it's you and me."

"Sure." They looked at each other with a little doubt passing between them as if they should be asking for something additional, something up front. But it was too late.

I have to admit, slitting that peckerwood's throat in the shower room did some good for my negotiating position within the walls of prison. You really can't go wrong killing a Nazi, unless you are negotiating with another Nazi.

Shawn Day stood filing her nails in the bathroom as I walked in without an appointment. Mr. Munro was in the handicapped stall in a meeting. He had the curtains down so that no one could see under the dividers, but I could hear soft voices speaking soft words, broken only by the sound of Shawn Day stabbing aggressively at her cuticles.

She had her hair wrapped in a type of turban, in a sexy Rosie-the-Riveter "We Can Do It" wartime-poster vibe, along with the red lipstick and big biceps thing. I could tell that Shawn Day was in a peevish mood and it was best not to provoke her.

I stood waiting in silence with her while Fourth Street spoke quietly and laughed with the man in the handicapped stall. Shawn Day did not look up from her nails but cocked her head and turban from side to side like a parrot eating seeds as she worked. Soon the man came out, tucking in his T-shirt, and awkwardly walked between us as if he were interrupting an argument.

"You can go in now, Mister Rogers," Shawn Day said, without looking up.

"Shawn!" Fourth Street admonished as I walked past her. "Be nice now!"

"Oh, you be nice!" she whispered.

There were jail mattresses folded like lounge chairs on the floor. The toilet was closed and covered with a pillowcase with a mattress set close by, so that the top of the toilet could serve as a desk. Street settled here and gestured for me to sit opposite him. "So, Mr. Teller came to see you after his client was pounded down pretty hard, yes?"

"Yes. I was wondering if you know who did that piece of work on Mr. Paul."

He smiled at me. I knew that whoever did the beating would have to have gotten an okay from Street, or they could be expecting a beating in return. "I only know what others tell me. I heard that you are going to put some money in some convicts' accounts so they'll watch out for him, but they need my permission first."

"Jesus, that was fast."

"They want the money, and they are very risk averse, so they got hold of a good friend who happened to get to me before you did." He showed me his phone, which apparently had a new text on it. "Who do you think did the pounding, Teacher?"

"Mr. Paul told me it smelled like Irish Spring soap in the socks."

"And what does that tell you?"

"All it tells me is that someone wants him to think it's white boys, the boys that like to put the shamrocks on their notebooks and on their skins—Aryan Nations types—but that doesn't mean it necessarily is. It just seems too obvious."

"You are a cynical boy, Teacher. You see conspiracies. Haven't you learned that conspiracies are for fools who want to believe in order?"

"What will it take to keep him safe?"

"How safe do you want him?"

"I need him to not be touched. I need him to be able to aid in his own defense and work with his lawyer and his legal team. I am a part of that team now. My daughter is part of the team."

"How long?"

"Right now, we are talking through his trial, through the verdict. He won't deal. If he is convicted, then we will have to renegotiate an arrangement."

"An arrangement?"

"That's what I'm here to discuss."

Fourth Street leaned against his makeshift desk and patted the mattress next to him. "Then let's discuss it."

"No, I can discuss it from here."

He leaned over toward me quickly and pinned me against the wall, kissing me hard. His tongue was in my mouth and his breath was clean with some sweet mouthwash. He leaned back and my face was cupped in both his large hands.

"I want to be part of your team. I have all kinds of contacts outside and inside. I will help you get information for the case. I will protect him."

All I could see was his face. I could not move; my shoulders were trembling and I felt as if I might pass out. "What do you want in return?" I gasped.

"What I want is physical and emotional intimacy with you while we are both incarcerated. I am not a homosexual. I know you are not a homosexual, and I will not force you any further than you want to go with physical intimacy. I will treat you with as much kindness and respect as I can . . . as long as you help me in understanding how to do that."

"If I stop showing you?"

"As in any relationship, if you pull away from me . . ." Here he looked around his office and for the first time I could see in his eyes he knew how pathetic his kingdom was. I thought I could see the desperation of his loneliness. "If you pull away from me . . . I will pull away from you and . . . our relationship . . . will have changed."

"Yes, I understand." Then I leaned in and kissed him back, tentatively, but on the lips.

8
THE THIRD RAIL

"Can we just dial down the drama? I'm having a DAY," the harried social worker said over the stack of folders she cradled in her arms as she stood on the dock. "My boss is getting flak from the governor's office. Do you hear me, missy? He is getting bad press because people are wondering why they haven't seen pictures of you reunited with your parents!" This was a Monday.

George squinted at her carefully. "Why in the hell did you carry those files down here to the boat to pick me up? You just carry them to look overworked."

"I'm running late. I didn't remember the freaking slip number of this miserable boat. I couldn't find your file, so I just brought them all and flipped through them on the way down here. Come on, just cut me a little slack now and grab your stuff. You are going to the Thompsons' for a couple of weeks. Right now. Pronto."

"Those files are just a prop," George whispered as she turned on the deck to go to her stateroom, "to let people see how hard you work."

"I heard that, girl! Let's move it. You are not my only customer today."

George jammed clothes, notebooks, toiletries, a phone, a computer, some cords and three books (one sci-fi novel by Lovecraft, one nonfiction about Alaskan whales and a book-sized notebook of evidence in her father's case) into a large duffel bag and wrote a note to Blossom and Jane Marie, who were out in the skiff looking for resident Orca whales. She placed the note on the galley table and lumbered out onto the deck, jumped to the dock and left to go stay with her biological parents for the first time in her life.

The social worker seemed to do nothing but sigh for the entire drive. When they arrived at the Thompsons' house, Mrs. Thompson and Lilly were sitting out in the backyard. George made a point of not speaking to the tired social worker and jumped out of the car waving to Mrs. Thompson and the girl. The social worker was already staring at the top of the next file when she drove away.

The small house was on the eastern edge of the flats, just one street up from the federal building at the foot of the hill that ran up to the governor's mansion. Gold Creek ran through a park just east of the house and along the edge of the property, but the creek was channeled into a concrete spillway and was partitioned off from all the yards by a metal fence. Most of the houses on the flats were built in the thirties or forties, but the majority had been remodeled. The Thompsons did not seem to have had much work done to their place. It was one of those old kit homes divided up into small dark rooms. The tired wooden floors sagged and announced every movement throughout the structure. Large window openings were filled by small panes held in place with soft wood and dark-stained putty.

They had pulled out the carpet long ago to keep the mildew smell down, but the oil-fired furnace had pooled up so many times there was always a hint of fuel in the rooms.

Mrs. Thompson came running to greet George from the yard, where it looked like she and Lilly were playing cards on a green metal table down by the creek. Lilly stayed at the table holding her cards in her hand and flicking them with her left thumb while kicking her feet back and forth.

"There you are. I'm glad to see you," Mrs. Thompson said softly. "I was worried that they didn't prepare you enough for this visit. Are you okay with it really?" She looked concerned.

"No . . . I was surprised. But I'm okay . . . ah . . . Mrs. Thompson." George put her duffel down near the gate.

"Well, we should talk about what we're going to call each other. But there will be time for that later. Would you like something to eat?" And with that, Kristy Thompson picked up the duffel bag and walked around to the back door and into the house.

The room they had set up for George looked to have at one time been the dining room. There were large windows that looked up the hill out back. There was a nice big bed, a desk and a small dresser. The odd thing was that there were two big glass doors that opened right out into the living room, which was quite small. There was a small dining-room table set up in one corner of the living room, near the door to the front steps and opposite the kitchen, which was long and narrow, with very little room. Besides the dining room, there was Lilly's room, a bathroom and then the parents' bedroom. The glass doors to George's bedroom had wool blankets covering them to give her privacy.

Mrs. Thompson set George's bag on the bed and then

sat in the desk chair with her hands resting on her lap. George came in and opened the zipper of her bag, then sat silently on the bed.

They waited.

Tears came to Mrs. Thompson's eyes. She cleared her throat. "It's strange, don't you think, to come to a new place and see things for the first time, knowing that soon they are going to be so familiar? Don't you think it's strange? How everything looks so weird and different, maybe even frightening, but soon it will all be"—she lifted her hands, palms-up, to her daughter's room, to the world really—"soon it will be so familiar and ordinary."

George saw the tears on her cheeks but didn't know what to make of them. "I hope Lilly isn't unhappy about this room, or about me."

"No," Mrs. Thompson said. She was about to say more but stopped herself for a moment before continuing. "We . . . we . . . will have some trouble with Dad." She paused again. Then she smiled. "He is so enthusiastic. He wants you to call him Dad, and he was the one who wanted you to move in right away. I told him you would need time, that you couldn't be forced into anything. You had to choose us. No matter what anyone says. You have to choose us. I know that, Georgianna." She wiped her eyes.

George reached across the short distance and took her hands in her own. "Thank you," she said softly. "Thank you for saying that just now."

They sat for a few more minutes without speaking. Outside, the varied thrushes sang in the trees out by the creek, and the leaves of the two mountain ash trees in the yard by the front of the house dappled the light that filtered into her room. Soon enough Lilly's voice broke through the window.

"Mom, can I have more cheese and crackers?"

Mrs. Thompson stood up and straightened the front of her housedress. "Yes," she said loudly through the window. And then to George, "Would you like to play hearts with us? I will open some salmon. Do you like smoked salmon?"

George nodded enthusiastically.

Mr. Thompson was at work at the capitol building. The legislature was not in session during the summer, but apparently he had a temporary job as a printing and publishing specialist in charge of manufacturing and distributing documents, so he was constantly updating software and tinkering with machines. But he would be home as early as he could to eat dinner with them. Mrs. Thompson explained all this to George as she took a glass jar of smoked salmon from her pantry, opened it carefully, drained it and laid the pieces out on a plate. She cut up some cheddar cheese and placed it on the same plate, and then took out a sleeve of saltine crackers and tucked them under her arm, so she could carry the plate with both hands down the back steps and out onto the porch. Reluctantly she asked George if she would carry two bottles of cold water from a plastic camp cooler before she nudged the screen door with her shoulder to step off the porch and into the sun.

Lilly sat patiently looking at a book, her feet still swinging. "Do you want to say hello to Georgianna?" Mrs. Thompson asked softly.

"Hello," Lilly said, barely audible.

"Hello, Lilly," George said, somewhat too loudly, she felt. "What are you reading?"

"Nothing," she replied. "Just a dumb book." Lilly put the book down under her chair as George set down the water bottles and sat in one of the three chairs around the small metal table. Lilly took a cracker and piled fish and cheese on it.

"I love dumb books," George said, and she too piled a cracker with fish while Mrs. Thompson smiled and sat down.

The morning wore on with the hearts game and snacks. Lilly soon started to look up at George, and then she started laughing at the jokes that would pass between her biological sister and her mom, and eventually she made some of her own. The sun climbed through the trees and the three of them ate lunch after Mrs. Thompson developed a commanding point lead in the game and Lilly lost all interest and decided to lie on the lawn and read her girl detective book. As George and Mrs. Thompson were clearing the table, a black bear sow and her two cubs walked down the concrete spillway, swaying their heads from side to side, looking for an exit. They would eventually walk down to the beach or up the side and over the fence into someone's unattended yard. The ladies stood and watched as the sow paused for a moment to sniff the air by their house. Mrs. Thompson said a sentence in Tlingit, then, after a pause, another. The sow checked on her cubs and shuffled along in the knee-deep water.

"I told her it wasn't safe for her to stay long where the human beings live. She should take her children back up into the forest for the berries." Mrs. Thompson smiled at George. "Did your . . . uh . . . dad teach you the language?"

"Just a few words—his clan name, thank you, you're welcome, some place names, things like that. He was a good storyteller."

"I know him. He is a good storyteller. He is a good man. You know, Georgianna, I do not hate the people you call your parents. You do not have to turn your heart against them. They did what they did out of love. It's hard to explain. But I know they did it because they loved you."

"Thank you," George said. "Does Mr. Thompson feel the same way?"

Mrs. Thompson turned and took the plates toward the house. "You are my daughter, George. I will worry about Mr. Thompson." When she got to the porch door, she put all the plates from the afternoon in one strong hand, used the other to open the screen door and walked into the house. George could look down the raceway and just see the basket-butts of the three bears wandering down between the houses of town, on their way to the tide flats on the channel.

George went into the little converted dining room with the blankets on the glass doors and put her clothes away. Then she lay on top of the bed, which felt as if it had never been slept in. She looked at the shadows on the old plaster ceiling, wondering if this room could ever be familiar to her, if it could ever be her home. She heard Mrs. Thompson working in the kitchen and then Lilly walking into the bedroom next to hers and locking the door of her room. George had to admit that she felt safe in the old house. The heater kicked on as the shadows lengthened a bit, but it was June and there would barely be any darkness at all until well past midnight. She started to feel sleepy and covered herself with a blanket from the foot of her bed, but she couldn't stop worrying about her father out at Lemon Creek prison. No matter how good Mrs. Thompson was, no matter how safe she felt in the little house, she couldn't bear the thought of him in an orange jumpsuit being held in a cell near where Ida Paul had died, away from their home, away from their . . . his daughter. His daughter now.

Soon enough, she was startled awake by the front door banging open. She got up slowly, pushed aside the blankets and looked toward the kitchen where she saw Mr. Thompson's stooped back as he handed bags to Mrs. Thompson. Lilly came out of her room and looked at the bags he had brought and exclaimed, "Russian dumplings!" in the happiest voice that George had heard her use so far. There seemed to be a quick consensus to add the piroshki to the meal that had already been prepared.

George stepped quickly into the bathroom and washed her face and brushed her teeth, then came out with some trepidation.

"There is our daughter!" Mr. Thompson burst out immediately, coming at her with his arms out to hug her.

"Hello, Mr. Thompson." George smiled and stepped back a bit.

He engulfed her in his big form. He was more than six feet tall and wore a white shirt and a wool vest with an old-fashioned tie and tortoiseshell glasses on a chain around his neck. "Dad. You call me Dad," he murmured.

"Tommy . . ." His wife's voice came from behind him. Her hands were on his elbow. "We talked about this."

"Oh, darn it now. Not in our own home. Not in my home. She can call me Dad, for Pete's sake." He let George loose from his grasp. Mrs. Thompson's jaw was set tight. Lilly was looking down at her shoes. The sunny mood of the afternoon was gone.

"Lilly, will you show George how to set the table?" Mrs. Thompson asked.

"Yes, Momma," Lilly said, and walked with her head down past her father. She took George's hand, leading her toward the table in the living room.

After setting the table, the girls took all the desk chairs

from the bedrooms and from the corners of the living room and set them around the table.

"It's a special night, so we will light the candles," Lilly said and smiled at George, and her sister could see the reflection of the flame in the girl's dark eyes. When everything was just right, Lilly went and rapped softly on her parents' bedroom door and then almost ran to get her own place at the table next to George, and opposite her father's spot at the head of the table. They ate baked salmon and homemade bread, along with the Russian dumplings, rice, cooked beets and onions from the garden, with blueberry cobbler and ice cream for dessert. They drank water and Lilly had milk with her dinner. They all had tea with dessert.

They talked about how none of them smoked tobacco or drank alcohol. Although both Mr. and Mrs. Thompson used to do both, they stopped when they learned they were going to have their first baby. There was an awkward pause after that. They talked about how they liked to watch Mariners baseball and Seahawks football. They had gone to the Catholic church at one time, but they gave that up around the same time they gave up drinking. Lilly said that she liked to read and play video games, but she didn't have her own computer or video console. She said she once wanted to save money to buy a horse, but figured that was not going to happen.

"Not for the price they charge to get hay up here on the barge," her father said with a half laugh.

Then a couple of minutes passed in silence with just the scraping of spoons against the dessert plates before Mrs. Thompson asked George, "What about you, sweetie? Can you tell us anything about what you like?"

George did her best to talk about her interest in whales

and marine biology, in forensic science. She liked baking and reading novels about girls having adventures. She didn't much like fantasy, though she liked science-fiction novels that had real science in them. "I don't like stories that change the rules right in the middle about what can happen and what can't, just willy-nilly, you know what I mean?" and here she looked at Lilly.

"I think so," the younger girl said.

"Like when somebody can't fly or turn invisible for half the book and then suddenly just when they need to, they find something that allows them to change the rules . . . that bugs me!" George said and shook her head from side to side.

"Well . . . don't you think that those stories sometimes represent an allegory of the character's journey?" Mr. Thompson said as he put his tortoiseshell glasses up on the bridge of his nose.

"I guess so," George said. "A writer could be saying something about the character, and the world that character thinks they are living in. But really it just feels like lazy writing."

Mr. Thompson thumped his knuckles down on the table. "But really, young lady, how would you know about any of that?"

"Tommy . . ." Mrs. Thompson's voice was soothing.

"I just meant that it's complicated," he said, taking his glasses off. "Maybe we should clear the table."

"Before that," Mrs. Thompson said, "I was thinking. George, you were planning on taking a trip with Ida before she died, weren't you?"

"Yes, ma'am," George said.

"Well, I was wondering if you would like to take a trip with me this summer. We could go to fish camp up past

Haines and you could meet some of my family. We could eat berries and fish and go to the big beaches up around the coast in my nephew's boat. Would you like that?"

"Momma, what about me?" Lilly said with panic in her voice. "I'd love to go too!"

"I thought you could go to horse camp this summer like you have always talked about. I have money I saved from the state fair."

"What?" Thomas Thompson asked.

"Yes . . . don't act all surprised now, Tommy. We discussed this."

Lilly was bouncing around on her butt as if she were dancing in her chair. "Horse Camp! Horse Camp! Horse Camp!" She had made up a little ditty like the chorus of a pop song to go along with the syllables.

"How long do you think we would be gone, Mrs. Thompson?"

"Mom," Mr. Thompson interjected, with just enough force to startle George. He brought his fist down hard enough that the silverware rattled on the table. "You should call her Mom or Mother or Momma in this house from here on out . . . Please . . . just choose one of those."

Silence enveloped the room, as if they were all goldfish in their tank and Tommy Thompson was the big eye looking in through the glass.

The three females stared down at their hands for a moment before Mrs. Thompson broke the silence. "Thomas, will you come talk with me in the bedroom?" The adults excused themselves awkwardly and left the table.

George stood up and as she walked around the table she put her hands on Lilly's shoulders. "If you clear the table, I will help with the dishes, okay?" Then she went into the makeshift bedroom and repacked her duffel bag, making sure she had everything. After double-checking she had unplugged her cords, she ran quickly into the bathroom and got her toothbrush and wash-cloth. She carried the duffel out to the front porch and then went to the kitchen.

Lilly was standing at the sink with her hands in the warm soapy water. The dirty dishes were piled on the side-board next to her, and Lilly was crying.

"I'm going back to the boat, Lil. I'm sorry."

"Take me with you."

"What?"

"Take me with you. Please."

"Is something going on? Does he hit you, honey?"

"If you go . . ." She was breathing deeper now, almost sobbing, and she made little quiet splashes in the soapy water. "If you go now, I won't be able to go to horse camp. It's all because of you I get to go. Don't you see? They have made some deal."

"No, Lilly . . . I'm sure you will get to go to horse camp. I promise. I promise." She put her arm around the smaller girl. Then they both heard raised voices from the bedroom. First his voice and then hers. Some-one's hand on the door. "I've got to go. I will come back. I will do everything I can to make sure you get to go to horse camp. I promise. But right now I've got to go."

Then she walked out to the porch, picked up her duf-fel and ran down the steps. She tried to make as little noise as possible as she crossed the short metal foot-bridge over the stream then pulled herself through the brambles of an abandoned yard in a spot no one would be able to find her.

She was jogging and pulling leaves from her hair. The

sun was behind the federal building and the heat of the day was fading in the shadow cast across the flats. The sun laid a slanted track through the consistently moist air rising up over the channel. George stayed off the streets, at first crossing the main road by the federal building and then skirting the remains of the old Native village across from the grocery store.

Then she heard Mr. Thompson's voice calling her name loudly. She ran behind a smokehouse that had a bloody cooler beside it and smoke easing out the top. Just as she turned the corner with her duffel on her shoulder, she heard a deep grunt and then a black shadow banged her hip, knocking her down, and two squalling forms scrambled over her. She lay dazed in the darkness. She listened to the black bear family scattering away from their raid on the smokehouse. She was barely hurt, but the cubs' claws left needling little red marks under her shirt. She crawled up under a blue tarp and then farther into the brush behind the old house as she heard Mr. Thompson's voice echoing around the flats. She jumped up and scrambled over the slope and back down the hill, onto the street that led toward the governor's mansion, in the opposite direction from Mr. Thompson's voice. She ran into Cope Park, where she lay by the stream for a bit. She heard the bears move past her on up the hill, back into the mountains behind town. George was not sure which direction to go. The street up toward the mansion was busy; it led downtown and to Star Hill, the capitol and restaurants. Blossom's aunt and uncle had a nice house up there, and Blossom would drive up that street soon enough to put her car away in her uncle's garage. Sometimes she would stay there and wash it as per his instructions. If she got to the top of the hill near enough to the aunt and uncle's house, she could call Blossom and have her meet her there, putting more distance between herself and Mr. Thompson in the meantime.

George picked up her duffel, still packed with her clothes and computer, phones and cords, and took the trail up the hill. Her cell phone battery was dead, so she could not call Blossom. She knew she could get to the upper streets and then work her way—using smaller streets, pedestrian walkways and staircases—to a place where she could get a good look down onto Blossom's aunt and uncle's house to see if Blossom was washing her car. Or at least she could maybe knock on the door there and try to stay there a while.

The woods seemed to be getting darker now, but only because of the angle of the sun. The summer sun gave beautiful haloes to the red huckleberries on the hillside, and the limbs of the red alders cast shadows like quill pens on the moss and lichen-covered ground. Then, George broke out onto the top of the little ridge above town, where the sun shone directly into her face.

Just as she'd hoped, there was the sporty little Renault Le Car parked in the garage with the door open. Blossom was scrubbing it down with a heavy mitt. A pile of towels was in a hamper and an old pressure washer was sitting near the boxy little grill of the car. Todd was holding the end of a green hose and spraying down the opposite side of the car from where Blossom was scrubbing.

George started jogging down the staircase; there were six flights down to the street, with landings that led to alleys for other houses and other residents. Two of the landings had benches where residents could sit and rest if they were carrying heavy loads on their way up, but George was bounding down. She started to whistle to get Blossom's attention.

"Wait," a male voice said on the landing just below her.

Mr. Thompson was sitting on the fourth landing down. George stumbled and her forward momentum, plus the weight of the duffel on her shoulder, caused her to fall.

Mr. Thompson lunged at her. "Here . . . here . . . Don't fall, please don't fall. I can't have you getting hurt. Kristy would kill me." He was holding her in his arms. George could tell he was immensely strong, and she could also tell that he was genuinely worried. But she wasn't sure why.

"Listen, Georgianna . . ." He straightened her up so she was solidly on her feet and he took the duffel bag and set it down on the bench where he had been sitting waiting for her, where she would be more comfortable, and where they would both be out of sight from the house down the staircase. "Listen . . . I'm sorry I raised my voice. I'm sorry. You don't know. You can't know what it was like to have a baby stolen. To have a child just disappear. It was so hard on us."

"Please just let me go talk with my friend."

"Will you just hear me out?" His voice sounded pitiful to George, as if he were going to collapse there on the steps.

"Go ahead," she said.

"I will admit I went a little crazy when they took you, and I have . . . some issues surrounding those circumstances, and I've gotten help. But I hope you realize that your mom and I are the victims here. We are the victims. We had our baby stolen from us. Our child . . . and now we are expected to be patient and understanding and . . .

politically correct? I mean, maybe Kristy can do it . . . but Georgianna, can't you see that I have a right to my own feelings too, my own frustrations, my own needs?"

"Yes . . . I do, and I'm sorry it is so hard for you. But don't you think it's hard for Lilly too?"

"Of course I do," he said, perhaps too loudly, perhaps too appreciatively.

"Do you know that she really, really wants to go to horse camp, even if I don't end up going on the trip with Mrs. Thompson?"

"Of course, I do. I overheard you talking around the table."

"But do you . . . did you know?"

"What difference does it make, Georgianna?"

"It makes a difference. Listen, I just want to go talk with my friend."

He took one step closer and put his right hand around her elbow. "You know they are not going to let you go back to the boat. That woman from Children's Services is going to pick you up eventually, when she gets around to it, and she is going to bring you back to us. Why don't you come back with me tonight, and I will swear on my mother's grave that I will let Lilly go to that horse camp, under any circumstances, if you come back with me tonight? How about that?"

Georgianna took a step back so she could see down into the garage. Blossom was under the car with a towel, drying off the undercarriage, which was one of her uncle's rules of use.

"Can I go talk with her?"

"Sweetie, we have to walk back home over the hill. It's getting late, I'm tired, and I've got to get to work early in the morning. Please, can we just go home and talk with your . . . can we go see Kristy? I know she is worried sick about you and mad as heck at me. Please?"

George had never been through as many changes as she had been in the last few weeks. She had never pushed back against adults, had never lost a parent or had one arrested, never shot a handgun, drunk a beer, been run over by a bear, or eaten family-style at Donna's Diner. Her head was swimming and she was completely adrift, so she picked up her duffel bag and walked up the stairs with this odd, angry man who was apparently her biological father.

"What the heck were you doing?" Blossom yelled at her the next day when they met at the park. "You were right above the house when I was washing the car, and you didn't come down? If nothing else, Todd and I could have used a hand with drying at least. For cripes' sake, you know how much I hate that part."

"I know, but Mr. Thompson was having a cow, and he wanted me back at the house."

"How's it going with him? I thought he was a creep."

"He is . . . at least I think he is. I don't know, B. His wife is so nice and the daughter is sweet, but he seems like a bully. But I don't know. He makes a fair point, you know? I mean, it looks like I'm their kid. The DNA says so."

"Can't jump to conclusions, George."

"Come on, B. Lay off me a minute."

"Listen, I know . . . this is weird for you and all, but you can't back out on your dad, on Mr. Paul, on the guy you grew up with. He needs you now."

"I know that."

They were in the high school parking lot leaning on

the front of the Le Car. They stood in silence for a few moments until Blossom cleared her throat and said, "Well, we can't just sit here. Let's go back to their house and find some evidence to explain why your mom stole you in the first place."

Lilly was at track and Mr. Thompson was at work. Mrs. Thompson was working in her garden. She was on her knees weeding and watering the small plants, which were beginning to take root and growing quickly in the long Alaskan days. She had on a traditional Tlingit-shaped clan-style hat made of cedar bark that blocked the sun, and she wore kneepads over her jeans. She had a milk crate with a tool bag hung on the inside for her gardening tools, and a hose that she dragged along the rows. George brought Blossom over and introduced her, and Mrs. Thompson stood up, removed her gloves, smiled, shook hands and offered to get them all drinks, but George went and got the drinks instead, while Blossom and Kristy Thompson sat in the dark soil and chatted.

"I am glad to meet you," Kristy said. "The social worker said that you work for Mr. Paul's lawyer."

"Not officially, ma'am." Blossom looked her in the eyes. "My sort-of boyfriend, Ned, has a summer job with Mr. Teller, but I do spend some time there and I'm interested in the law. My father is an investigator and I'm interested in the case. Does that bother you?"

"No, I know Richard Paul. He needs help . . . but the lawyers . . . my husband . . ." She looked up at Blossom, then back into the ground. "I made him a deal I wouldn't talk to the lawyers if he wouldn't talk to the police or the press anymore."

"Okay. I think I understand," Blossom said, but in fact

she didn't. All that was clear was that Mrs. Thompson had to manage and make deals with her husband.

"You are welcome here," she said softly, "but it would be best to come when Thomas is not here. He probably wouldn't like it."

"Okay."

"But I like it." She smiled at the sprouted plants and dug her fingers into the dark soil. "I want George to be happy. I really do. And everybody needs a good friend. I can tell you are a good friend. I know about your dad. That social worker told us about him and what happened. I'm sorry."

"Yes. Thank you. My dad is a good guy. I love him so much."

"That's good. It's a good thing that you do. It's healthy and good." A few tears came for both of them, then George came out with cold water and some cookies that Mrs. Thompson had made that morning, and they ate together in the sunshine.

George finished her cookie and asked Mrs. Thompson, "Kristy, I notice you have a basement. What is down there?"

"That is Tommy's workshop and his reading room. He keeps it locked up. He doesn't like anybody going down there."

"What kind of work does he do in his shop?"

"He does handicrafts with metal and wood—artwork mostly. He has some dangerous and sensitive tools, torches and cutting tools. That's why he keeps it locked. He sells his work, though." Mrs. Thompson started picking up glasses although she hadn't finished her water.

"Does he sell in the galleries downtown?" George asked.

"No, he sells to collectors, people he knows. You are not to go in there," she said over her shoulder as she got up. Then she walked through the porch and into the little kitchen.

"We are definitely getting into that basement," Blossom whispered. George kicked her softly with her toe.

When Mrs. Thompson came back out, she put her gloves on and went back to the garden. George and Blossom started walking toward the house. George told her they were going to her room to read, and Mrs. Thompson said that was fine. She asked if they would mind going to pick Lilly up from track in an hour and a half, and Blossom said that she would be fine with that if it was okay with Mr. T. Kristy said that she would just tell him that she was going to do it, and not to worry.

"Weird, don't you think?" Blossom said once they were alone.

"What's weird?"

"That she would lie to her husband about picking up Lilly so easily after she said it would be best that I not hang around."

"Not a big lie . . . I mean, is it?"

"But Lilly has to be in on it. She has to not tell her dad that you and I picked her up in my car. Isn't that a lot of pressure on the kid?"

George twisted her mouth around, thinking about the situation. "I get the impression that Lilly doesn't talk with her dad about much of anything."

"Maybe so."

They walked right past the old dining-room doors now turned into bedroom doors and straight to the front porch, where there was a very narrow staircase down to the basement. Six wooden steps led to a stone staircase from the outside, with an old barn-like door to the front yard, then a dark turn to a heavy door to the basement wall itself. The wall was concrete and appeared damp. The foundation was old stone with mortar, and the door appeared to be heavy dark oak, with ironwork that could have been handmade in a forge. It was probably relatively new in age but made to look old-fashioned, with long black iron hinges, massive pins and hardware.

"Let's get the fuck out . . . this is creepy!" Blossom said. "I mean, come on!" She backed away and took a wide photograph of the door with her phone. The flash illuminated the little grotto of the entrance. She tried the heavy lever handle on the door, but it wouldn't budge, and neither would the door. She noticed a modern silver lock above the old-fashioned one. Blossom took out her wallet and her student ID and dug around between the door and the frame until she found the dead bolt of the modern lock. Then she found the catch of the handle mechanism.

"We could easily slip this old lock with a jimmy or even a screwdriver and a block of wood, but we'll need my good pick set for the modern dead bolt." Blossom stood back studying the door.

"Who the heck are you?" George asked the girl she thought she knew.

"Wait a second . . ." Blossom dug around in her wallet and pulled out a thin piece of metal that looked like a bobby pin to George and another rusty fatter piece with grooves on the side. "I've got this in case I lose my boat key. It's a pretty good pick, but a shit sledge. It probably won't work. But it's worth a try." They heard footsteps up in the kitchen, water running in the sink, then it was turned off. They held their breath until the footsteps walked back outside.

"B, let's get out of here. Please!"

"Just one second and we'll be out of here." Blossom first put the tickler in and pulled it back. She could feel it push tumblers back. Then she pushed it in as far as she could. She put the sledge in, wiggling it to accommodate the tickler. She pulled the tickler back and forth, teasing the tumblers up into the lock, but the sledge was too small and the tumblers wouldn't stay. She held the sledge tight up into the lock and pulled the tickler up hard against the mechanism and twisted the sledge to turn the lock and—

Clink. The sledge and the tickler snapped off inside the lock.

"Oh, shit," Blossom said.

"What? What happened?" George was starting to get sick to her stomach.

"We've got to go. Now," Blossom said.

George didn't even remember what she told Mrs. Thompson they were going to do. Something about going shopping before going to pick up Lilly. Blossom was sitting in the Le Car frantically calling Ned on her phone. They agreed to meet at the office.

Ten minutes later they were sitting in front of a very stern-looking Harrison Teller and Otis Betts. Ned was sitting next to Mr. Betts in his leather riding jacket and was bouncing his helmet nervously on his knees. In another five minutes, Blossom had explained the problem of the broken tickler and sledge in the lock of the basement door, and that they had about an hour before they picked up Lilly and before Mr. Thompson got home.

Teller looked at Otis Betts. "We leave it? We know nothing, somebody, some fucking burglar tried to break in. We . . . I mean all of us . . ." He looked at George and Blossom, "ALL of us. We know nothing, and it blows over."

George raised her hand timidly. "Uh, I asked her what was down there just before we did it."

"Fuck a duck," Harrison Teller whispered. "Excuse me, ladies. Pardon my language."

"You have a lock-picking set and you used the wrong stuff?" Otis asked, looking at Blossom.

"Okay . . . yes . . . rookie mistake."

Harrison Teller threw up his hands and stomped around the office. "Otis, can you handle this for me? As always, I am forever in your debt, and I don't want to know how you will earn your big Christmas bonus this year. I've got to go pick up my family at the ferry, okay?"

"Okay, boss," Otis said, and he looked at his watch.

Teller headed out the door. "Either don't pick locks, or learn how to do it right." Then he waved over his shoulder and was gone.

"Yes, sir," Blossom said, devoid of her usual sarcasm.

Otis turned to the girls. "You got a picture of the door? Show it to me." He looked at the picture on the phone, enlarging it and squinting. He looked at his watch again. "Okay, do you think you can get hold of the key to this door? Tell me the truth. Before he goes down there, can you get the key?"

George squished up her mouth and wiggled it back and forth thinking. "It's a small house. Lilly and Mrs. Thompson are nice and I'm not afraid of them. I think I can find it if I start looking soon, but I'm going to have to go with B to pick up Lilly, otherwise she won't come home with her."

Otis Betts looked at them both. "Okay, you have to convince him he lost the key or the key got lost somehow. I will bring you the new key, and then he has to find it. You got it?"

"But . . . but . . ."

"You take care of your end." He pulled out a small Rite in the Rain pad and wrote some things on a piece of paper before ripping it out and handing it to Ned. "You have your bike, yeah?"

Ned nodded, his helmet bobbing faster now.

"Okay, I need this stuff downstairs in twenty minutes. Can you do that?"

Ned read the list carefully; he looked up at Mr. Betts. "You want these to be brand new?"

"Good question." He took the list back and pointed with his thumbnail at something. "These should be brand new. Hardware store. The big one will have them." Otis Betts pointed at something else. "And make sure this comes with three of these, okay?"

"Got it."

"If it only has two, get a blank one. But if it burns too much time looking for it, forget about it and just bring the two. Got it?"

"Okay."

Mr. Betts moved his finger down one space on the list. "This, get white or green, no writing on it, okay? No logos, nothing. Plain. Got it? I will take care of the writing. Once you buy it—large, my size—scuff it up in the dirt a little. Not too much, just so I look like I did some work, okay? Drive fast but not over the speed limit, no tickets. Twenty minutes. Out front. Go. Call me on my cell with any problems."

Ned was gone.

Otis Betts turned to the girls. "You two pick up Lilly. See if she can help you find the key, but make sure she doesn't snitch you out to the dad. If you think she will, forget about using her. We will do it another way."

He paused and looked at them both, then he smiled.

"Don't worry. I like that you tried to pick the lock. It's fucked up now, but that happens. Listen, I have to go. But we will have lock-picking lessons later."

"Okay," they said in unison but with voices close to tears.

Betts stood up and turned to the computer and the girls were gone.

9

IS THAT LIGHT IN THE TUNNEL GETTING BIGGER?

They had discussed it, and Blossom was in favor of trying to trick Lilly into talking about the stuff in the basement. George didn't feel good about it. George argued that Lilly was most likely going to be her sister one way or another and starting off with the truth would be the best way to deal with her. Blossom wanted to try some stunt—she had read that PIs called them "ruses." They'd tell Lilly they were doing a scavenger hunt, and they needed to find something hidden in the basement of the house . . . or something like that.

"No," George said flatly. "I wouldn't do that to you. I'm not going to do it to Lilly."

"Criminy, you are no fun at all."

"Nope."

They picked Lilly up at the school. Girls were enjoying the last few meets and relishing the camaraderie and strange fun of both school and not-school at the same time. Lilly looked as if she were talking to her teammates and might even be making friends. She laughed and waved to a group of tall girls and ran to the Le Car and jumped into the back seat. She recognized Blossom and said hello and tapped on her gym bag with her fingertips as they drove home.

"Why are you driving me home?" Lilly asked.

Blossom spoke right up. "Your mom asked me to pick you up, to save your dad some time."

"Oh," was all Lilly said.

"Listen, Lil," George said, clearing her throat, "I did something dumb. Really dumb, and I will probably get in trouble."

"What?" The younger girl leaned forward, more excited than worried, sticking her head nearly between the front seats.

"I wanted to try and see what was in the basement without asking permission. That door was so cool looking, so I tried to pick the lock . . . Well, we tried to pick the lock, and we jammed the pick stuff in it. Now I need to get the key to the lock to get it fixed before your dad or mom find out. Can you help me? Please?"

Lilly sat back in the seat and put her arms over her head and let out a soft kind of animal wail, a cross between sobbing and choking.

Blossom pulled the car over in a driveway; George jumped out of the front and got in the back seat with her sister. "Lilly, sweetie, what's wrong? It's okay . . . you don't have to do anything. It's okay. You won't get in trouble. I will take the blame. Sweetie . . . stop."

Lilly was trembling: her arms, her hands. She tried to cover her eyes with her fingers. "He will kill all of us if we go in there," she whispered, as if she were going to be sick.

"No . . . Lil, he won't," Blossom said. "It was all my fault. You didn't do a thing."

"That doesn't matter."

"What is down there, Lilly?"

"I can never ever tell anybody." She was breathing very hard, and both the older girls were worried now that she would pass out.

"Okay . . . you don't have to, Lilly. You don't have to do anything. We will take care of this. You don't have to do anything, okay? We will take care of everything. No need for you to worry at all. Okay? Okay? Lilly?"

Blossom asked Lilly what her favorite music was, and Lilly told her that she liked Taylor Swift. Blossom happened to have a recording of a local punk band doing covers of Taylor Swift songs. She had rigged her phone through a device wired up to the Renault's old stereo, which seemed to work well for the punk sound, so Lilly had stopped crying by the time they got home. Her eyes were red, but not so much so that it might cause suspicion.

Blossom opened her door and turned to Lilly. "Are you okay?"

"I'm okay. I won't say anything to anyone, if that's what you're asking?"

"Thanks . . . but I was really asking if you were okay. You had me freaked out a little back there."

"About what? I'm fine. Nothing happened." Then Lilly jumped out of the back of the Le Car and ran up to the house with her gym bag. Blossom and George followed her in through the front door.

Mrs. Thompson was in the kitchen. "Hello, girls. Thomas called and said he would be home soon. He's going to stop and get pizza for everybody. I decided to talk to him about you, Blossom, and he was fine. He doesn't know about you working around the lawyer . . . but anyway, he seems good today and he asked if you would like to stay for pizza with us. What do you think, Blossom?"

"Yes, ma'am, pizza sounds great."

"Should you call your mother? I could talk with her if you like?"

"I will call her, thank you. She is out on her boat tonight. I will let her know that you offered." Blossom and Mrs. T. exchanged numbers in case Jane Marie wanted to call or text, in the way of modern mothers.

Mrs. Thompson went back to making a salad with some herring eggs someone from Sitka had sent her. They had been jarred in seal oil, and she and Blossom were discussing the eggs when Lilly whispered from the corner of the room.

"Pssst. George . . . Hey."

George looked and Lilly was standing at the corner of her parents' bedroom door. George walked to the door and Lilly grabbed her hand. Suddenly both girls were in the parents' small, dark room. There was an iron bedstead and two small dressers. Lilly pointed to a small built-in panel above the closet door.

"Up there, push that panel in, and it will pop open. The key is hanging in there," Lilly whispered.

George could not reach the panel and looked around for a chair. There was nothing. The chairs were around the dining-room table.

"Lift me up!" Lilly said. George bent over and just as she did, she heard the front door open. "Hurry. It could be Daddy." Lilly clambered up on George's shoulders and sat astride. George was strong enough to stand up straight with Lilly's legs around her neck. She heard Mrs. Thompson talking to a man on the porch. The man sounded like Otis Betts. Lilly touched the panel and grabbed something, then clicked the panel shut again.

"Got it."

When George put her down, Lilly handed her a key on a leather fob. The fob was finely worked with the delicate image of a serpent wrapped around a naked woman. But the thing that made George almost cry was the tool work and painting on the key itself. The length of the key was plain with the usual hills and valleys that fit into the modern lock, but the grip that a person would hold onto while turning the key was incised and painted with the image of a human skull wearing old-fashioned dark glasses. The skull was well drawn, and the teeth seemed to be leering at her.

She took the key off the fob and put them both in her pants pocket. Lilly and George straightened their clothes and opened the bedroom door a crack. Otis Betts was still talking to Mrs. Thompson. He saw the girls over her shoulder. He made a point of showing her something on his clipboard. He was wearing white coveralls with some dirt scuffed on his knees. He wore a white hard hat, had some sort of official identification hanging around his neck and was carrying a bag of tools at his side. The girls sneaked into the bathroom, which was just two steps away. Then Lilly went to her room, which was another two steps. George took a moment, flushed the toilet, washed her hands, then stepped out and walked over to Mrs. Thompson and asked, "What's up?"

"This man is from the City and Borough and is here to test the radon in our basement. I told him the basement is locked up and my husband is not home, but he'll be here any moment and would be happy to help him then."

"I don't need to get into the basement, Mrs. Thompson, and I don't need to disturb your husband or look inside or anything. I just need to go down next to the door and get a reading. As long as I can see the foundation, that's all I need."

At that moment Thomas Thompson appeared on the stairs with an armload of pizza boxes, his briefcase slung across his shoulder. Mr. Betts gathered himself and ran through his lengthy and somewhat bureaucratic spiel one more time.

"I wouldn't think of going into your basement or disturbing your dinner, sir. Just need to take a reading and tap a bit on the foundation to make sure there is no radon pooling there at the entrance."

Mr. Thompson was irritated and quite clearly wanted to get inside. "For heaven's sake, Kristy, let's eat our pizza and let this man do his job and get home to his own family."

Mr. Betts went down to the basement, and Blossom and Lilly put out the plates and silverware. Mrs. Thompson brought out the salad and a pitcher of iced tea. The pizza was delicious, and Mr. Thompson was relaxed and happy. There were a few tapping noises from the basement and Mr. Thompson seemed happy when he heard them. "I bet he is impressed with that door. It took me months to make that thing and nearly a week to hang it properly." He smiled. "That's real craftsmanship, I tell you. Solid oak."

There was a loud thunk and a clatter from downstairs and Mr. Thompson started to get up, but George was closer to the door than he was. "I'll go see if he hurt himself," she said, "maybe take him a piece of pizza. I'll be right back."

She was out the door before anyone could object.

Otis stood next to the medieval-looking entrance. "I had to change out the lock. It was jammed up solid. Any luck with the key?"

"Yes, but . . ." She held out the intricately decorated key, which no new key could replace.

"Shit," Otis Betts said. "Well . . . Keep him away from here for as long as you can. Give me the key and the fob."

"Have some pizza," she said.

"Nice." He smiled at her and ate it. "See? Good things happen. Get going. I'll be back."

"What do I tell them?"

"Tell them 'no radon' and I will get them a report. No charge. It's all good."

And that's exactly what she did. As they were doing the dishes, the three girls had a huddle and all George said was they had to keep Mr. T. away from the basement until Mr. Radon came back. Lilly suggested that they all claim that they could beat him at chess, best out of five games. Apparently he was very proud of his chess skills. Lilly chose his favorite music, which apparently was obscure old Eastern European café-style jazz, while Mrs. Thompson binge-watched *NCIS.* There was a tense moment when Mr. Thompson went into his bedroom and stayed for several minutes. George and Blossom set up the chess board and were considering knocking on the bedroom door when he came out with a kind of flourish carrying a pipe and wearing a straw boater hat, gray slacks, a red cardigan with an ascot and some new old-fashioned wire-rimmed glasses.

"Ah . . . wow, Mr. Thompson," Blossom said in genuine surprise, "that is quite an outfit."

"These are my chess-master clothes. Something fun, I think. Do you really like them?" He turned around as if he were modeling. He held out his sweater a bit and he looked strangely thin, but he quickly put his arms down. Mr. Thompson went to his place at the head of the table and slid the window open. He had a big ashtray with wooden matches in the center and made a show of fixing his pipe.

"Come, now, girls," he said, with the slightest hint of an English accent, then lit his pipe, filling the end of the room with smoke, and tapped the end of the match on the table. "Set the board down here by the master."

If he intended all this to be a kind of fun show for the children, it really wasn't working for Lilly, who looked ashen, as if she were going to be sick. At first Blossom thought he was doing some kind of Monty Python bit, but when she saw Lilly turn white, she was worried. In the time she had known Mr. Thompson so far, he hadn't done anything really silly; instead, all his antics just seemed like weird little affectations that made her uncomfortable. She was beginning to see what George had meant about her new "dad."

Blossom played first and lost the first game, but won the next two, which caused Mr. Thompson to forget his accent and gamesmanship. He snapped at Lilly to bring him a cup of black tea, "with a small wedge of lemon please, dear." Mrs. Thompson got up and scowled at him and got him some plain tea instead.

When Mr. Thompson finally won his fourth game, he danced around the end of the table in a triumphant jig with both arms over his head, puffing his pipe like a steam engine. "A brew for the master!" he called, and Lilly got up immediately to bring him another cup of tea.

George then beat him three games in a row winning the best of five, and he was grumbling under his breath. Lilly had fallen asleep on the couch and Mrs. Thompson was dozing in her chair as the crew from the Naval Criminal Investigative Service went about solving yet another crime. Blossom had pretended to call her mom, who was motoring down to Pybus Bay. She was actually planning to stay at her aunt's with Todd and didn't need to call them because it was all set that she would come in late. Blossom had clearly been stalling as long as possible when the doorbell rang at ten forty-five.

“I’m going to forfeit this game . . .” George said, staring at the board. It had been picked off considerably, though she still had her queen and he did not have his. “I can see you have the best of me.”

Mr. Thompson stared down at the board. “I think you are right, George . . . in six moves, I do believe.” He added the last part as a complete fabrication. “Good game.” He shook her hand, then stood up to answer the door. “What in the dickens is someone doing here so late?”

Otis Betts stood at the door with the same white coveralls and hardhat on, his tool bag at his feet and the clipboard in his hand.

“I’m sorry to disturb you so late at night, sir, but I saw your light on and I was just headed home and I thought I would drop off your report.” He unclipped a nice-looking typed-up report from the clipboard and gave it to Mr. Thompson. “Everything is A-OK and of course there is no charge. Nothing to worry about. You can just show this to your realtor or a buyer or bank if you ever want to refinance or sell your property, and they will be perfectly assured that there will be no problems in the future.”

“It is awfully late, but thank you,” Mr. Thompson said, and went to close the door. Mr. Betts tipped his hard hat and quickly walked off the porch.

“Hey, Dad!” George blurted out.

“Huh?”

“He left his tools.” She was halfway to the tools when . . .

“Georgianna!” Mr. Thompson barked with a sharp voice.

“Yes, sir?”

“You called me ‘dad.’ That was nice.”

“Yes.” She smiled.

Blossom jumped up. "You stay here and start another game. I'll run and give him his tools," she said quickly, and she was out the door.

Otis Betts was waiting for her just around the first corner of the house, near the walkway crossing the stream, out of sight of the windows. He whistled softly as Blossom ran into his view.

"All right," he said quickly. "I found a guy who cut the original key up and put the new shaft onto the original turn. He pinned it and spot-welded it and polished it, but it still looks a little bit scabbed up and different, plus it will be weaker than the original. It all depends on how hard the deadbolt is to turn."

"Okay, I will get it back in its place."

"Good. Come see me tomorrow when you get a chance."

"What about?" Blossom looked at him. Something about how the streetlight a half block away was casting a shadow over his face made her shiver.

"I'm going to talk to Harrison . . . but you, George and that other girl . . . you should all get out of that house. We will talk tomorrow. He may get suspicious now. Go back to the house and put the key back. Remember, girl. You call me at the office first thing tomorrow." He gave her the key on the fob and picked up the tool bag, then walked away into the dark.

Blossom walked over the steel grating across the creek, then around the block, trying to clear her head. She was supposed to go up to her aunt's house, but her aunt never kept close track of her coming and going. Blossom was worried about what Mr. Betts had said, about how Mr. Thompson might be getting suspicious. She wanted to go back and check on George, but she stood on the bridge looking down. The water from the creek was racing down the pebbled concrete with a hissing sound. It was hypnotizing, the water rushing from the mountains down into the sea. She stood there wishing for that moment that she was with her mom headed down to the bay to look for whales. She didn't know how long she was lost in thought, but she realized she had been gone too long. She turned up the little dead-end street to the Thompsons' house, bounded up the stairs and ran into the living room.

The girls were cleaning up the living room. Mr. and Mrs. Thompson were in their room, and Blossom could hear an argument.

"Come on," George said, and she led them into her room. Lilly looked pale as a sheet. All three of the girls sat on the floor of George's room looking at each other for a moment.

"He knows the key is gone; he looked for it," Lilly said.

"Let's get out of here," Blossom said without hesitation.

"It can't be so bad," George said. "We will tell him we found the key in the morning while we were cleaning up."

"It will be bad," Lilly said. Her teeth were chattering.

"No . . . we will protect you," George said, and Blossom nodded her agreement.

All Lilly had to do was go to her track practice in the afternoon. Blossom fingered the strange-looking key and thought about going to see Otis Betts as soon as the office opened in the morning.

"I'll stay here with you," Blossom said. "We'll face it tomorrow. I'll pretend to find the key while cleaning up early in the morning." Then she stood up and folded the key inside the back of her underwear. "I won't lose it, and no one else will find it here. Let's just go to bed and I'll get ahold of Mr. Betts tomorrow, first thing."

The worried girls remained seated cross-legged on the floor. They looked at Blossom with worried eyes, but also complete trust. This was Tuesday night.

I had planned to split my time for the next two days between the greenhouse and the library. Users at the library seemed to be much more polite, and even the usually truculent libertarian jailhouse lawyers with their unending river of motions didn't want to fight me over finding the oldest and craziest documents to cite in their useless briefs. The time in the greenhouse was reserved for long discussions with Mr. Munro. We discussed what he meant by intimacy, what he believed was the nature of homosexuality, and what he thought was deviant sexual behavior.

"A true faggot is born that way. I got no beef with that. A prison queen is just trying to do easy time and they are usually weak—too cowardly to be a full snitch, so they just suck cock and pretend they are not gay. That's just the truth of that. They are acting against their true nature. They are betraying their nature, their manhood. They should be who they are, like Shawn."

"So, what are we?" I asked him, truly wanting to know what he thought.

"We are friends . . . colleagues. I respect you and I want to be more like you. You respect me and want to be more like me."

"I think that's true," I said. "I want to be as direct and truthful as you. I want to be as strong as you. But—"

"But what?"

"But sometimes I'm not sure you are honest with me. Sometimes I don't think you tell me the whole truth."

"Now you are talking like a bitch."

"When are you going to stop using that word, man?"

"Don't tell me what words to use."

"You wanted to know about women and we talked about respect, but you cannot bear to be disrespected yourself."

"Do you think I'm gay?" He stared at me as he asked this. He looked sad.

"What does that have to do with anything? Does it make you sad to think that might be true?"

"Fuck man, doesn't it you? Doesn't it you?"

"If I am a gay man, then I'm a gay man . . . but let me tell you this, Street. I like and admire you. But I have never had a sexual thought about you. I have never jacked off thinking about you. I have never gotten the slightest hard-on dreaming about you."

He shook his head and looked around bitterly as if the words were hurting his ears.

"Now . . . does it freak me out, would I kill myself, if someday that happened? No. Does your body sicken me? No. Does the thought of loving you or loving a man sicken me? No. Fuck, no. I think we need touch . . . particularly in a brutal place like this. But that doesn't make me hate myself, or doubt myself."

"Naw . . . you're a faggot. That's just called being a repressed faggot."

"So be it, Street. But if you are thinking about taking me by force, I'm going to fight you, man. I'm also going to hate you forever and our friendship will be forever dead. You understand that?"

"But I been playing you already." Here again, he looked at me knowingly: a steady and deep knowing, deeper than my smart-ass book knowing.

"I know that, and I went along with it because your power is attractive even to me. That is a real thing. So, too, your curiosity and your intelligence and our ability to have conversations like this . . . I will openly admit to you, these things make you attractive to me. That's true."

He backed away from me, and for the first time I think I saw him blush with embarrassment. His eyes misted. "I'm not sure anyone ever really loved me, Cecil. You know what I mean? My mom . . ." He stopped himself short. "Fuck it. I hate men's sad stories. They all sound so faggoty . . . like no story at all." He wiped his eyes.

"Albert," I said, calling him by his given name for the first time, "what can I do to really help you? You have a right to a different story, or at least a different ending to the story you've started. I'm serious. If you want help, I will help. Just tell me the truth. Honesty is what makes a friendship. That's what I think. I don't really know about anybody else, but I'm scared and confused most of the time. Honesty is the most important thing I want from my friends."

He laughed at me and took my hand. His hand was shaking. "I've been a gangster a long fucking time, Cecil. I don't know if I can tell the truth in that faggoty way you want to talk about stuff."

"Well, there is time."

"Yeah," he said, "time," and he squeezed my hand.

Just then a guard came around the corner into the greenhouse and told me I had a legal visit.

It was ten in the morning on Wednesday. Harrison Teller was sitting in the small visitor room, his investigator next to him in a second chair. As I waited to be buzzed into the room, I studied their faces, and an unexplainable anxiety gripped my body. They didn't speak to each other, but they each held their posture erect. Where usually Teller would slouch, now he was leaning forward as if he were ready to spring, and his investigator was punching his fist into his open palm. The guard just ten feet down the hall from me behind the mirrored window could see that I was waiting, but did not buzz me in. I suppose he just wanted to see what I would do: being anxious might indicate one thing about the visit, calm something else. The guard might make a note or might not. I might be waiting for a smuggled bindle of drugs, or the guard might be on a phone call with his wife and having a good time just watching me shift from one foot to the next, making me wait just because it was the only bit of authority he could exercise in his desperate ten-hour shift.

I was buzzed in after eight minutes standing outside the door, and I settled in front of the glass and the grating.

"Cecil, we have had a development, and I came right away to inform you about it," Harrison began. "Listen, you know Blossom is friends with George. We did not ask her to snoop around the Thompsons' house, and we certainly did not ask her to try and pick the lock on his basement door. But, well, she did, and she kind of made a mess of it."

"She tried to pick his lock?"

"Yes, and in doing so she jammed up his door. She came to us right away. Otis went and took care of it. He replaced the lock. George got us the key and Otis got a good key made because it was a special key . . . long story . . . anyway, everything was fine. But this morning, we went by the house and no one answered. We called the girls and no one answered. I think the wife and her daughters went to Haines in a smaller and faster boat of their own."

"Okay, so . . ." I asked, "how do you know they went to Haines?"

"They have a neighbor who watches their house and I

went by today, and she told me that Mr. Thompson said they were headed to Haines. The neighbor saw him loading stuff into the car."

"Okay . . ."

Now Mr. Betts spoke up. "I checked with some people on the ferry system. They did not get on the ferry today. This morning they found the Thompsons' car burned up on the side of the road by Tea Harbor. Still hot. The cops said it just happened. They said some witnesses saw a big skiff leaving the scene."

"Bodies?"

"No bodies."

"What aren't you telling me?" I asked.

Otis Betts leaned back in his chair and punched his fist into his left palm looking at Harrison Teller. Teller was looking at a piece of paper he had in his hands and said nothing for a moment, then leaned in close to the glass.

"Listen, Cecil. I think this thing with the car is a bullshit move. I think Mrs. Thompson took off in a boat with two of the girls, and Mr. Thompson is holed up somewhere else. Maybe he is still in his basement with the other one."

"What do you mean the other one?" I said slowly.

"Listen, Cecil. Blossom never showed up at her uncle and aunt's house last night. Her car was found at the harbor. I know she would never leave it there. Mr. Betts talked to the uncle, who got it hotwired and took it back to his garage. He said he moved it because he wanted to scare the girl for leaving it parked outside. He wasn't worried; he just wasn't sure where she was. He had no reason to think things had gone nuts."

"Where is Jane Marie?"

"She is on her way out to Pybus Bay recording whales.

We spoke to Jane Marie on her cell just a few minutes ago. Last night she got a call from Mrs. Thompson saying they were ALL going to fish camp in Haines. But Jane Marie said Mrs. Thompson sounded weird, and she definitely said Haines, but I don't think they all went. The neighbor said only two girls left in the car with Mrs. Thompson. She said she assumed it was their two girls but she wasn't really sure."

"So . . . call the cops. Now."

"Cecil, we can't."

"Why the hell not?" I slammed my hand down on the metal countertop in front of the document port.

"Well, Mr. Otis here changed the lock on the basement door. He looked in the basement just briefly. Technically, he broke in. He committed a crime. If the DA's office found out about that, we would be sanctioned and thrown off Mr. Paul's case. It would hurt my client. I can't do it, Cecil."

"What the fuck? Why did you come talk to me, then?"

"I want to know if you found anything out on your end here."

"Found anything out about what?" I wanted to climb through the iron grating.

"About Thomas Thompson, Cecil. We are going to find Blossom and the girls, I promise you. We are going to get this sorted. We just need a little information."

"What did you see in his basement?"

Otis Betts looked at Mr. Teller and the lawyer nodded, then Betts leaned forward and said, "I didn't do a thorough search. It just looked like an old-fashioned library with an old bed in it. There were manacle-style handcuffs on the bedposts."

"What do you mean 'an old-fashioned library'?" I asked.

"Nice wooden shelves with hardback books. Leather

bound. Lamps with colored glass shades, pictures of old-timey men with bowler hats and high collars, women with full hoop dresses."

"You bring Blossom to me by tomorrow. Call her mother again and have her come back to town. I will find out what I can. Tomorrow. Bring her to me." I stood up and started buzzing on the door to get back into prison, and this time the door opened immediately.

It was probably a testament to Harrison Teller's and Mr. Betts's reputations that I was taken immediately to security and strip-searched, complete with the squat and cough to check if I had anything keistered in my butt. But there was nothing to be found.

I went directly to Fourth Street's office. Shawn Day was doing her lashes in front of the mirror when I banged through the door.

"Goodness," she said, "*someone's* in a mood."

"Can you give us the room for a while, Shawn?" Street said from the handicapped stall. She made a pained face at herself in the mirror and capped her eyeliner, then brushed by me, leaving me in a cloud of her strong scent.

As Shawn Day started to walk out, she pulled my arm toward the door and whispered into my ear, "He's messing with your white ass, you know that, right? You ain't shit to him."

I shook my head and walked back to the Street, who was rolling his eyes. "Man, you got to cut her some slack. She just gets that way sometimes. She thinks it makes her more womanly, you know what I'm saying? I think it just makes her more of a pain in the ass."

I didn't smile. I started right in and explained that I was worried about my child on the outside. I wanted to know what he knew about Thompson and if there was something he could do, if there was someone on the outside he could send to find her. I realized as I was speaking that I sounded distressed. My voice was probably pitched higher than usual, and I might even have been tearing up. My hands were shaking.

"Cecil, man, calm down," he said, putting his hand on my shoulder. He led me into the handicapped stall where he had mattresses laid out and a reading lamp set up on the toilet along with his cell phone and notepad. We sat down next to each other. He still had his arm around my shoulder and was rubbing my neck.

"Calm down now, brother," he said softly.

I pulled his arm away, roughly. "Stop that."

"What?"

"Stop trying to seduce me. I'm coming to you as a friend with a real problem with my daughter. If you want to fuck me in exchange for helping me with this, let's talk about that, but I'm not going to be sweet-talked or fooled into fucking you or falling in love with you . . . not now, not at a Goddamn time like this. Can you help me? Yes or no?"

He wasn't used to inmates talking to him like that, and he moved away from me. He looked me up and down as if he were reassessing. Moments passed. Then more. I started to get up.

"Thompson is a freak," he said. "I've known it all along. I bet your boy in here knows it too. I suspect it had something to do with the case and why the mother took the child. I was going to see if I could use it . . . you know, in exchange for something in here." Street had his forearms on his knees and his hands draped down. His head hung as if he were sad. But I could never be sure with the Street.

"What kind of freak, and how good is your information?" I asked.

"Solid. I had girls who went to him. He paid them. I

knew men that he hung out with. He started out with just light bondage and kind of dress-up games . . . you know, white people games. Frilly English kinds of games. Accents and riding crops and shit. Then he got into young girls and more serious pain . . . not just light leather whips but serious beatings. My girls wouldn't go back no matter how much money he was willing to pay. I suspect he thought he was intellectual; he talked about pre-war Nazi shit and occult stuff. I don't know. It was a mishmash of bullshit. I cut him off when he called me a bunch of racist names, and I sent a couple of guys to collect some money he owed me, and when they roughed him up . . . you know . . . he started calling them the same kinds of names but . . . you know, he had a hard-on . . . sick fucker."

"If he has my daughter, what are the chances he would hurt her?"

"Jesus, Cecil . . . I don't know . . . Did she do something to make him mad?"

"Probably. She was snooping around his house for the case . . . She was pretending to be a private eye."

"Then yeah . . . he would probably get off on hurting her. I'm sorry, man."

"Why didn't you tell me this earlier?"

"It didn't come up, man!"

"What else aren't you telling me?"

He sat there staring at me. "Nothing."

I got up to leave again.

"Your girl—the mother—I don't think she killed herself. I can't prove it, but I think someone helped her out of this life. You know what I'm saying?"

I grabbed his phone off the can. "Call somebody, have them find my daughter, grab her. I don't care what happens to him."

"Man . . . Cecil . . . you don't understand. That is a big ask. Grabbing somebody. Possibly killing the freak. That is making a big noise . . . it is definitely going to attract the attention of the police . . . That kind of thing is both expensive and dangerous for me. I got a parole hearing coming up, like I told you. The few people who I could talk to about something like this would drop a dime on me in a second if the cops ever got word of this. You would drop a dime on me. You wouldn't want to, but if they threw another ten years on you . . . ten more years away from her . . . you know in your fucking heart when you got back in that room with your lawyer you would cut that deal."

I looked at him. I was breathing hard. I reached out and took his hand. I had to admit that he was probably right.

"There has to be something I can do, Street."

"Maybe there is," he said, and he squeezed back firmly.

Earlier that Wednesday morning, Blossom had woken up groggy, drugged and tied to the bed in George's room. She had a ball gag stuffed in her mouth with a tooled leather strap holding in in place.

Mr. Thompson was standing over her. He was wearing black stockings, a garter belt and an impossibly tight lace-up bustier, which made his waist possibly fifteen inches around. He took the key fob to his dungeon out of the top of his bustier and dangled it in front of her.

"Thank you, darling, for leaving this right where I could find it." He looked down at her with a clownish smile. "Things are moving too fast. Lots of sneaking around and drama. I can't deal with it all at once," Mr. Thompson said softly as he snuggled next to her on the bed, fiddling with a hypodermic and a bottle. He tightened a small leather strap, which looked to be made just for the purpose, around her arm and slapped the underside of her elbow hoping to make a vein stand up. Blossom began to struggle against her bonds, and the gag started to make her choke.

As he leaned over to inject her with another large dose of ketamine, she could hear George's muffled shrieking behind the closed door at Mr. Thompson's back. Mr. Thompson bent over her, and she could hear the leather of his outfit creaking. He said, "I will see you soon. Now sleep tight." Then she started to relax, and she fell into a strange, dream-filled sleep.

Thomas Thompson had attacked all the girls in their sleep, drugging them first and then binding them up. Kristy had pleaded for their lives, and Thomas had promised to get Blossom safely home, but of course he didn't. Kristy was desperate, and whether she knew what he was going to do to Blossom is unclear. Kristy was not thinking straight. After Thomas left with Blossom, she called family and arranged for a nephew in Haines to pick them up in a boat on Juneau's road system to the north. She knew that without bodies, she couldn't fake their deaths and disappear, but she thought it would give her more time. She didn't understand Thomas's ultimate plan. Did he think he could just get a bunch of cash and leave town before his wife and faithless children came home from Haines? But she couldn't bring herself to think about it too much.

But why did Thomas Thompson attack all the girls at once? What made him want to blow up his entire life at that particular moment? To say that he was a "freak" didn't cover it. The truth was, getting Georgianna back had flooded him with satisfaction. He was vindicated; a *thing* of his had been stolen and now it was returned. He was bursting with a kind of emotional high, similar to the feeling of wicked sex. He was getting what he had always wanted. It made him feel powerful, but more than that . . . he felt invincible. That sweet feeling was exquisite for the first days of the discovery that Georgianna was *his,* then two sensations entered this world of glowing satisfaction. He saw that George was willful and smart; she not only backtalked but she ran away from him. It was obvious Georgianna didn't love him and wouldn't obey; she beat him at chess for God's sake, and this enraged him. Then when he sensed a newfound willfulness in Kristy, that she was on Georgianna's side, that Kristy was able to love the child and the child apparently loved her back, Thomas began to sense that he could not dominate their combined energies. This realization was like dropping an anvil in a particle accelerator, and Thomas exploded. His darker desires collided with his hatred of the weak, and his rage blossomed like a fireball.

Kristy put everyone's cell phones in a duffel. She thought about going to a shelter, but she worried he would find them there. She didn't know what to do other than to flee the man she had married. All she could think was that she had to put distance between them and not let anyone else find them for a while. Anyone who would bring the police into it.

Kristy and the two girls made it to fish camp late Wednesday afternoon, and the rest of her Haines relatives had already set up and stocked the camp by the time they got there. Kristy hugged her girls and cried. George kept arguing and wanted someone to contact Blossom, but Kristy forbade it. Things didn't get really worrisome with Kristy until Thursday afternoon when she saw that there was no satisfactory endgame, and started drinking.

◙ ◙ ◙

It is hard for me to write these details. My own sweet daughter told me what happened through her tears, and I could not write it down at first. Truthfully, at first, I could not picture the events without phasing out into a kind of white-hot haze of gut sickness, rage and finally tears. But later I told myself, and her, that there would be no recovery from this kidnapping without facing the devil himself and looking at him clearly with our own humanity intact.

Blossom woke up again as Thomas was lugging her down the basement stairs. She felt sick to her stomach, and she started to moan. Thomas flopped her down on the iron-frame bed surrounded by bookshelves. When she started to yell, he fitted her with the ball gag again, and she choked, then vomited. He cleared her mouth that one time. Then he tucked the kerchief back into his sleeve and took the wooden handle of an elegantly tooled strap with both hands, and said, "I'm going to tie your other hand now, and I don't want any more of your sassiness."

Blossom lay still and he tied her left hand without trouble. She had no idea how long she had been tied up. Thomas Thompson took a drink of water and looked her over. She was sobbing, her face twisted away from him, doing her best to move so that whatever blows would be coming would land on her back. He flipped her faceup and started to undo her belt. When he began to pull her pants down, she kicked him in the face.

He shrieked like a girl, and she cut her bare heel on one of his canine teeth. He stood up, wiping blood from his mouth with the back of his hands and licking it with his wolfish tongue. Then he stripped down, revealing another red lace-up corset constricting his waist to an impossibly narrow girth. His whole body was shaved, including his legs. He wore black leather shorts and strange leather lace-up boots that came just above his knees. The whiteness of his skin glowed like lanterns against the black.

He flipped the tooled strap with the wooden handle over his shoulder and said, "Now, shall I begin again?"

There was only pain. Everywhere. Fear. Helplessness and pain. She went somewhere else. Her old room in Sitka, then the skiff offshore with the whales surfacing and blowing vapor, the great seabirds, the albatross chortling on the water after they had folded their massive wings to land and feed on the discarded bait. The gigantic swells rolling up under her dory as she took photographs. The slap of the flukes of the big male sperm whales when they would dive after she had taken a skin sample before rolling under her tiny boat. The great blue wilderness of the North Pacific, the endless expanse of the sky above it. She tried to disappear into it all.

She heard voices, another man maybe . . . a higher voice. Upset. The beating stopped. Everything stopped. Someone else was scared now. Then there was an explosion . . . and the smell of gunpowder and hot metal. Like that time out at the gun range, with the lawyer . . . and his investigator. After breakfast. Who was that guy?

Then there were lots of people—lights—and people asking questions. People untying her. Cameras taking pictures. Someone lifting her up and tilting her over, a strange jouncy lift, being carried in something like a cradleboard. Then blue lights and a bright box with tubes that jostled and bounced while a nice lady she didn't know held her hand, stroked her hair and couldn't seem to stop crying. She had gone to the Thompsons' on Tuesday afternoon, and now it was late Thursday night, and she was on the way to the hospital.

10
THE WILDERNESS

Blossom remembered that when she got to the hospital, Jane Marie called her. She remembered that her mom wanted to come take her home, but the doctors said she needed X-rays and a bunch of exams, and there were lots of people there asking questions, and would it be all right if Jane Marie got her in the morning. Surprisingly, Jane Marie said yes, and Blossom was grateful for that.

Blossom didn't want all the drama of her mom freaking out when she looked at the marks on her body. But inside her head and chest B felt as if she were coming out of some kind of narcotic deep freeze. She was filled with hard blue ice, and she was terrified of what it would feel like when she began to thaw. Blossom just told her mom that she would be all right and not to worry, but in fact Blossom felt as if she were really going to break into a thousand crystal chips. Her mom said, "Of course, sweetness, but I'm coming down to see you now for just a second" in a really sweet way that made Blossom want to cry so long and hard that she calmed down thinking about her mom. But after Blossom hung up, she started gasping for breath, believing for whatever reason that her lungs were filling with ice. A nearby nurse grabbed her hand, rubbed her back and asked an orderly to help move her to another room. When she got back from her tests, her breathing was better and Todd was sitting in her private room. Mrs. Feero had apparently given him some prayer beads and he was clicking them when she came in. He hid them quickly.

"Hello, Blossom," he said with a bright smile. "I wasn't praying for you, I was just thinking about some things I would tell God if I could."

"Wow . . . okay, Todd," she said, "I am so glad to see you." She started to cry, which made Todd anxious. He took out his beads and started having a speculative conversation with God once again, which continued for the next ten minutes or so until Jane Marie showed up and cradled her daughter in her arms.

"I'm sorry, Blossom, I know they still need to do some more tests, but I just had to come, because I love you so much," Jane Marie said between her kisses. "Please forgive me. I promise I will be a better mother to you. I won't hound you all the time. I . . . I just love you so much."

"Mommy . . ." Blossom said weakly, "I love you too."

That night the cops debriefed Blossom and her mom for a few moments. They told them what little they knew. Blossom found some solace in the fact that Mr. Thompson hadn't beaten her face too badly, though she did have a pretty bad black eye. Her face was nothing compared to her torso—front, back and legs—which he had gone over pretty hard with the lash. She was bandaged up. Mr. Thompson was in a locked down ward at the hospital. He had been arrested and the cops assured her that he was not going to bail out. They had a lot of photos. The cops had interviewed her for a while and asked her about the shooting. Thompson had been shot in the face. There was no gun found. No shell casings. Apparently no footprints or fingerprints that belonged to anyone else but Thomas. Blossom told them what she dimly remembered. Two other voices . . . one voice higher . . . or different in tone than the other. Man and woman . . . man and a boy? She didn't know. They had argued with Thompson. She didn't know how long they had been there. The owners of the voices didn't untie her, but apparently one of them had called the police. They played her a copy of the 911 tape and though the caller had done his best to disguise his voice, Blossom's stomach clenched up with a suspicion that she recognized who it was. She said nothing to the cops.

They also grilled Blossom and Jane Marie about where the girls would be hiding out with their mom. They gave the cops nothing at the time. Jane Marie wasn't sure why she wanted to get to Kristy Thompson first, but Blossom wanted to help Georgie and get her out of whatever trouble she might be in.

Jane Marie left soon after the briefing. If Blossom noticed anything strange in her demeanor, she mentioned it to no one. Blossom wanted no more drugs and did not sleep well. She had one dream about being calved off a glacier and woke up with a start to the crashing sound of waves. The next morning Todd pushed her in a wheelchair to the front door when Jane Marie came to pick her up. The nurse helped her get into the car, and Blossom winced as she sat down.

"Oh, baby girl," Jane Marie said softly.

"Hey, Mom." Blossom started to say something more, what might have been the beginning of an explanation or a speech, but she just stopped, lost for words. “I was trying to help Georgie, Mom. Then her new dad . . .” Blossom stopped again. Tears came to her eyes. “The woman, the new mom, she can’t have known what he was going to do to me. She is really nice. I think he was planning to kill me. Or kill them. I don’t know.”

“I don’t know either, baby. Do you remember that I was there last night with you? I talked to the police? All the tests at the hospital . . . all the swabs they took, came back negative . . . for . . . you know . . . genetic material from . . . you know . . . him. They told me that, because, you know, I’m your mother.” Then Jane Marie paused and muttered an apology, awkwardly.

“I know, Mommy,” Blossom said, but still it wasn’t clear if she remembered.

They hugged in the car very, very tenderly, because there were few places on the girl’s body that were not bruised. Then they drove to *The Winning Hand*, where they wrapped themselves in quilts and drank tea until Jane Marie got the boat underway to go up Lynn Canal to find Kristy, Lilly and George. This was what Blossom insisted she wanted to do. She maintained she needed to find George before she could think straight about anything. She did not cry, and she did not shake. Her jaw was set and she stared forward out over the compass in the direction of their course. Soon she lay back in the steering station berth and slept.

About twenty hours later, after making many phone calls and calls on her VHS radio, Jane Marie set anchor in a shoal area near the mouth of the river near Haines and gingerly loaded Blossom into a rugged inflatable skiff with an aluminum hull and a center steering station, to navigate as far upriver as they could. There were many fishing families that used the river and one of them gave them the location of Kristy Thompson's family's old camp.

Jane Marie had sealed buckets and a large backpack with food and camping supplies for the two of them in case the skiff got stuck on a mudflat within tidal range, and they had to spend the night. She also had a shotgun with a legally shortened barrel. Not a sawed-off, but more like a riot gun for bear protection. Jane Marie favored one round of buckshot carried in the chamber and five more full of slugs. The gun was well oiled, and every year Jane Marie tested it before the fall salmon run, when the bears were sure to be along the rivers. Currently eulachon, the small oily fish, were just finishing up their run, and though bears enjoyed their taste, they didn't gather for them in the numbers they did for the large salmon runs. Still, it was best to be prepared for a curious brown bear to be walking along the river, or perhaps a moose with a calf, which could be dicey if you caught a cow moose in a protective mood.

The engine ran smoothly and they pushed up the river. Jane Marie stood up on her seat to get a good look at the unfamiliar channel. She revved the engine higher than normal to push against the current and make headway but didn't zip along the way the Natives did heading to their fish camps, familiar with every bend and rock in the riverbed. Blossom sat on cushions in front of the steering station; she was grateful for the slow speed and the lack of bouncing. Most of her body was showing black and blue under her bandage dressings. She was taking a few over-the-counter painkillers and some aspirin to thin her blood. She hadn't eaten much, but she hadn't developed an appetite yet either. She loved the feeling of being in the skiff. She loved the smell of the air, the roll of the boat.

Two moose walked through the willows along the river's edge. The large one waded out into the shallows and stopped, watching them, then turned to look back. As they passed, he turned his big head and the long wattle under his throat dangled like a watch chain toward the current. Jane Marie smiled and nodded over at her daughter.

Soon a plume of smoke came up from the trees ahead, and Blossom's stomach growled with hunger. Someone had been cooking biscuits over a fire. There was a big flat-bottomed wooden skiff with an outboard pulled up on a sandbar next to the bank and Jane Marie eased her skiff toward the bar. She tied up and unloaded their gear, then helped her daughter, first up onto the sides of the pontoons, and then gingerly out onto the bank. They held hands like two old women with their rubber boots on as they waded through the little side stream and then walked gingerly up the bank through the low overhanging branches of some red alder trees, and under the mossy canopy of the larger trees of the estuary.

Jane Marie wore her pack and slung the shotgun over her right shoulder. She had left the sealed buckets of food and cooking gear in the skiff. She walked slowly, a few steps ahead of Blossom, toward the smoke and the camp noise. The moose had trotted downstream once their hull crunched the rocks of the beach, but Jane kept an ear out in that direction. Up ahead she could hear girls' voices and the sound of someone cutting kindling. She pulled a branch away from her face and ducked underneath to take a step toward the river, then she heard a clattering of brush and a deep, woofing kind of bark: more enormous than any dog could have made.

Just ten feet ahead and to their right was a large bear with tiny cloudy white eyes. His hackles were raised all the way down the ridge of his back like a racing stripe, and he appeared to be about the same bulk as a race car. The head appeared to be almost twenty-five inches across. The boar twitched, then snapped his teeth in their direction. Moose are either bulls or cows. Bears are similar to pigs in that they are boars and sows. Knowing the sex of any wild animal can be important because in almost all species, males are more aggressive. Especially dangerous are brown bear boars, who will sometimes attack young or weaker bears, then consume them.

Jane Marie chambered the buckshot round, making a metallic clatter. "Hey now . . . Hey bear," she said loudly.

The blind boar clawed the moss with his front feet and bellowed. He jumped like a thousand-pound puppy, all four legs off the ground and coming down in the same spot. He snapped his jaws louder this time, with a sound like a rifle shot—his growl as low as an aftershock of an earthquake.

"Hey! Hey, big boy . . . we just want by!" Jane Marie yelled, but her voice was pinched and audibly higher. She shucked off her pack and whispered to Blossom, "Can you hold the pack over your head? Make yourself look bigger?" Blossom did her best, but she could only hold the pack about shoulder height, hiding her face. The blind boar roared again.

"If he charges, I will shoot. Give him the pack and try to climb a tree." Jane Marie's voice was more halting as she gasped for breath. She raised the shotgun to her shoulder. Then . . .

Suddenly from upstream Lilly came bounding out of the brush with a large air horn in her hand that ran on pressurized gas of some kind. It sounded like a boat horn, or a European football fan. The young girl yelled out after each blare and waved a towel in the air above her head.

"Grandfather!" she called out. "Go down to your bed by the river. Go on now. Move it!" Lilly's voice was stronger than it had been in town. She seemed more confident here in the woods. "Go to sleep, Grandfather. Just rest and then eat your fish." They listened to the old bear amble down toward the river, groaning and farting, before disappearing into a dense bower of brush.

Lilly wore canvas shorts, a T-shirt and flip-flops. Her hair was wild and undone. Her legs were dirty and covered in bug bites. She looked as if she had been camping for weeks, but it had only been a day and a half.

"He's okay," Lilly said to Jane Marie. "He's old and almost blind. He comes down here every afternoon. He doesn't hurt anything. He's almost like our family bear."

Then Lilly looked up over Jane Marie's shoulder and saw Blossom.

"Oh my gosh! I'm so glad to see you. We have been worried sick. Mom, especially . . . she's not doing well. Come on. I'll show you around."

Lilly signaled Jane Marie to back up and walk around the tree behind them and take a little game trail to the left. Jane Marie kept the shotgun at the ready, just in case, and mother and daughter walked backward with their gear to the game trail, where Lilly met them.

Georgie then burst out of the woods and wrapped Blossom in her arms and gently held her. No one said a word about what had happened back in town. No one mentioned Thomas Thompson.

◘ ◘ ◘

The camp was made up of two-wall tents and a tarp strung partially over a fire pit area. There were plywood tables made for cutting fish and several short trails that led to smokehouses, one to the river and another to a cache tree where they had built a small treehouse-style platform to store their food and fish coolers. There was a burnt-down fire barely smoking in the center of the camp, and the two girls were working to build it back up.

"Oh my God. I was so worried about you, B. He didn't let you go, did he?" Georgie said with wide red-rimmed eyes. She had Blossom lie down in a hammock filled with sleeping bags and pads that was strung close to the fire. Jane Marie sat in a folding chair. The other girls perched wherever they could find a dry spot.

"No," Blossom said.

Lilly gave a little shriek.

First Blossom recounted what had happened to her in the basement of the house. Lilly and George hung onto her gently in the hammock. Jane Marie made herself a cup of tea and discreetly wiped a tear from her cheek.

"Do you know who came in and stopped him?" Georgie asked. "Was it Mr. Betts and Mr. Teller?"

"I don't think that's the important thing now . . ." Jane Marie spoke up quickly, trying to interrupt Blossom before she answered. "Right now I need to speak to your mother, girls. Before the police do. I don't doubt that she is involved in all this, and I'm going to get her to turn herself in to the police and give them all the information they need. Enough secrets."

Blossom tried to sit up as best she could and blurted out, "How do you know she is keeping a secret? We just have to talk with her." She lay back down, and Lilly stroked Blossom's hair.

"Mrs. Thompson put you in danger, B. She has to answer for that. She has to talk to the police about how she was involved in all this . . . But first she has to talk to me. She needs to talk to me."

For the first time in this ordeal, Jane Marie was finally showing her daughter real anger, which felt good.

Suddenly they heard a yawping sound out in the woods that ended with a retching noise, then a woman's voice called, "Oh, my . . . NO! Lilly! No. Who is that? Who is that? Don't come over here!"

"My God," Jane Marie said and looked at the girls.

Lilly looked at the fire. "Mom got into the whiskey."

"Where is she, honey?"

Georgianna spoke up first. "She is up in the cache. She climbed up last night to get another bottle. She tried to pull the ladder up with her, but she was all crazy and the ladder fell down, and we didn't put it back up."

"My mom doesn't drink," Lilly said urgently, needing them to believe her, to understand the situation. "At least I've never seen her drink."

Georgianna cleared her throat. "There was an old, old case of whiskey. The family must have kept it there. I don't know. Before you got here, we were just talking about what to do—whether we were going to climb up there and get the bottles away from her or try to lower her down on a rope and keep all the bottles up there."

Lilly said, "We hadn't heard from her for a while and thought she might have passed out from too much liquor. Thought maybe we could sling her down. It's only about fifteen feet."

Jane Marie stood up and made sure there was a cartridge in the chamber of her gun, then started to walk toward the trails. "Is it this way?"

The girls jumped up and helped Blossom out of the hammock. Lilly bounded ahead of Jane Marie and ran the fifty feet to the old cedar tree.

Before Jane Marie arrived, she heard Lilly give a shriek. "Momma, NO!"

There on the edge of the platform sat Kristy Thompson, in dirty three-quarter cutoff jeans and a rolled-up flannel shirt. She wore old rubber boots that had been cut off to make slippers. In one hand she had a bottle of whiskey and in the other she had a commercial-grade fillet knife. But the most concerning thing to Lilly was the rope knotted around Kristy's throat and tied off to the thick branch above the cache platform.

"Oh, great," Kristy slurred. "More fucking perfect fucking white mothers." She waved the long knife around as if she were conducting an orchestra. "Let's go look at the drunk Indian lady who's fucked everything up. Efffrey thing UP!"

Georgianna and Blossom arrived, stared up at the tree, and gasped. Lilly ran back to the camp.

"Mrs. Thompson?" was all Jane Marie said as she stared up into the cache, then she set her gun against another tree. She saw where the girls had laid the ladder on the mossy forest floor.

"Go ahead and shoot me, white lady. Perfect fucking person. You perfect fucking mother. Shoot the drunk Indian lady!"

"I have to tell you the truth now. The truth is that I'm really mad at you, Mrs. Thompson!"

This scared Mrs. Thompson, or at least startled her drunk mind.

"Faa?"

"You put my daughter in danger by leaving her with

your crazy-ass husband. You also put your own daughters in danger."

"So shoot me! Gowan shoot me, perfect person!"

"Will you stop that?" Jane Marie shouted up to her. "I'm not going to shoot you." Then she looked over and saw something that resembled a giant mushroom made out of sleeping bags, tarps and sleeping pads wobbling up the trail. It was Lilly with a plan.

All the girls huddled and Lilly discussed something she had seen on TV. Jane Marie had her reservations—she didn't like the part with the razor-sharp hatchet—but she couldn't think of anything better.

Lilly explained that it was important to establish dialogue with the person attempting to commit suicide.

Jane Marie took her cue. "I want a drink," she shouted up.

"Fuck you," Mrs. Thompson said, but then a bottle came flying down. When Kristy tried to go get another bottle, she found she was all rigged up to hang herself and was too unstable to get up, so she plopped herself down, dangling her legs over the platform again.

"Mrs. Thompson?" Blossom asked.

"What?"

"Why did you come out here?"

The Tlingit woman recognized Blossom's voice and appeared to try to pull herself together. She pushed back from the edge—perhaps to get out of sight—and she lay on her back looking up into the trees. "Oh . . . I suppose . . . I wanted to run away. I suppose I wanted to break all ties with the gosh-darn man." She closed her eyes. "And . . . I wanted to talk to my two daughters. Two daughters . . . I wanted to tell them the effing truth about all this mess, and I was going to let Georgianna make up her own mind about what she wants to do, about who she wants to live with. I wanted to tell her everything, and I wanted her counsel on what she and I should do as mother and daughter." Kristy was blubbering now. Drunk in that bleeding-heart way.

Blossom stepped under the platform and looked up at the legs swinging above her. Jane and George arranged the pads and whispered about how to hold the tarp, while Lilly quietly set up the ladder on the back side of the tree, away from Kristy's line of vision.

"Mrs. Thompson, don't you want to come down? We have some soup for you and you could have a good, long rest," said Blossom.

"Oh, baby . . . you are a good girl. I'm so sorry I didn't bring you with us. But that son of a bitch was going to hurt all of us." Now Kristy was openly bawling.

"Mrs. Thompson, it's okay now. Everything is okay here. Your husband is in jail."

Now Kristy Thompson let out a wild animal wail. "He's gonna kill me."

The sound of her broken heart echoed down the valley. I can imagine it riffling through the matted fir of the old blind boar snoozing down in the bracken by the river.

"He's gonna kill me . . ." She sniffled. "No, he won't . . . because I'm going to end it here."

Everyone was taking care of their jobs. Lilly was moving up the tree, and the other two were trying to determine where to pile the cushions. Jane Marie gave B the signal to keep Kristy talking. Blossom kept saying she couldn't hear her and eventually Mrs. T sat up and looked down at the battered teenager.

"I better get to it," Kristy said as she wiped her nose on her sleeve. "I better tell you all what you need to know."

She loosened the knot around her throat as if she were loosening a necktie.

Essentially, Mrs. Thompson said this: "Thomas was SOO smart when I met him. He had been to college and he had studied history and literature down in Seattle. That's what he told me. He told me he was a professor and had a PhD, and I believed him. The TRUTH was, he never got his degree, and he was just a teaching assistant. Meeting with students after the REAL professors lectured. He never finished his big, long paper. HIS DISSERTATION! His fucking dissertation. He never even passed his oral exams. He was sooooo pissed off.

"He just kept telling people he was Dr. Thompson, and he taught Victorian literature at a little college in British Columbia. We were okay for a few years. We tried to have children. We really, really, really wanted a family, but . . . pffft . . . it didn't work. Then he got in trouble at the school with an undergraduate student—a female student, wouldn't ya know—and the administration found out about his credentials—his LACK of credentials—and we moved home to Juneau. Juneau, you know, was where I had lived before.

"He was VERY angry. I suggested that he get a teaching certificate and teach high school or teach lower-division classes out at the college, but he would have none of that. He was angry all the time. He said he was going to write a book. He began to say that the real problem was that the administration of the college was bigoted against him because he had a First Nations wife."

"Mrs. Thompson," Blossom said, "he's awful. I know that. But you have to throw the knife down. Please don't let him cause any more pain—for you, for Lilly, for anybody. Excuse me, Mrs. Thompson, but Thomas is a fucking monster. I'm sorry for my language. But he is. Please just chuck the knife into the woods, and we can be done with him hurting us."

Jane Marie was standing under the cache. "Easy . . ." she said softly to her daughter.

"Oh, sweetheart," Mrs. Thompson said, as if the whole thing—her future, her impending suicide, the past—was all an absurd drunken joke. Then she threw the knife away. "Love makes you crazy. You will learn that. It will make you do things against your own self-interest, against people you care about. You don't realize it at the time, but you will look back and think, 'I must have been fucking crazy!' Now excuse *my* language."

Blossom could see Lilly climbing up above her mother, hooking onto branches with her left hand and carrying the hatchet in her right.

"Yes, it was a strange thing . . ." Kristy continued, as if she were just sitting around the living room drinking tea with some girlfriends. "He became a champion for Native rights and mixed marriages. He acted quite militant, at the same time making it clear that none of his bad luck would have happened if it hadn't been for me." She looked down at Georgie, tears coming to her eyes. Up in the trees, an eagle flapped through, wings hitting the branches, and landed high in a spruce. A raven called in its ragged voice. "Hey . . . Hey Mrs. T. look at me! Blossom said because she didn't want her to look around and see Lilly. Mrs. T did looked down and tears streamed out her eyes, and if there is a difference between drunkards tears and sober ones then perhaps these were sober ones.

"And . . . he got . . ." She closed her eyes tight as if she not only didn't see Blossom, but she did not want to let any light into her memory at all. "He got increasingly violent . . . at first I didn't mind it. I found it kind of thrilling. But . . . but you know . . . we were never equals."

Lilly was over her now. She took the razor-sharp hatchet out of its sheath.

Mrs. Thompson took a deep breath and continued. "So when he wouldn't stop—even when I asked him to—when he wouldn't stop when I begged him to, that's when I knew . . . I'm so sorry, darlings," she said to the open air.

At that moment Lilly brought the hatchet down on the rope tied off to the tree, and she vaulted down onto the platform where her mother sat. She tugged the rope off of her neck, then sat down on her butt and pushed her mom off the edge using both of her feet.

Mrs. Thompson hit the tarp that Georgianna and Jane Marie held, and they all tumbled into the pile of mats, pads and sleeping bags on the forest moss. Kristy hit with the distinctive "woof" of a drunk person falling out of a tree, and after a moment it was clear that no one was seriously hurt.

Lilly scrambled down and threw her arms around her mom. "She's okay. She is okay. Don't anybody hurt her. Don't anybody *dare* hurt my mom." The girl kissed her mother's tears, and her own dirty face rubbed dirt into both their cheeks.

They stood around the fire the next morning, not saying anything for a while. Ravens called to each other, and flies hummed close to the women's ears.

"So, what do we need to do now?" Jane Marie asked the group as she looked at the fire. It was early in the morning. There had not been much talk that night. Soup. Aspirin. Lots of bottled water, hot tea and oatmeal with yogurt and dried cranberries.

"Well, we are too early for the fish," Kristy said solemnly. "I would like to stay and wait for them, but I suppose I need to go to town and talk with the district attorney about your dad," she said, looking at George. "I mean talk to them about Richard Paul and the child-stealing charges. Then, Georgianna, I suppose you need to work out where I fit into your life now that you know what kind of a woman I am."

Both Georgianna and Kristy stood quietly and looked at the ground while the river sang and ravens clonked under the canopy of the ancient trees.

Jane Marie wanted to help Kristy, wanted to say something to console her, but just then she looked at the young girls, and she heard the blind boar rustle through the brush near the riverbank, heard the sounds of his massive paws slapping at the water. Jane Marie, for some reason, felt miserably sad and still angry, as if nothing could possibly be said or done to make things right. Blossom looked at her mom with a newfound understanding; somehow, she knew her a little bit better now. Given Cecil's position, Jane Marie knew she shouldn't be one to judge another woman because of that other woman's husband. But here she was pissed off and rearranging the weights on the delicate scales of justice in her mind. Blossom also knew that her mom didn't like being angry at anyone unless it was her dad.

George got a glimpse of mother and daughter looking at each other with that "now what?" expression. George got up, walked over to Kristy, who was standing on the soft black ground, then wrapped her arms around her. "Let's pack up camp and get in the boat. We can work some of this out later."

11

THE CASE OF THE BADASS BOYFRIEND

They left the tents set up and most of the camp in place because Kristy Thompson was serious about returning as soon as the fish started running. She had an uncle in Klukwan who knew the blind boar and would peek in on her camp from time to time to make sure no one else was sneaking in to use up her wood or take any of her food supplies.

It took a couple of trips in the skiff to get them all back to *The Winning Hand* with everything they wanted to take home. The women had enough room on the boat to sleep comfortably. There was a high-pressure system blowing through, which meant a north wind and following seas all the way back to Juneau. The autopilot could easily handle the steering as long as there was someone at the helm to watch for any drift logs from the river systems or any ships coming up Lynn Canal on their way to the northern ports for the interior.

Blossom stayed wrapped in her blanket in the helm chair looking out as she listened to the steady thrum of the engine. She had slept plenty on the way up, but she traded off every three hours or so during daylight hours with George, who enjoyed wheel watch. Blossom taught her friend about all the engine gauges and the navigation equipment. Since the rules on the boat were that the person at the helm got to choose the music in the wheelhouse, *The Winning Hand* was blasting Dude York, Superchunk and Father John Misty at full volume as whales breached off their eastern beam.

While the girls listened to tunes, Jane Marie took Kristy into the upper steering station and sat her down.

"We have to talk some of this out. Now what is going on with these girls? What is going on with your damn husband?" Jane Marie demanded. She took the seat that gave her the best view of their course.

"Yes . . ." Kristy said. She looked down Lynn Canal, where the waves were piling up ahead of them like windrows of wheat. Because the wind was coming from the north, the boat tracked well despite the waves, and the stern only slipped around a little bit as the bow lunged through the seas. "Yes . . . I owe you that, plus an apology for my horrible behavior yesterday."

"Yes, let's just mention that. Do you do that . . . I mean do you drink like that often, and have you threatened to kill yourself before?"

"No," Kristy said, "I swear to God. I am so sorry for the spectacle I made of myself. I haven't had anything to drink since a few weeks after I got married. I quit. I swear. I don't know what happened. I don't know what happened to me. I don't know how I got here."

Jane Marie looked at her skeptically, then handed Kristy a mug of tea. She took a deep breath. "My husband is in prison. You know that, right? Cecil is . . ." She paused, watching gulls curling in the air to the north. "Cecil is a goofball . . . and he seems to always be putting our daughter in danger . . . but . . ."

The boat hummed underneath them. "No," Kristy said, "don't compare your husband to mine. Mine is a monster, so much so that I gave my first baby away because I was scared of him." She took a deep breath. "There. I've said it. That's the first time I've said it to anyone."

"So tell me about it from the beginning."

Both of the women took drinks of tea and settled in.

"We couldn't have babies, or so I thought," Kristy started. "Then I got pregnant. I mean, really! What was I going to do? He was still into bondage, but I wasn't. I knew he was going out with other people and having people over to his basement, but after I got pregnant, Thomas said he was going to change his ways. He promised me and made a big deal of it. We knew Ida and Richard Paul. Ida became our birth coach and was going to be our nurse.

"But as the months went on, it became obvious that Thomas wasn't going to change. He kept going out to see his 'friends,' and it was clear he was the center of a group of like-minded people who enjoyed the same kinds of things. I tried not to mind it. I had my own life. He had started teaching. He was making money. He kept working on the basement, saying he was remaking it for the baby. Then one day I went down there. I got a look at what he and his friends were doing down there, what kinds of photographs he was looking at, the age of the girls he was fixated on, and I knew I couldn't bring a girl into the family. I couldn't. I know that makes me a terrible woman—a terrible mother—but I couldn't."

Below deck the engine churned, and the boat rolled into the waves coming up Lynn Canal. The women and the girls were warmed by the burning heat of the oil, sucked from the earth and polluting the air. Yet there they were warmed against death and the violence of men. Jane Marie looked down the course they were headed and knew that this pleasant ride wasn't going to be long enough to solve many, if any, of the real problems they faced.

"So . . ." Kristy went on, "I worked out this plan with Ida and Richard. They would be the perfect parents. I knew they would. I asked Ida if she would do it, if she would raise my baby. She would pretend to be pregnant at the same time as me, and I would give her the baby at the hospital. She could have a home birth. She agreed. She took care of the paperwork. I took care of my testimony, throwing the police off track."

"Did Mr. Paul go along with all of this from the beginning?"

"He never openly acknowledged the plan, at least to me. But he knew. He is not unsophisticated. They had both wanted a baby for a long time—a baby that would be half Tlingit and half white. This was their opportunity. For Richard, it was basically a 'don't ask, don't tell' fake pregnancy. The planning and the carrying out were all Ida and me."

"Wow," Jane said softly. "But what about Lilly? She is yours too, right? How did that happen?"

"Yes, I know what you're thinking . . ." Kristy said, and took another breath. "Once George was born, Thomas had a whole new campaign . . . a new cause. He was the victim of a horrible crime. His baby had been stolen. He was not going to rest until he brought the kidnappers of his baby girl to justice. Ida's and my plan was for me to be kind of her best friend and the baby's auntie. I was going to be involved in George's life all along. Birthdays, picking her up at school, taking her to events, babysitting.

Almost a co-parenting kind of thing. But Thomas was suspicious right from the start. He felt Ida was a prime suspect from the beginning. I told him it was ridiculous, but he wouldn't let it go. He tried to break into the Pauls' house, to find evidence of the birth. He tried digging up the tree where Ida said the placenta was buried, but was scared off by the dog."

Below deck Blossom sat at the helm and watched the controls and the course ahead of them. The boat was still on autopilot, and the navigation system showed where it was at all times. But Blossom stayed alert.

"You think your mom is telling my mom the whole story?" She turned a bit to Lilly, who was playing cribbage with George.

"Geez, I don't know. I don't know that *I* know the whole story. I just know that my dad is a control freak and is pretty mean." She laid down her cards and counted out her points.

"Ah . . . yeah . . ." Blossom said.

"I'm so sorry, B," Lilly said. Her voice trailed off, and her shoulders slumped.

"Lil," Blossom said, "it's not your fault, what your dad did."

They sat listening to the Screaming Females for a moment as Dall's porpoises cut the bow wake.

"Can I ask you something, honey?" Blossom reached her hand over to Lilly.

"Yeah . . ." Lilly said in a small voice.

"Did he ever do stuff like that to you? You know, what he did to me?" B lifted up her sweatshirt to show both girls the yellowish-purple bruises and cuts on her back.

Lilly nodded and a tear fell down her cheek.

Blossom squeezed Lilly's hand. "Well," she said, "that's

never gonna happen again. Not to our superhero girl who cuts ropes and knocks people out of trees. Super. Fucking. Hero."

Lilly wiped her eyes and picked up her cards.

Back on the covered flying bridge, Kristy took another aspirin and drank another bottle of water before continuing her story.

"I watched Georgianna growing up from a distance. Ida would sneak me pictures; there is a hole in the outside of my garden fence where she would place photos and drawings she made. I didn't dare keep them. I would look at them and then either burn them or cut them up and throw them into the ocean."

"Why would you risk having Lilly around him?" Jane Marie asked in a tone that she regretted as soon as she said it.

"You are right to question that. But . . . he did change. When he was the victim, he stopped with the freakish stuff for a good long time. He was crime-fighter Thomas. He stayed home with me. He didn't run around with his friends for years. He was self-pitying and depressed—maybe self-centered still, but sad and more sensitive. Attentive to me. I thought things would get better, and having a baby, just knowing I had a daughter in the world, made me want another one all the more. The yearning was there. I think it was in him too. I got pregnant again and we were happy.

"But once Lilly was born and the real demands of fatherhood came along, once he was no longer a victim, once Lilly started to speak for herself and make demands—once I started to make demands—that was too much for Thomas and it all started up again . . . if it had ever really gone away. The plans for the basement to be turned into a playroom were gone. The new heavy door was built. My figure changed, and he became obsessed with my having a slimmer waist.

"Then he got obsessed with his old Victorian literature and wanted me to start calling him 'Doctor' Thompson. He said he was going to complete his book, and he became incredibly vain about his looks. He started to combine his crime-fighting identity with his odd sex fantasies. I don't know. I don't know."

Jane Marie checked the course they were on and scanned the seas ahead for any dangers. Her eyebrows were knit tight with worry. How could two people get so off course? she thought to herself. Then again, she never expected that she herself would be married to a convict and she would be living in an old boat while her husband only saw their daughter in jail and kept getting involved in crimes.

"Then when the whole story about the theft of a baby came out, and his suspicions about Ida and Richard were vindicated, he went crazy. I think he went to George's mom and dad's house and said something to them that caused Ida some incredible anxiety. I don't know. I think he threatened her. I just don't know. And although I had my suspicions for a few years, I became certain that he was emotionally abusive to Lilly.

"Then all this happened. He became paranoid. He thought he was owed a happy life. He felt entitled to a happy life, but he was sick. He wanted us all to be like a happy family in an old book, but it was not possible."

Kristy was crying again. She looked up and saw the black-and-white porpoises swimming through the wake. She smiled through her tears.

"How long can you go on not knowing who you are? How long can you go on, hungry for pain? He is narcissistic and in thrall of a sick identity. He thought he was some kind of Victorian intellectual and I, I of course was a kidnapper, and I think he knew that too. It drove him crazy. When Blossom discovered his secret room, he thought it was all over. All of it was going to be on the front page of the paper and everything had to come to an end."

"What does that mean?" Jane Marie said, more sharply than she intended. She stood up and gave Kristy Thompson a look that was surely the outrider of a hostile reproach.

"I thought he was going to kill us all," Kristy said.

By the time the boat had pulled into its permanent slip, the sun was coming up on the next day, and the girls were asleep in their bunks. Jane Marie and Kristy had slept through the early evening and taken the helm around nine-thirty at night, while the girls were starting to watch videos on their computers and becoming more and more oblivious to the finer details of navigation.

The boat was tied and the engine was shut down. Jane Marie plugged the shore power into the boat and came back into the main cabin. The girls were up, making breakfast and listening to "Learn to Surf" for the third time.

"You are up early." Jane Marie looked skeptically at all the sleepy girls, who appeared to be in the early stages of making either French toast or scrambled eggs.

"I'm gonna talk with Ned. Got to find that boy." Blossom yawned, holding an eggy fork in front of her eyes.

"You really think seeing your boyfriend is a good idea? Why not give it some time, sweetheart? You need to rest and take care of your injuries."

"Mom, what's with you? I don't know what Ned is to me."

"Boyfriend!" Lilly barked out behind her.

"All right, little Miss Nosey. Boyfriend." She turned back to Jane Marie. "It's not like I'm never going to talk with him. He's probably worried about me."

"I know you texted him before the boat left town." Jane Marie poured the two of them some coffee.

"Yes, and he acted all weird and cool or something, like he wasn't worried enough about me being missing."

"What do you mean?" Jane Marie asked, probably too quickly.

"I mean, he was like all . . . 'Glad you are all good . . .' and, 'Good thing you are spending some time with your mom on the boat' and stuff." Blossom squinted suspiciously at her mom. "He was not acting normal for the situation, not like, 'Oh my God, I was so worried about you. I will be right there,' and all lovey, goopy like he usually is."

"Oooooh," George and Lilly said in unison this time while George put some vegan sausages in a hot frying pan and bread on a toaster rack above the iron stove.

"Okay . . . enough, you two," Blossom said. "I'm just going to go talk with him. I want to see him . . . first, because I want to see him, okay . . . I admit it . . . but then I want to find out what he knows about how I got out of that basement. Don't fucking tease me right now!" she snapped, and her eyes filled with tears. Blossom was close to breaking open, but Jane Marie saw that was the last thing she wanted to do.

"I don't suppose I can stop you, B," Jane Marie said, "but please don't grill him. Don't get him to confess to something that might get him in trouble . . . or get anybody else in trouble. I don't want . . . I just don't want you to get any more entangled in . . ."

"Mom. You worry too much." She poured the eggs into another hot pan.

"Worry too much? Are you freaking kidding me, young lady? Should we go down the list of things you have been through lately? If anything, I am beating myself up for not worrying ENOUGH! You will be lucky if I let you out of my sight ever again."

Blossom slumped down at the galley table and cried like a little girl. Both Lilly and George sat across from her and reached over and took her hands. Jane Marie sat at the helm chair and sighed.

"God, help me," Jane Marie said out loud.

"We will help take care of her, Mrs. Younger," Lilly said softly.

"Of course you will, Lilly. Just keep your hatchet with you," Jane Marie said, looking at the youngest girl with a kind of exhausted admiration.

It wasn't a long walk up to the law office for Blossom, Kristy and the two girls. Kristy had called and spoken with Darcy, Harrison Teller's assistant, and made an appointment for that morning. She asked if Mr. Betts was in the office and he was. She then asked if Ned was around and sure enough, he was too, so all four of them walked up toward the flats together to take care of their business.

Otis Betts met them at the elevator. He gave Blossom a soft pat on the back as soon as she got off. Then he shook hands all around.

"Harrison is waiting to talk with you, Mrs. Thompson," he said to Kristy, before turning his attention again to Blossom. "I was worried about you, girl. I talked to some cops, and a friend at the hospital told me what happened to you. You okay?"

"I'm getting better, thank you, Mr. Betts. Is Ned around?" Blossom stared at Otis Betts to see if there was any break in his poker face, but he showed no tells, only genuine concern and relief at seeing her walk in.

"I think young Ned is back at his desk off the copying room. You know where that is?" He pointed down a narrow hall. "Let me get these ladies situated back with Harrison, and I'll catch you later, all right?"

"That would be great." She waved at Lilly and George, but she kept staring at Otis Betts as he walked away, as if she wanted to crack his unbreakable demeanor.

When she opened the door, she startled Ned.

"Heyyyy!" he said, and he put down the file he was reading and sat for a moment just staring at her. "Wow. I thought you were going to stay out camping a lot longer!" He didn't stand up.

"You don't sound happy to see me," Blossom said.

"Of course I am. Jeez. I'm really glad." He got up and walked around the tiny desk, which was squished in the corner of the room, and gave her a hug. Blossom noticed that Ned had a hard time looking at her. His eyes seemed to dart around, landing on anything that wasn't her. The hug was short and awkward. He backed up quickly and he had his right hand around his neck.

"Um . . . how are you, Blossom?" Another thing: he didn't usually call her that. "I mean, um . . . how are you feeling?" Then instead of looking at her, Ned hugged her again—this time hard, so hard that it hurt her. This time, she could feel that he was starting to cry.

"Neddy . . . what's wrong with you, man?"

"Dude . . . nothing." He backed up and went back around to his desk. "I'm just surprised you are back so soon . . . is all."

"You are like a mass of weird tics, Ned. Relax." She leaned over the desk and hugged him kind of tentatively, like she really wanted to kiss him, but Ned seemed to want to pull away. "I missed you," she said into his ear. "I wanted to see you. I wanted to talk with you and thank you for what you did for me."

"I didn't do anything, Blossom . . . really."

"Okay. I get it. I'm not going to give you the third degree. My mom told me not to." Here Blossom turned the old reading light on a spring lever over his desk around so it shined in Ned's eyes. He squinted and ducked away.

"No really, B! I didn't do anything to get you out of that house. It wasn't me. Get that out of your head."

"Jeepers, you are a bad witness, Ned. I never mentioned the house or getting me out of it. You just blurted it out."

Ned stared at the floor. A few tears leaked out of his eyes. He tried to use his tough-guy Bogart voice. "Give me a break, doll. I'm about to crack this new case wide open." He tried to smile . . . but not up at her.

"I'll meet you after work, then?"

"How about the soda shop for a malted, Jughead?" he said softly as he wiped his eyes.

"You betcha, Arch." Then she hugged him, all elbows, across the desk again. He closed his eyes and started crying again, almost sobbing. She stood up looking at him quizzically.

"Hey, buddy, don't cry. It's all right. Nothing bad is going to happen to you. I already soaked up all the bad karma around here." And here, her hands were shaking and her voice started to crack. "I'm just hanging on here, Ned. But the hell with it, you saved me. I'm not going to say anything to anybody."

"You're swearing a lot," Ned said and smiled, looking

tired, and suddenly Blossom thought she could see her boyfriend as an old man, and it frightened her. She thought she was going to go crazy right there in the law office and that scared her. Ned looked old.

He said, "Oh, B, everybody thinks they can keep a secret . . . you know . . . but damn it . . . it's just not that easy." Then he lifted his eyes and looked right into hers. "Let me finish up this stuff. I will meet you and we will get something sweet. You know, you are my best friend, and I don't know what's gonna happen to us . . . But I love you like crazy, B."

"Yeah . . . me too," she said, "but don't scare me, dude."

"Check me later, man."

"Okay, later."

B later told me that after this meeting with Ned, she walked outside and threw up her breakfast on the sidewalk, and cried hard enough that a tourist lady stopped to ask if she should call someone for her. Blossom wiped her mouth on her sleeve, brushed back her hair and said, "No, ma'am, I just ate some bad clams my dad dug this morning," then walked away quickly.

A few minutes later, back on *The Winning Hand*, Blossom was helping her mom clean up the boat as best she could. She was washing dishes and placing them in the drying rack near the oil stove as her mom had the hatch to the engine room open and was checking all the fluids on the engine and the gen set. Jane Marie had a small bucket and some old paper towels, and was wearing disposable surgical gloves as she squeezed around the engines. Blossom had to raise her voice to be heard.

"Mommy, why would Ned be so sad? Let's just say, for the sake of argument, that he was the one who got me out of the fricking basement, why would that make him sad? Why would seeing me again make him cry?"

Jane Marie poked her head, with her hair wrapped in a bandana, up through the hatch. "Honey . . . it's probably complicated. It's a trauma for you, right?"

"That's right. It's a trauma for *me*! So why is *he* crying?"

Jane Marie told me later that Blossom's voice was almost frantic at this point. She was close to tears all the time and Janie was sick with worry on many fronts.

"Sweetie . . . I'm not saying it was him. I don't think it was . . . but like you said, for the sake of argument, if it was, it would be traumatic for him to see you like that. To be hurt so badly. He wouldn't have known how . . . you know . . . how badly you were hurt."

"Oh, JESUS CHRIST!"

"Blossom, please."

"Do you think that's it? It's because I had my pants off? He's never seen me like that."

"Please, calm down, honey. I'm not trying to pry into that with you."

"Mom . . . GROSS, NO! We are not like that. I mean . . . no. Gross."

"Okay . . . but skipping over all that. Ned loves you, honey, and knowing that you have been hurt and threatened . . . possibly raped . . . we know you weren't, but he wouldn't have known that at the time . . . he still doesn't know how to help you. That would be traumatic for him too. Not like it was for you, but still, enough to make him a little crazy."

"Okay, I get that, Mom. But why didn't they cut me loose right then? I mean, Jesus, I had suffered enough. Why didn't they cut me loose?" Here Blossom started to crack and cry in front of Jane Marie for the first time, and

Jane Marie patted her daughter's toe with her greasy black-gloved hand.

"That's why I don't think it was him, Blossom. If it was Ned, I think he would have. Ned wouldn't have shot anyone. Ned doesn't even hang around with anyone with guns. He's not good with guns, is he?"

Blossom wiped her hands dry with a dish towel and started in on the dishes in the rack. "Otis Betts has plenty of guns, Mom. They would have done it together."

"And if they had . . . and I don't think they did . . . Mr. Betts wouldn't be so stupid as to get a child caught up in that kind of caper, and Betts didn't need him. Betts knew where you were and Betts could have gotten in without Ned. Betts wouldn't take Ned, and Ned wouldn't get involved in gunplay, Blossom. That's what I think."

"For the sake of ARGUMENT, Mom!"

"Okay, the reason they . . . the reason anyone wouldn't cut you loose right away is because they committed a crime. They shot Mr. Thompson."

"Thompson is a major criminal and a pervert."

"Still, they broke into his house and shot him. Whoever they were, they weren't cops on official business. They were probably wearing hoods, at least that is what Thompson told the cops. Hoods and jumpsuits held together with duct tape."

"All of which Otis Betts has access to," Blossom yelled down the hatch.

"And everyone in Juneau, Alaska, and America," Jane Marie yelled up. "So they left you tied up so they would not risk you getting loose, following them, or hearing their voices any better."

"And identifying them as Ned and Otis Betts . . ."

"Possibly . . . or any number of people who hated

Thomas Thompson and were involved in his weird little sex club . . . someone like the guy at the bank or one of your teachers!"

"EWWWW . . . disgusting, Mom."

"Anyway. That's all I'm saying. I don't think Ned was involved. I don't think it was anyone . . . anyone you know. I think you should cut Neddy some slack."

Blossom finished putting the last plate on the rack and then started storing things in the cabinet without having to take a step. "Neddy? When did you start calling him that?"

"Never mind—NED. Ned loves you, B. He has strong feelings and what happens to you affects him deeply. You like acting like a badass all the time, but it's important that at some point you admit that these things affect you, too, and don't degrade the soft feelings in others."

"Oh, like you don't do that to Cecil!"

"I do not. I don't degrade your father's sensitive feelings." Jane Marie's voice had a bitterness that was much different than her parental tone. She also knocked her bucket over and dropped the transmission oil dipstick in the bilge. "Oh, fuck it!"

"Mom?"

"Never mind . . . I do not degrade his feelings."

"If you say so," Blossom said.

"There is a lot about your father and me that you don't know, young lady. Hand me a paper towel, please."

Blossom bent over and handed Jane Marie the loose flopping end of a roll of paper towels. Jane Marie ripped a couple of sheets off and started cleaning the dirty dipstick. From that angle Blossom could see up through the window, and she noticed a figure walking along the bridge in the distance. As she got a good look at the figure, she dropped the entire roll, which landed on her mom's head, then bounced onto the grate above the bilge.

"Blossom!"

"Sorry, Mom!" Then she grabbed her mom's good binoculars and ran to the back deck and trained them on the figure on the bridge. It was Ned, walking quickly. He was walking toward the Douglas Island side, which seemed strange for several reasons. One, it was close to five o'clock and their ice cream appointment was coming up, and two, why wouldn't he be driving his motorcycle if he was going to Douglas for an errand?

When he got to the middle of the span, he stopped and took out his own binoculars. He started scanning straight down into the water. The tide was relatively low, and he didn't appear to be looking at any particular point; instead, he was covering a wide distance to the north in the middle of the channel, as if looking for birds. Then Ned started scanning the coastline south of the harbor and slowly working his way up on the Douglas side and then the Juneau side. Blossom began laughing and stood closer to the bulwarks of the boat so she would be clearly spotted watching him through her binoculars. When he caught sight of her, she waved a seat cushion from the skiff over her head and started screaming, "Ahoy, Ned! Ahoy! Studmuffin off the port stern!"

Ned put his binoculars back in his coat pocket and started running quickly back toward the Juneau side of the bridge.

Blossom waited out in her mother's skiff, thinking he was coming to see her, but he never showed up. He never showed at the ice cream/coffee shop near the federal building either. Blossom called Darcy on her cell phone and was told that Ned was still at the office but was not able to take any calls. His cell phone went right to voice mail.

Blossom reasoned that if he was coming late to their appointment he would come out the north side of the building, but if he was trying to avoid her completely he would come out the east or south side. She pulled up her hoodie and waited at a nearby bus shelter through an entire round of buses. Finally she saw him come out. He was wearing a sweatshirt she had never seen him in and sunglasses that made him look like someone in a daddy band. Jesus, Ned. She gave him a long lead and fell in behind him on the opposite side of the street in case he crossed inland. He walked past the bridge, which for some reason surprised her, then he took a right on her side of the street and over by the high school. Then he doubled back, and she cut past the swimming pool and watched him go back into the flats. She followed him again at a safe distance, but this time she turned her sweatshirt inside out so it was a different color, and she pulled a ball cap out of the lost and found at the pool. She wore a ponytail, which she never did. Ned walked across the Egan Expressway into an area where there were state-operated buildings; there was a surplus warehouse and a laundry distribution center that was still operated by the Department of Corrections. Blossom could see old DOC vans parked nearby.

She watched Ned glance up at the cameras mounted on poles, and as he studied them, he noticed that there was a pile of bricks—large concrete blocks, actually—piled just out of the area under camera surveillance. Ned, who was hardly looking casual, stumbled and slunk over to the pile, removed a brick, and awkwardly and quite obviously retrieved a revolver from the pile and put it in his pocket. Then he bolted away from the surveillance cameras. Blossom hid behind a utility pole. Ned stopped and looked around as he made it back to the sidewalk up along the expressway. He started walking toward the bridge.

Blossom had read about doing a close single-person tail. She had to change her appearance so she wouldn't stick out to her "target." Ned would probably recognize her face, but his eye might not pick her up behind him if she changed basic "target values of appearance." She had her shorts on under her pants, so she took off her long pants. It was a warm Juneau summer evening, and shorts were perfectly appropriate. She put the pants in her backpack, took off her sweatshirt, unbuttoned her long-sleeve shirt and walked with her yellow tank top showing. She slung her mom's good binoculars around her neck and twisted her ball cap backward. She put the water bottle in the outside pouch of the backpack and pulled her socks up high, trying to cover as many bruises as she could. Except for the yellow and purple bruising that was so ubiquitous on her legs, she must have looked like a touristy nature nerd off a cruise ship. She crossed the expressway and jogged painfully along the parallel street, then set up on the other side of the bridge to either catch up to Ned or to watch him.

Down below the bridge and off to the side, she had a perfect view of Ned walking along. When he got to the midspan, she could see him reach into his sweatshirt pouch and, without stopping or missing a step, he flicked the black revolver over the side of the bridge with almost no motion of his arm.

Two gulls lifted from the gray-green surface of the channel and took flight, rising up into the air just above the concentric rings of the gun's wake widening toward the shore. Ned turned and started walking back toward Juneau.

Blossom put the binoculars in the pack and hid beneath the undercarriage of a delivery truck until she decided Ned was far enough ahead that he wouldn't catch sight of her. Then she ran to her car and drove out to the prison.

My lovely daughter once asked me what I considered to be the most valuable talent an investigator needed, and I told her there were several. Just to get in the door, all investigators had to have doggedness and skepticism and be okay with double-checking everything and plain old hard work. But the one talent that I thought was exceptional, which most people didn't have, was attention to others, or what your elementary school teachers called "paying attention and being a good listener."

Now being a good listener is not just hearing the words and thinking about them. It's about much more than that. Being a good listener as an investigator means not thinking about yourself, or thinking about your case or about anything else, but trying to feel wordlessly empathetic toward the person you are speaking to while noticing everything about them, and then trying to understand what the heck is going on. If you don't understand, keep asking questions. Eventually, if they are lying (or you are doing a bad job at the interview) they will spin you in a circle so you come back to where you started like a lost person. Or . . . if they are lying and you have done a good job with the facts, they will become frustrated and just stop talking. They will get mad at you and blame you, pull rank or accuse you of being stupid or wrong. That's when you know they are lying to you. That's when you know you have out-listened them. If they tell the truth, the facts come out like a river to the sea, and the facts fit perfectly with everything else you know, with no need to stall or swirl.

This is what happened to me when Blossom came to visit me in jail just after she had seen Ned toss the gun off the bridge. She caught me in a lie, and I shut her down.

"My God, it's good to see you, B. How do you feel?" I asked.

"I feel horrible actually. Pops . . . I checked on your visitor list. Shows that Ned came to see you yesterday. Why would he come out to visit you?"

"He didn't know where you were. He was worried."

"So he comes to ask a man in jail?" She stared at me for a long moment, then she added quickly, "What did you tell my boyfriend, who you don't particularly like?"

"I like him," I said, trying not to stare at her injuries. I was breathing hard.

"What did you tell him?"

"I told him I didn't know how you were. He told me you had been in the hospital. How are you, darling? I have been worried since I heard you were hurt."

"So he told you I was hurt?"

"I got a note from the police department. They told me you had been the victim of a crime. It's a thing they do if a family member is injured. I can apply for extra phone privileges. I tried calling your mom, but I couldn't reach her. I don't have clearance to call your cell."

"So Ned told you more than you knew?"

"Yes."

"So why did he really come, if he knew more than you did?"

"Blossom, are you mad at me for some reason?" I deflected.

"Pop, why did Ned come to see you?"

"Ned is worried."

Blossom leaned in close to me. We were sitting near

the vending machines. There were only two other people in the contact visiting room, two Filipino men who were speaking Ilocano and playing cribbage. They slapped their cards down hard on the table and counted their points quickly on a board, each time exclaiming "Ieeeee!" and laughing.

Blossom whispered, "Cecil, did you tell Ned to dump the gun he carried when he rescued me?"

"What the hell?"

"Cecil, I just saw Ned throw a gun off the Douglas Bridge in broad daylight."

Now, I know I should have said something other than what I did, but what I said was, "The hell he did . . . the big dummy." As soon as it came out of my mouth I realized it sounded bad and just like something any number of my public defender clients would say, so I added, "But I don't know why you would ask me about it, B. I'm here locked in jail!"

"Cecil, at first I thought it was Mr. Betts and Ned that came and shot up Mr. Thompson. But I get back from talking to Mrs. Thompson up in Klukwan and Ned is all crazy, and Otis Betts is all cool."

"What does it matter who got you out of there, B? You are out. You are safe. Just let it lie."

"Pop, Ned seems all messed up. He was crying when I saw him. He said something about how 'everyone thinks they can keep secrets but no one really can' and he can't look at me. I love you, Daddy. You know that, but if you got Ned hooked up with another one of your goofy clients to bust me out of there and now Ned has to cover for this client and run from the police, then I want to know. I will have to help him." She looked at me with her sad almost-grown-woman eyes, and my guts hurt so bad.

"No," I said to my only child, "you have to believe me, darling. Ned is right about secrets. They are not something you want to keep." Then I got up from my cheap plastic chair. I wanted to run from her. I wanted to run, because I knew I couldn't keep her from digging deeper into this, and I knew that if I took her into my confidence, I was risking not only more prison time but perhaps a death sentence at the hands of someone in jail.

I walked over to her and hugged her gently. I kissed her cheek and whispered in her ear, "Ned did a good thing for you B. Don't blame him. Don't get him in trouble." Before we both started crying, I walked away from her and rang the buzzer to call the guard to take me away for my full cavity search.

12
THE UNOFFICIAL FOURTH STREET FURLOUGH

The truth was that Ned was scared. Scared by what he had done and scared of the consequences. Not just of the official consequences of having a conviction on his record, but, more frighteningly, at the idea of doing any amount of jail time with Thomas Thompson. Because, on the night of Blossom's rescue, Thomas had ripped off Ned's clumsy pillowcase hood and gotten a good clear look at his face. Not only that, Ned had admitted, "You hurt the girl I love," before he shot Thompson but didn't kill him, giving even the most amateur detective a pretty good chance of figuring out who he might be.

I happen to know these details because I was right there with him.

How this happened starts with a prison guard known as T. Rex. T. ran the off-site laundry and pick-up detail in the downtown facility. Back in the old days when the ferry dock was downtown and the state capitol building only used linen hand towels, and the governor's mansion got all its linens, sheets, tablecloths, napkins, etc., from the prison laundry, the off-site laundry was much larger. But now there were only a few deliveries in and out of the downtown shop. The union kept it open more out of pride than function. T. Rex (not his real name) had one trusted inmate assigned to him in his small security area. He and the inmate managed deliveries to the capitol and up and down the road system to other state facilities that still had the long roller-style linen hand-drying machines, as well as extra towels for ferries and machine shops, and sheets and bedding for the governor's mansion.

For a single cash payment of ten thousand dollars directly to T. Rex, an arrangement could be made to have another trustee moved into this single inmate position for a twenty-four-hour period. T. Rex would take care of all five counts that would be required for the institution. The inmate was free to go anywhere in the city for twelve hours. For twenty-five thousand dollars, they could be out and about for twenty-four hours. If the inmate was not back exactly on time to ride in the van back to Lemon Creek, then T. Rex would report an escape. If the inmate was seen, caught or captured during the twelve or twenty-four hours that T. Rex had vouched for them, T. Rex would, of course, lose his job and pension, but there was two hundred and fifty thousand dollars in a locked box in a downtown bank for which he was one of the authorized key holders. Our own Mr. Fourth Street was the other. These unofficial furloughs presumably would end when Fourth Street left prison, and if his quarter of a million was gone without his knowing it, nowhere on earth would be safe for T. Rex.

There were some details necessary to make this happen. Rex needed a photo to send in for one count, so he took a photo of me the night before in his van and told me the rules. He used an old phone with a bad calendar so the wrong data was imprinted on the photo. He would send that the next night. He gave me the locations of the drop-off and the pickup, and he warned me of all the cameras in the downtown area, telling me in no uncertain terms to avoid them unless my head and face were adequately covered.

He also advised me to commit no “flashy or loud crimes.” He specifically said, “If I hear any fucking sirens, I’m not fucking picking you up. So you better hope that there is no fire tomorrow morning. Got that, Jocko? No drama. No sirens.”

It was Tuesday that Blossom was fussing with the lock. Wednesday she was tied up, and Thomas was moving her car around back to the harbor—which was a mistake—and negotiating with his wife. Wednesday was also the day Harrison and Otis Betts visited me in jail and I started in on Fourth Street to arrange my furlough, which happened on Thursday. I had worked out a deal and a price for a drop-off at 6 P.M. and a pickup at 6 A.M. So that Thursday at six in the evening, T. Rex let me off on a street on the north side of the flats. I was dressed in jeans that were too big, a black T-shirt, white sneakers and a Juneau-Douglas swim team sweatshirt. I had a Seattle Mariners ball cap. I could not have looked more generic. I had two twenty-dollar bills in my pocket from my own prison account, and I had two prison-issue pillowcases stuffed into my jacket pocket. Rex had told me to be back to meet him at 6 A.M. under the bridge. The street he was on would not be a suspicious place for him to be seen, and it was also not busy. He pulled into Cope Park and slowed down. I jumped out and ran into the trees and sat down to collect myself for a moment. I walked through the neighborhood of the flats, very close to the Thompsons’ house.

My nose stung with the strange smells of the stream and the cottonwoods, and the summertime smell of barbecuing. I heard kids playing in their yards. TVs with baseball games on. Pop music. I heard a woman laughing, and I wanted to follow the sound for a moment—it was intoxicating—but I kept walking, not quickly enough to draw attention to myself. Just fast enough to look like I was late for a party.

I timed my approach to the office building for when someone was coming out. Stragglers were leaving late, and I grabbed the door before it closed and locked. There was a handwritten sign on the reader board by the elevator giving Harrison Teller's office number, and I went to the stairwell to go up the three floors.

There were no lights showing under the main door, but down the hall a lone thin thread of light was coming from under a door and shining onto the carpet. This would be where an intern or an underpaid secretary would work. Teller had no underpaid secretaries, so I walked down the hallway and knocked.

Ned answered. "Jesus. Mr. Younger. What?"

"You are not seeing me. Understand, Ned?"

"Ah . . . no."

"Just tell me where you think Blossom is and then never tell a soul you saw me or spoke to me, okay?"

"I was just going over there myself. It's not far," he said, and he walked out, locking the door behind him, pulling on his jacket at the same time. I asked him if he had duct tape and a knife. He acted clumsy and patted his pockets like he might have had a roll stashed away and didn't know about it, like a kid does sometimes just to impress you. Then he unlocked the office door, rummaged around and came out with a whopping roll of tape and an equally impressive folding knife. He must have gotten the gun at that time too because now his *Magnum, PI* Hawaiian shirt was untucked when it wasn't before, and he walked kind of awkwardly—self-conscious, as if he were wearing his Halloween costume in front of his parents for the first time.

Now, did I know for sure that he was carrying a gun when we walked to the Thompsons' house, where I knew that there were probably going to be some blows struck or at least some serious trouble coming? I probably did know that the kid had a weapon besides his knife. Sure, he looked as suspicious as a drunken shoplifter coming out after stealing Thanksgiving dinner, but maybe I was telling myself it was just the roll of tape, and he was a good kid. Or maybe I was telling myself it would be good to have a gun in the area if things got stupid and all the better if I didn't bring it.

As we got closer I told the kid, "You don't want to break into this house, Ned."

I was going to go on with a lecture about civic responsibility and maybe keeping a clean record so he could get into a good college, but he interrupted me and said, "You can't break in. I already tried. But Mr. Betts has an extra key. He doesn't know I took it. Don't worry."

"Trust me, that's not what I'm worried about."

Ned looked at me quizzically.

When we got to the house, we walked down the stairs to the basement. I could vaguely hear the sound of my daughter retching and choking on the other side of the thick door, and all thinking or planning stopped. I grabbed the keys from Ned, forced them into the lock and shouldered my way in.

I saw the flash of her body from just inside the big door. I stopped and quickly put a pillowcase over my head and one over Ned's. Thompson had not reacted to our entrance yet. His back was to us. I took the knife out of Ned's pocket, pulled away the fabric and slashed a messy hole at his eye level and one in mine. It was a chunky knife with a four-inch blade and a heavy handle commonly used by hunters back in the day. When I clicked the knife shut, Thompson turned around. I took four quick steps toward him, then clocked him over the head with the butt of the closed knife and knocked him down. Thompson was wearing an extreme corset that took his waist down to about twenty inches. He had pale white skin that bulged out of his black leather shorts and boots.

I didn't want Blossom to see me, but my hood was so badly made I wasn't sure if she could see me through the eyeholes. Thompson wasn't quite unconscious. Ned didn't know what he was seeing. Blossom was naked. She looked to be unconscious or drugged; she was beaten so badly neither of us wanted to look.

I pulled the shitty hood around so I was sure she could not see my face, and I told Ned, "Sit on this asshole." He did, and Thompson gave a big "woof!" as Ned put his weight on him. The corset could not have helped. I went to the bed where my daughter was bleeding and tied. I put my hand on her neck and felt that her pulse was strong. I undid the ball gag. I brushed her sweaty hair off her face.

"Oh . . . B. Sweetheart," I said. "Should I kill this piece of shit?"

Her voice frightened me and I jumped back a bit. "No, Daddy . . ." she said. "You never get away with anything." She moaned. Her eyes never opened. I was almost certain she would not remember me being there, would not remember my words or my voice, but I turned and walked quickly back to Ned squatting on Mr. Thompson. I kicked

Thompson in the genitals. Gratuitous, I know, but it was a fatherly instinct at that point.

Ned handed me the roll of tape and I fixed my hood so it wouldn't come off. I turned around to fix Ned's hood, and just as I did, Thompson flung out an arm out and pulled the boy's hood off.

"I see you! You broke into my house and attacked me. I'm going to have you up on charges!" Thompson said, in a voice that was strangely calm for the situation he was in. It almost seemed as if he were enjoying himself.

And this is where Ned acted inadvisably. He turned his head for a moment in silence, looking at the lit space just above Blossom's body on the bed, as if he could sense something, her essence perhaps floating above her pain-riddled torso. I could tell he was deep in thought. There in the dark, listening to my daughter breathing hard, I thought Ned was working on some withering comeback. Finally he just whispered, "You hurt the girl I love."

"You poor sap," Thompson said. "There are only moments of pain and moments when pain ends, and let me tell you, your girlfriend knows both of them are delicious."

Ned let his head hang down for several seconds. I will admit, I wanted to kill the bastard, but I didn't. I moved to get Ned out the door, but before I could do anything, Ned simply said, "Oh, fuck it." Then he pulled the gun from his pocket and shot Thomas Thompson once in the face. The blast from the muzzle flared. I blinked my eyes several times. I didn't look at his face, but sadly, and I say sadly because this is how my mind works, I thought of that long-ago shooting in the Lamplighter Motel, and how it became legend among the tough boys of Alaska. I'm also ashamed because thinking of that old shooting made me almost say, "Put another one in him," but I didn't.

Thompson's legs were limp. My ears must have been ringing from the blast. I didn't hear Thompson's burbling breaths. I looked at Blossom. I knew we couldn't cut her loose. She would cling to Ned until the cops came and got him for the shooting. I told him to run. He shook his head. He said he would stay and take the whole thing, he would explain it to the cops. I told him we would call the cops soon, but I was going to take him out of there, while Thompson, I snuck a peek at him then, was still breathing and spitting up blood through the hole high up on his jaw.

As I turned to walk out the wooden door and up out of his little torture chamber, I didn't hear Thompson breathing anymore. I looked on the back of the door where someone had carved a nice image of the planet Earth and underneath the globe, carved in intricate Gothic script, were the letters: W.O.P.

We ran out of the basement and down a dark street that goes through what the locals call "the Indian Village." Some young men were standing around a barrel fire near a mobile home. I gave a kid twenty bucks to borrow his phone. I called 911 and had Ned use his shocky tear-filled voice to say that there had been an assault and a shooting at the Thompsons' address and they would need two ambulances there at once. He did not give his name. I threw the cell phone back to the kid. I hoped the lighting was bad enough and we were too far away for them to give a good description of us. Besides, I hoped the twenty bucks would help cover for us with these guys who were used to being harassed by the cops.

I walked Ned back to the office. I told him where I was going to temporarily hide the gun, for I never like to hide a gun until it is absolutely necessary. The office complex had a shower and Ned had extra clothes there for when he went running after work, so I told him to shower and change. I told him to stay strong and keep quiet. I told him that he had done the right thing. Except for maybe the shooting part, but I didn't say that, because it was too late for regrets. I thought it was best for both of us to stay positive at this point.

I told him I had to hide out and that I was going to go back to jail. I was going to have a pretty solid alibi for the night, but unfortunately I was not going to be able to help him with an alibi. Did he understand? He nodded, but clearly it was too much to take in. I hugged him hard and thanked him for saving my daughter, and told him she must never know what we had done. I had spoken to her, but I doubted she was in any state to remember, and she would not have seen Ned's face either since she had her eyes closed the whole time. Then I ran straight to *The Winning Hand* to do another completely foolish thing by putting a person I love in an impossible position.

As I walked down the ramp toward the harbor, I had my hood pulled up and my hat pulled down. I looked away from all the security cameras that I knew were placed in the area. But as I came around the corner of the main finger from the ramp, I ran straight into Todd, who was coming from *The Winning Hand,* where he had had dinner.

"Cecil, you are out of jail! I knew it. Does this mean we are going back to Sitka?"

I stopped dead in my tracks and looked squarely at my oldest friend.

"Todd . . . Jesus . . . No, not quite yet."

"Why not? I have been doing some research, and it's

perfectly appropriate for you to return to your main residence, to the jurisdiction where you were arrested, and check in with a probation officer there. You have a right to go home, and Sitka still has a probation office. You know that. I called them and they said they will be happy to work with you. Isn't that great? I can even get my old job back at the senior center serving lunch. I can see Carl and Mary and Louis and everybody. I think we should go right away!"

"Oh, Todd," I said, "I would love to, and I'm sure we will soon enough, but I've got to take care of some things first."

He slid his thick glasses up the bridge of his nose and his big shoulders slumped down in disappointment. "Oh" was all he said, looking straight into my eyes.

"The first thing I have to do is ask you not to tell anyone—no one at all—that you saw me today. You see, I'm not supposed to be out of jail. I'm going to go back tomorrow. I just had to take care of something. But you can't tell anyone. Especially not Blossom, okay? I can't explain it all now. I will explain it next time you come to see me. Got it?"

"I think so," he said in what we called his Eeyore voice.

"It's really, really important you not tell anyone. Okay? I know you are good at keeping secrets."

"Yes, I am. I won't tell anyone. Not even B."

"Especially B. She could get in real trouble if she knew. I know it's hard, but there will be a time soon when we will all be able to talk about it and I will tell you when that is, okay? But for now . . . tell no one."

"Okay . . ." he said again in the donkey voice, "but then we can go home?"

"Yes, pal. For now, I want you to walk out to the

hospital. When you get there, Blossom will be there. You sit with her and make sure no one messes with her. No reporters, no clergy, no social workers. The cops will want to talk with her and that's okay, you can't stop that, but if anyone else wants to talk with her besides a doctor, a nurse or a cop, you say you are family and her family says she is to rest and not talk with anyone. Tell them you are her stepbrother if you need to. If they argue, have them call Jane Marie. Yes?"

"Yes, and nothing about seeing you or talking to you."

"Perfect."

"Then soon, pretty soon, we will be going to Sitka."

"Exactly . . . I promise." I didn't hug him because I was worried about blood transfer onto his clothes, but I waved and walked away. As I walked toward the boat, I could hear Todd mumbling under his breath, and I assume he was praying, for he had a slow and sincere tone.

Jane Marie had just returned from the aborted trip to Pybus Bay and stood at the door of her wheelhouse. Behind her on the galley table was a tangle of cables attached to her phone, her laptop and a small printer stored under the helm instrumentation panel. She had papers scattered over the table with phone numbers scrawled on them and a carton of tissues near at hand, used tissues wadded up like wilted magnolia flowers on the floor.

Her eyes were rimmed red and they widened considerably when she recognized me.

"Jesus fucking Christ, Cecil, what are you doing out of jail? I got calls from my sister that Blossom never showed up and B wasn't answering her phone, so I turned around and I came right back. I called all of her friends but no one will call me back."

"Pull the blinds down, Janie." When she didn't move, I started pulling down the blinds so I couldn't be seen by anyone walking down the dock. Dock walkers are notoriously nosy.

"Oh my God, you broke out of jail!" she screeched in a shrilly loud whisper.

"I'm going back first thing in the morning."

"What do you mean you're going back? Are you some kind of library book? What the fuck, Cecil?" She pulled the final shades down on the forward ports looking out the bow. "Does this have something to do with Blossom being missing? You have something to do with that, don't you?"

"No!" I said probably too loudly, then "no . . ." softer this time. "At least I don't think so."

"Cecil?" she said, drawing it out like she was about to sock me.

I sat down at the galley table opposite where she had set up her command post. "Look, first things first. Any minute now you are going to get a call from the police that they have found Blossom."

"Oh my God." Her shaking hands were in front of her mouth and she flopped into her seat, tears in her eyes.

"She is going to be okay, Janie, but they are going to take her to the hospital. Thomas Thompson had her. He beat her up pretty bad."

"What? Why? Oh . . . Goddamn him . . . why would he hurt her?"

"He is a sick and twisted man. But Janie . . . you can't know anything about it. You can't tell them about me. I'm not supposed to be out. I swear I'm going back tomorrow morning at six. Don't ask me questions right now. The call is going to come and you have to act surprised, okay? I probably shouldn't have told you, but I had to get off the streets."

"Did you . . . did you rescue her again, Cecil?" Jane Marie was trying to pull herself together.

"Me and that kid Ned, yeah. We went in and stopped Thompson and got hold of the police. Ned got a little carried away . . . I don't know, but again . . . Janie, you can't tell anyone. Ned might have killed him. He didn't mean to. I swear. He's just a kid and when he saw Blossom was hurt, he just lost it."

"What did he do?"

"He shot him, baby."

"Cecil, did you give him a gun?"

"No, I didn't. But trust me, if you had had a gun you would have killed Thompson yourself."

She sat at her desk, picked up a screwdriver and started stabbing into the tabletop. Another boat was coming into the harbor and her boat rocked against its mooring lines. "Yes," she said, "I'm sure I would have. So what now? I've got to go see her."

"First you have to take the call. No mention of me or Ned. Act surprised. Todd is walking out there. He will take care of her tonight."

"Blossom knows it was you and Ned though?"

"I'm not sure. She was out of it. She spoke to me, but I doubt she will remember it. It was pretty traumatic. Plus we were kind of masked . . . it got pretty confusing and Thompson pulled Ned's hood off. That's when the gunplay came into it."

She just looked down at her hands and didn't say anything. She took long deep breaths for perhaps two minutes. I leaned back in the padded corner seat that ran around the galley table. I closed my eyes. I listened to gulls cawing in the channel and I could feel the slivers of late-evening summer sun slanting through the cracks in the shade across my face as the boat bobbed on the ripples coming into the harbor. Ravens walked on the upper deck looking for bits of food that might have dropped from the table up above, and I got the very first thrill of the sensual delight of being out of prison and someplace familiar.

My body responded to being in a boat, for one thing. Being in something that was not rectangular felt odd—the womanly shape of a boat hull, just that in itself was erotic. The noninstitutional food, the bowl of apples on the table. The smell and look of it was exciting. The tea left out for who knows how long in an old hippie-style mug seemed like a fine-art painting. The forest of kelp under the barnacle-covered pilings—all of it was sensual and erotic to me now. All of it was starkly not prison, and just then it was startling. I closed my eyes and relaxed into this feeling of being outside for a moment.

When the call came, Jane Marie handled it well. She cried with relief and asked the right questions. The police told her that the suspect was in custody and that everything else was currently under investigation. She asked if she could come see Blossom but was told that she was being examined and that she would be able to visit her and probably pick her up from the hospital at eight in the morning. Jane Marie tried to insist on talking with her daughter, but the police said it was impossible. They knew Jane Marie had been looking for Blossom because Jane had been calling them after she had turned around. The police had no questions for

Jane Marie and they ended the call, telling her that Blossom was in good hands.

Then she stood up and said, "I'm going out there to see her. I will call her on the way. I don't care what they say. You should go below. I'll bring some bubbly water and dinner down to the V berth when I come back. No one can see you down there."

She took her phone and cord, plus a bag of picnic supplies she always has at the ready in her refrigerator, and she left. The picnic supplies, she always takes. Jane Marie is the kind of woman who usually takes a tent, a shovel and an ax when things go wrong.

There were so many details I wanted to discuss with her. How I got out, where we were in our relationship, our marriage. Who I had become in prison and what my experience there had been. And then some questions too: How is her life in Juneau? Was it true that she had been seeing women?

But when I got into the warm front of the boat, I lit the oil stove, which cast a small flickering light. We had paneled that berth with hemlock tongue-and-groove boards from Ernie and Gaylen's mill in Sunnyside before I went to prison. The bunk was the width of the entire space with about a three-foot spot to stand up in toward the stern. The walls were a compound curve with a small skylight hatch. On this evening, the lighting was a warm amber jewel. As I mentioned, there was so much to discuss, but my mind went blank and I lay down, then disappeared for a moment into the dark.

When I woke up, Jane Marie was coming down the ladder with a roasted chicken from the store, some warm bread and butter and a bottle of soda water.

"She looks horrible, Cecil, but she is alive. She seemed drugged up to me. He must have loaded her up on something like a sedative, but maybe she is just in shock. I don't know. She just seems different. Todd is staying there with her. I thought that would be best."

"Did he say anything about seeing me on the dock?"

"He saw you on the dock?"

"Okay . . . that's good."

"And I heard some good news at the hospital . . . two things actually. That bastard did not penetrate Blossom. That's what the doctors think the rape kit shows. She shows no tearing, bruising, injury, redness or any foreign organic material. Of course, she will have the last say on that."

I shook my head and said nothing. I just let the rage rise up and subside.

"What else did you hear?"

"I heard that the bastard is going to live."

"Jesus . . ." I said, trying to figure out if this was good news or bad news for me and the kid. I tore off a piece of bread, slathered butter on it and bit in. I started working the problem, but thankfully my wife interrupted.

"Cecil, let's get her through this, okay? But no more of this crime bullshit for our girl." Her voice was stern but not accusatory. She knew she had custody of Blossom. She knew Blossom had been living under her roof when this all happened and had been trying to help her best friend; and I knew that if I pointed out these facts to Jane Marie, nothing good would have come from it.

"Yes," I said. "Let's just get through this first."

We ate some warm chicken with the French bread and butter. Drank some cold soda water. I don't know if it was the food, or the shape of the boat, or the look of her face, but I leaned over and kissed her greasy lips and she started taking off her clothes. When I saw her broad shoulders and womanly wide hips, strong arms and familiar breasts, I couldn't think of anything more to say.

I shed my borrowed clothes, then clambered into the bunk and curled around her. The first thing I felt was gratitude. Gratitude that our daughter was safe, gratitude to be here with my wife after so long apart. Happy for how we fit together so perfectly. When I kissed her, her mouth opened and her breath was warm. When she kissed me, I gave way in exchange. She moved in circles and those circles moved, as Theodore Roethke once wrote. Where my hands were hard and broken, her breasts were soft and forgiving. I ached and burned, and she was wet, pliant. I pushed in and she fell back. She swung up on top of me holding onto the grips above the bunks for getting up in rough seas, and she pulled herself up and down on top of me, her beautiful body, a lovely fecund shape, strong, moving up and down on my hips as I rose perfectly in time with her as if we were one and the same machine. A four-stroke engine. Sweat now, running down her neck and torso, her biceps taut.

"You . . . are . . . beautiful," she said to me, her breath puffing now. Something she had never said to me. I stopped and grabbed her hair, graying now from its jet black when I first met her. I sat up, staring into her blue eyes, which caught the flame of the stove like the diamond I never gave her. I pulled her down by her shoulders as hard as I could, pushing myself up. "Everything . . . everything . . . I want . . . starts . . . with . . . you." Then the solitary, narcissistic cliché of orgasm.

It was a mess, necessitating a run above deck for the tissues and then a towel, washcloth and a metal wash pan for the little stove. “My God, Cecil, don’t you masturbate in prison? I thought that’s all men did in stir.” She was helping me with sheet cleanup.

“Well, Janie, there is not a lot of privacy and not really a lot of support for furtive, sensitive feelings.” I smiled.

“Huh” was all she said.

As is often the case with long clean-up processes in a V berth, I found myself cleaning Jane Marie in an intimate way, perfectly situated, standing at the union in the middle of the V. Feeling that I had not quite been as generous to her as she had been to me, I rediscovered my love of the smell and taste of female sexuality. Again the amber light lit up her entire body as I used my mouth, tongue and fingers to cause her to writhe on the bunk and say my name over and over again. Jane Marie has a beautiful belly and throat when she rolls her head back, stiffens her body and laughs. She also has an amazing aptitude to maintain this orgasmic pulse, this stiffening, for some two or three minutes at a time if the right touch is maintained and not rushed too much. I might breathe her name in her ear or lightly scratch her nipple with a fingernail. I sometimes end this period lying next to her with her holding my hand, letting her put my finger where she wants, telling me what she wants, as she is quivering, moaning, as I do her bidding.

This of course leads to another round of cleanup and perhaps some more sex. On this night we went through four cycles of this process before we got down to any substantial conversation about prison. She asked me about the details of my unauthorized furlough, and I told her all about Albert Munro or Fourth Street. I told her everything I have detailed here, except the two kisses and his apparent feelings for me.

She was leaning on her elbow, naked under the sheet, and still tinkering with my penis and a tissue. "But what are your feelings for this man, Cecil? It sounds intimate, this protection."

I was lying flat on my back. "Oh, you know, he is smart and we do talk about art and poetry. I suppose it is intimate in a way. He didn't have to help me get out to do this for Blossom, but he did."

"What's he gonna want in exchange?" she grabbed down hard on my hose.

"I don't know. I might have to pay him ten thousand dollars eventually. I told him I didn't want to fuck him."

"Is that true?" She leaned over my chest and looked at me hard in the eyes. "I'm not judging you. I don't know what it's like for you in there. I just want to know the truth."

"This is the truth. I'm desperately lonely in there. The truth is I am confused. He is interested in things I am interested in. He is also strong of character, you know. I think you would like him . . . if he wasn't such a gangster and didn't refer to women as bitches."

"Yeah . . . that could be a problem."

"But . . . you know, he does that to get my goat. I have no desire . . . you know . . . for physical intimacy . . . but . . . I don't judge the men harshly who do hook up in prison. Most of them are hungry for sensual pleasure. It's hard to explain, Jane."

"Tell yourself any story you want." She rolled over on her back.

"Yes," I said. "We all tell ourselves any story we want. Particularly when it comes to sex."

Then I asked her about the women she had been

seeing. I explained that Blossom told me about it. She told me haltingly about the two women. She explained that they were intimate, but not physically. I asked if she was in love with anyone else, and she said no and then laughed. How does anyone know about love when your lover has been locked up?

Then I said, "If you want to become bisexual or a lesbian, just tell me about it, okay?"

"Gross," she elbowed me. "I know what you're thinking . . ."

"No . . . listen, Janie, I know my going to prison is hard. I may have to do more time for this shit with Blossom tonight." She raised herself up on her elbow again. "Wait . . . I just said maybe. I think it's going to work out. I think it's going to be fine. But what I'm saying is, I know it's hard on you. But the rock-solid truth of my life is this: I adore you. I love you and Blossom more than anyone and anything else in existence. That includes myself. Got that?"

She lay on the bunk in that same amber light, which earlier had been erotic but was now the atmosphere of some holy devotion. My heart was as bursting as Saint Teresa's, accepting the arrows of God's angel. I looked at her directly now.

"If God is love," I said, "I am your disciple and I'm not fucking around about this."

"How eloquent, convict," she said, while rolling over and kissing me. "But I'm serious. You have to promise me that you will not let Blossom do any more messing around with this investigation business."

I kissed my wife again. "I think the truth is, my darling, that you are going to have to get that promise from Blossom herself."

Jane Marie made a face at me as if she knew I was right but didn't like it, then opened another bottle of fizzy water.

We ended the evening with more tired kissing and fondling and agreeing that going to jail was hard on a relationship but good for the homecoming sex. We ate our picnic and drank the bubbly water. We also agreed to communicate more frequently and to always try to tell the truth when fate and prison security would allow. Then she set two alarms for 5 A.M., and we wrapped ourselves in each other's arms and slept the sleep of the dead.

13

THE CASE OF THE TWO HOMECOMINGS

As promised, T. Rex was under the bridge at 6 A.M. exactly, where I was waiting for him. I hadn't taken a shower on the boat, but lay next to Jane Marie until the very last possible moment. There was no more sex; we simply spoke intimacies in the dark. We spoke about plans for the future and about Blossom. We talked about taking care of her so that nothing like this would ever happen to her again. We would keep her safe to the best of our ability, realizing that she was already off to a rough start and had become a person who was not averse to taking risks of her own which, try as we might, we couldn't completely control.

I held onto Jane Marie for as long as I could, then I dressed and ran from the boat to my appointed spot. I smelled of her. I was thinking of her when the prison laundry van rolled up.

"Hop in quick," T. said through the window. "Strip, put the old clothes in the garbage bag, then get back into the green jumpsuit of a trustee. We got a delivery, then it's home again, home again, jiggety-jig." And just like that

I was back in jail, where all the angles are ninety degrees and all statements are commands.

We got back to what T. Rex called the "main campus" before first lunch. I got in through all the gates without any interest from anyone. T. wanted me to report back in the evening just to check on the schedule and see if anyone was asking about me. I got into the chow line as usual. One old guy asked what working off-site with T. Rex was like, and I said it was okay, but kind of dull. T. Rex liked having a reputation as a hard-ass and a stickler for rules, so I told the old guy who asked that Rex was kind of a hump, and he snorted as if I needed to say no more.

I got a bowl of something hot and a ham sandwich with a cup of fruit punch, and sat down with Street and Shawn Day, which was not something I normally did. Shawn was not allowed to dress as a woman out in population, but she wore her hair slicked back in a hairnet and had just the slightest touch of makeup on—it could be said to be face cream—with an almost imperceptible beauty mark under her lip. Her medium-security prison orange was gathered somehow at the waist and unbuttoned down her shiny chest.

Street appeared to be talking business with some other Black men. I sat down quietly and murmured, "Gentlemen . . . Shawn. May I sit?" Street looked at me as if he didn't recognize me at first, then said, "It will be a moment. Why don't you talk with Shawn Day for a bit?"

We moved over to another table and two older white pedophiles moved down toward the end, as is customary. We sat across from each other. Shawn Day looked me straight in the eye. "My God, you couldn't smell any more like sex, Cecil. Jesus, did you bathe in it?"

"Jesus, Shawn."

"I'm just telling you, girlfriend. Here, cover it up, or the bulls will start getting randy if you know what I mean." And I swear she winked at me for the first time as she handed me a tiny squeeze-bottle of some kind of scent.

I took the lid off and sniffed. "Really? You think this will be better?"

"No . . . maybe not." She frowned. "You will just smell like some freshly powdered old slut. Make it worse probably." She stared at me for a few more seconds without saying a thing. Then, "So, did you take care of that thing with your daughter or did you just fuck your brains out and forget about the poor dear?"

"No, I took care of it. If everything goes according to plan, Thomas Thompson will be pretrial in here as soon as he gets out of the hospital."

She pursed her lips. "Hospital, how butch of you. Jesus, I never took you for a fag basher, Cecil."

"Thompson is not a homosexual, is he?"

"No . . ." She slapped me on my hands. "I'm just joshing you. He's just a freaky straight man. He's got a couple of his club members in here now. The bent boys, I call them. One of them is very dangerous. Very, very bent. He is under my protection, in my crew, if you will."

"I didn't know you had your own crew, Shawn," I said, trying to make conversation, looking over to see if Street was finishing up his business. This was a mistake, for I must have come across as condescending.

She reached out and enfolded my hand in hers. It is easy to forget that Shawn Day is six feet five inches tall and all muscle. She squeezed my hand until it felt like my knuckles were going to all come loose and jumble around like marbles and sticks in a skin sack.

"You are fucking right I have a crew," she said in an uncharacteristically threatening voice. "You would be mistaken thinking that I was someone's bitch. I provide Mr. Munro with protection for a very good price. Plus . . . my own . . . personal considerations."

"Of course!" I winced and tried to pull my burning hand away. "I meant no offense to you."

She released my hand, then tapped it lightly. "I'm sorry, dear. I thought you knew." Her voice had gone back to normal now. "I provide information and protection to Mr. Munro. You know little bitches. They love to talk, and I love to listen," and she chuckled in an almost mannish way.

I massaged my hand to get the bones back in order and the blood flowing. "What can you tell me about Thompson's club?"

"You know, Cecil, ever since I was a young child, I knew I had a dick and all the biological characteristics of a boy but the inner life of a girl. My mother caught on quickly. My father threw up his hands and split, brother. I don't really know why, but I always suspected it was because of me. Anyway . . . I played with dolls. I wore dresses in my room. I wore my mom's makeup. She prayed over me. She tried to help. She sent me to an uncle who she thought would help, but he was just a regular old faggot. That didn't help. Anyway, I moved to the Magic Kingdom as soon as I was able. Sixteen."

"What? Disneyland?"

"No, silly. New Orleans. I loved it . . . Never mind that, baby. The point is I always knew who I was. These white boys, these bent boys, they don't know what the hell they are. The one from Thompson's club, Kenny Walters—he is so straight, you tell him he might be gay, he will bash your head in . . . but he loves him some rape fantasies.

That's all he is into. He wants big old hairy violent men to beat him, tie him up, or hold him down and take him from behind."

"Are you shitting me?"

"Girl, I am not."

"So what kind of protection do you offer him in jail?"

"I basically schedule his appointments and make sure nobody kills him and make sure he doesn't turn anybody in. Girl, I tell you, he likes it rough, so he will make the boys mad. He will call a man a nigger just to get him riled up and beat on him extra hard. It's crazy shit, I'm telling you. He wants to be debased, girl."

"He wants this?"

"Oh, you poor baby, am I shocking you? Yes, he wants this. He wanted it out in the free world. He wants it in here. He was a fucking dentist or something. He was a straight white man. Re . . . spect . . . a . . . ble. No. Shit. A stone-cold freak." Shawn Day was leaning over me and gesturing with her hand as if we were two ladies gossiping over our coffee in the morning. "Talk about burying the lede, sweetheart. I have something big to tell you."

"Okay." I waited.

"You should have killed that motherfucker when you had the chance, because he just made it through isolation in record time."

"Who?"

"Your boyfriend, Mr. Thompson. All the bent bitches are having the vapors. So exciting!"

"How'd that happen? You telling me he is population already?" I whispered. "That can't be possible."

"Apparently his head wound wasn't all that serious. Went down through his cheek. Took a couple of teeth and hurt like hell. But he's got some friends in admin, and they put him right through. Walters is his main guy in here and will run interference."

"Wonderful," I said.

"Got something else for you too. You know your man . . . Mr. Paul? Well there is a rumor that my man Kenny did his wife, Ida, when she came in here."

"Wait . . . wait . . . Ida Paul? The woman who was charged with stealing the baby?"

"Yuh . . . hmmm."

"I thought she hanged herself in the women's shower?"

"No, sir. They found her in a closet just off the law library. You know how women have library hours. They found her in that fucking closet where they find, you know, men and women sometimes. She was dead, hung with a belt from a mop hanger or some shit. But word from the bitches is that Kenny got money coming in on his account from Thompson for that."

"You're not making this up just 'cause you don't like me, are you, Shawn?"

"Cecil, I'm not saying it's true, I'm just saying what the bitches in my set say, and"—here she sat up straight and fussed with her hair and the buttons on her jumpsuit as if she were getting proper—"as far as not liking you, that's not strictly the case. It's just . . . it's . . . now if you tell anybody this, I'm gonna take all of yo teeth out, okay?"

"Okay . . ."

"It's that I just love Mr. Munro. I love him. I do, Cecil. He is the first man I've known and worked with who treats me with real respect. He knows who I am. He knows me deep down. And he respects me. At least I think he does. I love him. But you know this, Cecil. He is smart. He is smarter than me. That's why he likes you and that is what kind of pisses me off about you. It's not personal, girl."

Suddenly with the knowledge that Thompson would soon be out in population, I wanted Shawn Day to have no doubts about my loyalty to her. "Shawn." I touched her hand. I gently squeezed her fingers. "I'm sorry. I really am." She dropped two big fat tears on the greasy tabletop between us.

I looked down at my tray and realized that my food was probably cold, but it didn't really affect the taste of it anyway, so I lifted the bowl and drank whatever it was straight away, aware for the first time how hungry I was, having forgotten about the ratio of exercise to calorie intake I had had on the boat with Jane Marie. I looked at Shawn Day as she finished her cottage cheese and fruit salad, trying to think of something to say that wouldn't make her feel any worse.

"I'm not trying to vie for his affections, Shawn. I . . . like Mr. Munro. He is good to me, and you know I need his protection in here . . ."

"No kidding, Tarzan." She snorted. "Not many people get to swing out of jail for a day." She made a sour face.

"But you have to . . . I mean, you should try to believe me when I tell you that I don't have the same kind of feelings for him as you do, and I have been honest with him about that. I wouldn't do anything to undercut you or sell you short to him either."

"But you think I'm stupid."

"Lord, I do not."

"Don't . . . what is that word you say? Don't act like a father to me!"

"Don't patronize . . . that's the word."

"You see! Fucking stupid!"

"Listen to me." I was stage-whispering now, shrilly, so that the old pedophiles cast a slow eye toward us. "You may have formed an opinion of your own intelligence, but since this is probably the longest conversation you and I have ever had, I have not. So, one, my opinion has not been formed and doesn't matter anyway, and TWO"—I slapped my hand on the table a bit too hard because I caught the eyes of several inmates—"your opinion of your intelligence is the only one that matters. You know you are both sexy and scary as shit, so don't play the pity card with me, missy . . . But ask yourself, do you really think he respects you, or does he just think of you as a tiny bit better than you think of yourself? I'm just asking."

And just then, praise God, Fourth Street sat down at our table. "What is going on over here? You girls having a problem?"

"No, sir. We just gossiping, you know, like a couple of bitches." Shawn Day smiled sweetly at me and for a moment I felt a genuine kindness in her smile; then she patted my hand again.

I ate my sandwich.

"Cecil," Street said to me, "I heard things went well with your daughter. You got her out of the situation at least. I'm sorry she was badly injured, but sounds like Mr. Thompson took some injuries as well. We are still good, and Shawn and I have your back in here. But . . ." he paused and bore down on me from above. "Where did your boy get a gun, and what did he do with it?"

"There was a second party. It was his. He knows nothing about you."

"Did he get rid of the gun?"

"He said he was going to."

"Do you trust this person?"

I paused a bit too long before I said, "I do."

"Cecil," Street asked, "I have to ask you. Is this second party the kid who works at the lawyer's office? The boy Ned, who also goes out with your daughter?"

"Jesus. How . . ."

"Don't ask. Please just get word to him to be sure to get rid of the gun. Some people in here were asking about you. It's not going to be a problem. T. Rex is going to keep you on his off-site laundry detail for a week or so. Just so it won't look funny you coming off and on just at the time of this incident, okay? Rex will let you use a phone in the capitol building. Call the lawyer's office and talk with the kid. Tell him to get rid of the gun. That gun ties him to the crime. The cops get the gun, they put pressure on the kid and he flips on you . . . and then me. Tell him to call from the capitol. So many phones in that building, no one can trace that call."

"Street, what about this business about Kenny doing Ida Paul at Thomas Thompson's behest? Anything to that?"

Street looked straight at Shawn Day and smiled an affectionate smile. "I see you two girls are finally making friends, huh? Jesus, when does it stop with you bitches?"

"Street, you realize I'm not a bitch, right? And Shawn Day I believe is too valuable to be disrespected. I'm just saying . . . as your teacher, you know."

"The teacher I am sticking my neck a very long way out for, in case you don't know it."

"I do know it, and I'm very grateful. The favor, though, does not make me a female dog, just to be clear. Not Shawn Day either. We love you, Street. But love has terms. So ends the lesson for the day."

"Fucking guy . . ." Street shook his head. "Eat your sandwich and check with T. Rex at two." Then he walked away.

Shawn Day got up to go after him but then stopped and said, "Cecil, let me ask you something."

"What?"

"Do you really know what you are?" She looked at me with serious, sad eyes, and started after her man.

"I'm a man in prison, doll. Doing my best," I called out after her.

I went to the library and checked work assignments and didn't see my name there. I checked the mail and didn't see any notes or write-ups, nothing from the probation office at all. Around two, I went to the security lock-up and checked at T. Rex's cube, where I saw my name on his work-detail sheet. I knocked on his secure door and got buzzed in. There was some big hairy mook slouched in a chair also waiting to see T. I saw on the tag that his name was K. Walters. He looked like an old-school Black Irishman with curly black hair and the heavy stubble of a beard, six-one, probably two-sixty. His orange suit fit him like a sausage casing. He had cuts and bruises across the knuckles of both hands, and it looked as if he was getting over two black eyes and cuts on his protruding brows. I didn't envy anyone who wanted to hold him down to enjoy a romantic moment with him.

T. Rex came in from the outside where his truck was parked in the locked yard. "Younger, you are here. Good. You are on my crew for the next couple of weeks at least. You did good on your probationary trial." He slapped down a file on his desk. "You, what the fuck? Walters, you can go. Keep checking the lists. If you see your name, you see your name. Got it? Until then, I already got a crew."

Walters stood up and stretched his shoulders like some kind of cheap hood trying out for a bit part in a boxing movie. “Who is this guy? I was here before him,” Walters said.

“This is the guy who had the job before you did. Scram. Watch the lists.”

“Watch your back,” he said before walking out the door.

“Hey!” T. yelled at the closed door. “I could write you up for that . . .” He turned back to me. “How do you like that guy?”

“Cheaper the hood, the gaudier the patter,” I said.

“That’s not you . . . who said that?”

“I dunno. I read it somewhere.”

“Tremendous . . . anyway, that big guy is too pushy. He wants on my crew a little too bad. I don’t like him.”

“Why don’t you just tell him that?”

“Jesus, what am I, a therapist? I don’t have to tell that hump shit. You just show up here the next couple of weeks. You and I are going to do our thing. You okay with that?”

I told him I was, and I walked out through the labyrinth of halls that led toward the main campus, past the main security entrance where they processed the new fish, and back around the loading bays. I quickly walked into a short hallway that I knew was a black spot on the camera layout. As I was buzzed in, I turned right, then walked straight into a hard fist coming right toward my chin, and I went down.

“Your boy should . . . have killed me,” a voice said—someone whose mouth must have been stuffed with cotton. Blue sky seemed to have poured into the jail somehow with dazzling stars racing through. Then my vision cleared a bit so I could see the horribly bruised and stitched-up face of Thomas Thompson above me.

“That I think we can agree on,” I said, which was probably insensitive of me because he kicked me in the crotch, which was justifiable payback.

Speaking must have been painful, for he was economic with his words.

"I'll cut your nuts off."

"Really?" I sputtered through my bloody lips. I must have bitten my lip when I took the groin shot. "Did someone ask you to geld me? The Future Farmers of America are hiring in here now?"

Thomas Thompson must not have been a country boy because I don't think he understood the reference, or else the word "geld" was giving him a problem. He stared at me with a quizzical look like a monkey who didn't get his treat after hitting the right button.

"Not. Funny." Bits of saliva and blood spattered on me.

Just then the opposite door buzzed open and magically, it seemed, Street walked in. He looked at me laid out on the floor and then he looked over at Thompson. Shawn Day was not with him. It was just the three of us in the little blacked-out section of the hallway. Thompson reached down to lend me a hand up.

"Be careful." He took a tissue and wiped the bloody spittle on my shirt. My chin was red; the bruise wouldn't rise up for a half hour still.

As Thompson was leaning toward me, Street grabbed him by the hair and in an instant had somehow created an inch-long cut through Thompson's right nostril. The heavy iron door buzzed open on the main campus side. Street held Thompson's head away from him so that the blood spray fell to the floor and not on his shirt.

"Take off," was all Street said.

The oddest thing about this entire exchange, besides the fact that I never saw Street's shiv, was that Thompson kept smiling the entire time.

"Not scared," Thompson said, looking up into Street's

eyes as if he were about to kiss him. I later found out that Street carried a small hooked knife that closed into a kind of ring that could fit on his finger or inside several orifices. With a flick of a thumb and forefinger a razor-sharp talon would appear, which could be used to slice open a nose or, when used properly, could open up a belly.

"You sicken me. Walk." Then as the door was shutting, Street threw Thompson through the opening just as it was about to close on his legs.

"You all right, brother?" Mr. Munro helped me up off the floor.

"Yeah," I said, "I guess so."

"He's scared shitless. He knows life is going to be hard in here. Listen"—he paused and tenderly put his hand on my shoulder—"I am going to have to make a show of keeping my distance from you for a bit. It will be better for you. Better for me."

"Okay, but . . ."

"Don't worry," he said. His voice was soft and he pulled me close in a side arm hug. "It's nothing personal."

Then the buzzer blared, and a correctional officer came in and politely asked about the blood on the floor. Surprisingly polite, I thought, but then he was only looking at Mr. Munro, who said, "Hell, I don't know, officer. It was here when we got here." And the buddy just nodded and called on his radio for a mop and bucket to be brought to his location.

Later that afternoon I met with Shawn Day in Fourth Street's office. Street was doing some business on the phone when I came in, giving me a moment to talk with her.

"What's up with this guy Thompson?" I described to her the scene in the camera's blind spot earlier, along with his threat to neuter me.

"Maybe he wants you to have sex with him," she said as she was putting some lip gloss on, staring at herself intently in the mirror.

"It really didn't feel like a come-on, Shawn. It legitimately felt like a threat."

"Oh, you can't tell with some of these bent bitches," she said as she dabbed at a smudge with the very tip of her little finger. "But I will tell you his man Kenny has been trying to pump me"—just a quick smile here—"for information about you. Lots of questions. So, if Mr. Munro knows all the details about what happened when you took care of things with your daughter, I bet that someone else does too." She snapped the cap on the gloss, stood up straight and smiled, checking her teeth. "Also, I know that Kenny is desperate to work on the truck with T. Rex."

"Why do you think he wants to do that, Shawn Day?" I was becoming frustrated with how kittenish she was being.

"I'm sure I don't know," she snapped back, "but I understand that Mr. Thompson has phone privileges. Of course he doesn't know that they are letting him use the phone all he wants so that they can listen in to everything he says."

"Ah," I said.

"Yes, girl, 'Ah.' And apparently he has mentioned something about having your tender little bits cut off, but nothing about why. People are just assuming that you might be 'an acquaintance' of his."

"Terrific . . . but nothing about . . . a second party, a younger person?"

"No . . . nothing about killing your boy downtown, or your daughter. Just that Mr. Thomas Thompson is not worried about his trial, for the assault on your girl."

Street walked out of the handicapped stall. "You two spend way too much energy gossiping. There is nothing to worry about. Shawn, you have control of that freak Mr. Walters, don't you?"

There was an awkward pause while Shawn looked down into the sink and picked up all her cosmetics.

"Well, don't you?" Street said, this time a little more forcefully.

"Of course," she said. Then she said under her breath, "Sometimes I don't know why I bother."

"Are you talking back to me?" Street blurted out.

"No, sir."

"Wait, Street."

"I'm not talking to your ungrateful ass, Cecil." He stepped forward with his fists balled.

"Hold on, now. I'm grate—" and for the second time that day I felt the sky go dark and the stars come out. I didn't see Street hit me, but he did. I was down on the floor. Eventually the ceiling tiles came back into focus. Shawn Day was crouched in the corner, and Street was yelling at her through her tears. I couldn't make out what was happening over the ringing in my ears and the guttural choking of Shawn Day's sobs, which sounded poisonous in my head. I got up and walked out.

No one in my housing unit asked about the bruises. They knew who I hung with and they knew not to ask. A good kid gave me one of his magazines to read. It was a prison-approved rag on Western history and I just scanned the photos until lights-out. My face hurt, but more importantly, I knew I wasn't going back to Street for protection, and I wasn't sure what this meant.

◙ ◙ ◙

It was just a few days after my unofficial furlough. I had committed an illegal break-in and my young partner had committed felony assault in front of my daughter. At the same time, an apparently bent sex freak knew that I had escaped jail the night of this felony assault, and to make matters worse, this information was apparently widely known to a number of convicted or accused felons who might possibly want to use that information to leverage some kind of advantage, either with law enforcement or criminal organizations, neither of which apparently shared any love for me anymore.

Also it seemed there was a bounty on my reproductive organs. So, the red, red robin was not exactly bob, bob, bobbing along, in my desire to do quiet jail time.

I spent most of the days working with T. Rex on his off-site laundry job. He did allow me to use a phone in the capitol, so I called Ned and told him again where I hid the gun and said in no uncertain terms that he was to throw it off the bridge. Like a kid, he whispered, "But Mr. Y, it doesn't belong to me. What should I do? Buy it from Mr. B?"

I told him he would make a terrible spy. "Just make sure no one is watching you and throw it off the bridge." Then I hung up.

Blossom came to visit me. I was crazy happy to see her and relieved. I kept trying not to look at her injuries and just be nice to her but she was all nosy and acting suspicious. I told her that I knew nothing about her boyfriend. But Jesus H. Christ, I am a terrible liar, to her in particular. I might as well have just said, "Okay, to start off, I'm going to lie and say I know nothing about this . . ." It was like pouring gasoline on her curiosity, I'm sure.

◎ ◎ ◎

One day I was walking down the long hall by the legal visiting rooms when Shawn Day came toward me, then suddenly gripped my hand in her big mitt. She squeezed mine affectionately, or at least that's what I thought the gesture was, but as I walked away without looking at her, I felt a note in my hand that read, "*Thompson and Kenny planning something big. Escape?*" Then there was a heart with a little smile in it. I swear to God.

The next day, I saw Shawn Day in the chow hall sitting by herself. She had a black eye. I sat down next to her and at first we didn't speak. Then all she said was, "I left him. He can protect himself for all I care."

We ate in silence for several minutes. I had been working for T. Rex for more than a week and just before she got up to return her tray, Shawn Day asked me why I wasn't off-site working with him.

"I got there early this morning and he had already left. My name was on the sign-up sheet, but he was gone. I don't know what happened."

Shawn Day scowled. I could tell she didn't want to say the next words. She shook her head quickly as if she had been bitten by a fly. "I would talk to Street. I bet he knows something. All I know is both Walters and Thompson are planning something that is going to shut this place down hard."

I stood up and walked over to where Street was meeting with some white inmates. Three of the men were beefy, with shamrocks and SS insignias tattooed on their arms and necks. One had "88" in black ink on the back of his hand. Street was doing business with a neo-Nazi prison gang. I excused myself, from the group while Street made it clear that he was dismissing me.

I grabbed his arm, stood him up and said, "No. You can do it now. I won't keep you long." Street snapped his eyes over to Shawn, but she was not meeting his gaze anymore. The Aryan brothers were not going to be seen taking his side in a beef with a white man, so we walked to a corner for a polite chat.

"Listen, I'm sorry. I really won't keep you . . ." I started off.

"Save it." He seemed sullen.

"What do you know about Walters?"

"Call your lawyer friend. Tell him to keep an eye on that kid."

"What do you know?"

"That's all I know. I can't believe neither Walters nor Thompson has money to pay T. Rex for a furlough. But they apparently plan to kill your boy and maybe your daughter."

"But Shawn said—"

"Listen, Cecil, things change. I will take care of what I can. But I have to do something I hate doing."

"What's that?"

"I'm going to talk with the cops before this shit gets real, and comes back to me."

I looked at him, genuinely curious and genuinely panicked. "What's going on with you, Street? You sound scared."

"I got my parole hearing coming up. They moved it up, and all this stuff with you and your kid is messing with my future."

"How? I don't understand."

"Never mind," he said, as if he were a sulky teenager.

I excused myself and ran to try to get a place in the phone line. It was crowded. It seemed like every hump in the joint had decided they had to use the phone that very second to talk their lawyers through a rewrite of a Court of Appeals brief. I was beginning my second hour in line when Shawn Day walked up. This time, she slapped a note into my hand and walked past me quickly, clearly angry, clearly not wanting to stop and talk.

The note read: "*Cops found T. Rex and Walters dead in the van, down by the harbor. Thompson did not come up in the last count. Take a piss right now, 'cause we are going on lockdown.*"

There was no smiling heart on the note this time.

Lockdown came down hard and fast. I learned nothing new for hours. I did not learn that Walters had forced T. Rex to go back to the prison and pick Thompson up at the loading dock, and then apparently they both tortured T. Rex to give up his key to the safety-deposit box where Street had stored the money to secure the unofficial furloughs. T. Rex kept that key in his office safe, and Kenny Walters had to use some box cutters and a ball-peen hammer to encourage T. to give it up. When they got back on the road, Thompson slit Kenny's throat with a box cutter, which reassured T. Rex that things might be going his way until Tommy Thompson did the same thing to him. Rumor was he did it so fast that when they found T. Rex's body, he apparently still had a smile on his face, but I don't believe that. Thompson then parked the van near some dumpsters and abandoned cars under the bridge near the harbor. He hid the bodies as best he could in the truck's laundry bins. But when the cops found the van, there was blood spatter outside on the ground where blood had flowed out from under the locked doors onto the mud.

Even though I knew he did horrible things to my baby, part of me was surprised he'd killed two men; but then again, Thompson got off on suffering.

◘ ◘ ◘

Blossom had been investigating Ned for several days now, no matter how much her mother tried to talk her out of it. Rather, and I suppose I could have told Jane Marie this, the more Jane tried to hint that it was not a good idea for B to look into who had freed her from the basement, the more our daughter wanted to find out.

Blossom was spending time with Kristy and Lilly at their house. Blossom would talk with them, but no one took a step toward the basement. George was sweeping and carrying garbage bags of evidence tape from the upstairs out to the cans, and Lilly was cleaning up fingerprint dust with window cleaner.

Blossom had tried to do everything she could to get Ned to tell her about that night, but Ned stuck to his vow of silence. She had snooped through his journal, but there was nothing, for apparently he had started a new journal that summer, and he was keeping it at work. She visited him at work every day. She spoke with Otis Betts about how Ned was doing and Betts revealed nothing suspicious. She asked Betts whether they had gone out shooting again, and Betts said no. When everything went to pieces and Todd decided to move back to Sitka, sirens were blaring out of the valley like wolves. Otis Betts walked briskly around the office suite whispering with Darcy and trying to get a word in with Harrison Teller. Everyone seemed agitated, but no one would say a thing to Blossom. Ned was going through his office drawers and looking around as if he were trying to hide something.

"Ned, why is everybody acting so weird?"

"No one is acting weird. Jeez. You are acting weird," Ned said. He was not looking at her. Then he asked her to look outside to see if there were fire trucks pulling up to the building.

Blossom scrunched up her face at him like she wanted to sock him. "Fire trucks?" But she walked over and looked out the windows. She could hear the sirens, and far down the expressway she saw the flashing lights of an ambulance and several police cars that were all pulled over. "No fire engines, Ned . . . EMTs and cops."

Otis Betts came over into Ned's area and said, "You guys better take off."

Ned was standing up looking like he was tucking in the back of his undershirt, which again seemed weird to Blossom.

"There is nothing going on here now. Take Blossom out and go for a walk somewhere, Ned. You know, don't go driving out the road or anything. Just go for a nice walk, and check back in later. Just get out of here."

Ned looked at the big Black man for a few seconds and Blossom could see that Ned wanted to ask him some questions but didn't because she was standing there.

"Go on now, it's fine. Really. Call me later," Mr. Betts said and gestured toward the door.

Ned grabbed his ball cap and his leather riding jacket and walked past Blossom into the hallway.

"Take the back stairs." Betts's voice followed him out the door.

"See ya, kids," Darcy said as the door swung shut. "Be careful."

"Ned? Come on. Tell me what's up." Blossom chased after him once they got into the scrubby back alley.

Ned was almost jogging. Now they could see police cars pulling up around the front of the building as they rounded the corner.

"Okay, B. Mr. Betts is nervous because the police have been questioning him about the shooting of Mr. Thompson. I think he is afraid they are going to come arrest him today," Ned said.

"Arrest him . . . and maybe you?" Blossom added, trying not to be overdramatic.

"He said he wasn't going to let that happen. But I'm not sure."

They crossed the street and Ned held her hand. They walked down toward the waterfront. They walked through parking lots and around dumpsters and boats on trailers. They walked hand in hand and tried not to look as if they were skulking or hiding from police, but more like a couple of teenagers looking for a place to make out, which seemed natural.

"Do you want to go to my mom's boat?" Blossom asked him.

"I don't think we should get her involved in this. I like her and all, but you know how she can be with advice. I just want a place to talk with you, and a place where we can think."

"Okay," she said, and she squeezed his hand harder and pulled him closer to her body. He shifted for a moment and gave her a quick side-arm hug.

Soon they were walking down the floats in the harbor. They went past Jane Marie's boat and past several other houseboats that were liveaboards, and then out toward the end of one finger, where there were some empty slips. This section of the harbor had not been maintained for a few years and the planks were still covered in dry algae. Someone had been cleaning them off and one section was extremely slippery. They stopped just short of the wet planks and lay down on the warm dry wood.

There were no boats around in the nearby slips. This was where most of the small fishing fleet moored, and most of the boats were out on the grounds. The sun was warm and the air smelled of fish guts, gull poop and tarry pilings. The breeze that blew through kept the smell from being overwhelming. It was a comforting atmosphere for both of them, Blossom especially; boats and harbors had always meant both home and fresh adventure for her. For Ned, the harbor had always smelled like romance and Blossom.

"Ned, are you in big trouble because of me?" She put her head in the crook of his arm.

"I don't think so," he said, but his voice went to a lower register, which was something that her father had told her was indicative of deception or ambivalence.

"Ned . . . do you really think that two people who really, really like each other . . ."

"Blossom, can I tell you something?" he interrupted her.

"Yes."

"I love you," he said as a glaucous gull wheeled like a Chinese kite over their heads.

They both watched the gull for several moments. Blossom thought of the albatross out at sea folding their great wings as they land to eat the bait from the fishing boats while the sperm whales rise to feed on the black cod. Her heart lifted when she saw the whales' great blocky heads split the waves in half.

"Yes," she said, "I love you too. Do you think it's possible for two people who love each other to keep a secret from each other?"

"I don't know," Ned said, still watching the bird. "What if keeping the secret protects the person you really love or someone really important to the person you love?"

"Well," said Blossom, lifting her head a bit, "I suppose . . ." and she was going to try to say something profound about love and honesty, or love and complete understanding, but instead she rolled up on one elbow and leaned into Ned's body, then kissed him full on the mouth for a good long time. A colder wind than usual blew from the south, carrying the scent of boiling coffee and frying bacon from one of the fishing boats in the harbor.

If I am lucky enough to grow old as a free man and if I ever dance at Blossom's wedding, the moment before I walk her down the aisle toward whomever she chooses, I hope she tells me that she counted that kiss on the dock as her first real romantic adventure, and that Ned was her first true love.

They dozed for a bit on the dry section of the floats. Jane was on *The Winning Hand* in the same harbor, and she heard the squelch of a police cruiser giving a short burst on the siren. She looked up and saw the cruiser in the parking lot. The officer had seen Ned and Blossom lying on the dock and was getting out of his car. He was speaking on his handheld radio. Blossom nudged Ned and he woke with a start. They both got to their feet and started walking toward the end of the float, worrying that the police would block them in. Blossom said, "Let's go to Mom's boat. If we go there, we can lock the door. Won't they need a warrant to come in?"

"Unless they think we are in imminent danger. Then they can bust right in. That's what Mr. Teller told me. Cops use 'juveniles in danger' to search all the time."

They started jogging toward *The Winning Hand* while they both considered the legal niceties of search and seizure.

Suddenly a wild-looking man with a Department of Corrections jacket and orange pants appeared in front of them. His face was horribly bruised and seemed misshapen. They certainly didn't recognize him. Tommy Thompson saw them and slowed down. He was glaring at them both.

"Ned," Blossom said, "he has a prisoners' jumpsuit on. It has blood on it."

"Hey kids!" Tommy raised his hand in a friendly wave.

Both Ned and Blossom were sick to their stomachs.

"I've been looking for you. I have a message from Mr. Younger. I'm afraid he has been hurt and has been moved to the hospital."

Both of the teenagers stopped. There was no way to move past him without coming within arms' length. There was no way to walk off the moorage float, but they backed up anyway.

"Thank you, Mr. Thompson. I will give him a call right away." Blossom took out her phone and dialed 911. Immediate response. "Yes, there is a man from LCCC down here in Aurora Harbor on float C saying that my father, Cecil Younger, has been injured at the prison."

The dispatcher said only, "Keep the line open, miss. Help should be there immediately."

"Hey! No time, troublemakers. Need to fly away." He was spitting blood from his mouth. His voice was hard to understand but it was clear that nothing good was planned for that afternoon. He started walking quickly toward them. They ran the other way. Ned ran past where they had been lying, turned, reached into the back of his pants and pulled out the new .44 caliber handgun that Mr. Betts had lent him.

"Stop, Mr. Thompson. I will shoot you again. I will kill

you this time. I swear to God," Ned yelled in a quavering voice.

"You shouldn't . . . shoot me . . . first time. You make . . . me . . . look weak," he mumbled through his broken mouth.

Ned pulled the hammer back on the gun.

"Ned, don't," Blossom said. "The police will be here in a minute."

Blossom was standing by the stern of an old wooden trolling boat. Thompson was on Ned quickly, and Ned fumbled with the gun, then fell backward. Blossom reached into the back of the trolling boat and pulled out a gaff hook—essentially a baseball bat with a sharp spike on the end of it. Ned and Mr. Thompson were rolling around on the slippery deck.

"Oh my gosh!" Blossom shrieked, because just then Todd appeared from around the corner. Amazingly, he didn't slip on the slick deck; instead, he reached down and lifted Mr. Thompson up by the nape of the neck and shook him so that he spat blood and flopped his limbs wildly. Thompson managed to slash Todd up high on the thigh. More bright-red blood. Blossom was screaming and sliding toward the pile of them holding the fish gaff over her head when suddenly the .44 Magnum went off.

Ned had somehow shot himself in the left foot, removing three of his toes. Ned's leather motorcycle boot was shredded at the end: blood red with sparkling white chips of bone. This stopped the action for a moment. Thompson was as stunned as anyone, for his chest was covered in Ned's blood and his first thought was that he himself had been shot. He tried to squirm out of Todd's grip, but Todd is monstrously strong.

Ned was moaning and sliding on his ass down the dock

on a slick of blood, swearing like a frantic coast logger, patting himself looking for his own wound, while Blossom just stood there silently holding the gaff above her head.

Finally, Todd looked down at his leg and saw that he was bleeding. He threw Thompson roughly down, kicked his box cutter away, stood back and said, “I’m sorry, Blossom, but I’ve decided I’m going back to Sitka by myself if I have to.”

This all happened in a matter of seconds. The running steps charging up the float to rescue them had stopped at the sound of the shot, then started up again much more cautiously.

Then Mr. Thompson made a move for Ned’s gun, grabbed it and pulled the hammer back. He lumbered to his feet on the slick deck, pointing the gun at Ned’s chest. Blossom walked over and hit him with a full roundhouse swing square at the base of the spine, apparently burying the spike of the gaff straight into his spinal column, which caused the man to collapse like a sex doll with a ripped seam.

“Oh, Todd,” she said, “you did great. Don’t apologize.” She left the gaff where it lay with the long handle wobbling back and forth like a dog’s tail, as the police, along with Harrison Teller and Otis Betts, came up the float to secure the scene and get everyone to the hospital.

“Goddamn children!” Thompson screamed. “You didn’t thank me.” He sniveled.

His voice echoed around the boats in the harbor and perhaps up into the parking lot. He was gulping for breath.

“You. Stole. MY daughter. You. Broke into. My house.”

He was running out of breath now, his voice becoming weak; he was, about to pass out, but he would not die.

He spit blood and saliva onto the deck as he rasped,

"You wanted into my world of pain. I didn't force you to go in there. You wanted to be there, and you never even thanked me."

"Did he really just say that?" Otis Betts asked as he skidded onto the scene, with yet another gun in his hand. "Wow. That is sick," he said in a monotone. "I mean, really."

As soon as the EMTs had Ned wrapped up and the bleeding stopped, one of the patrolmen asked, "Why in the heck did this guy want to kill you, do you know?"

Harrison Teller stepped between them. "This young man is my client and he is availing himself of his right to silence. Do you understand that, officer? He is looking forward to fully cooperating with the authorities, but he will not answer any questions without me present. I assume you are recording this conversation?"

"Shit, man, I was just curious," the cop said. "Would you like me to record it?"

Soon enough Jane Marie was there to smother her daughter with kisses and hugs. She looked at Ned and Blossom, who were both shaking their heads, and before the police could start in questioning Todd, she led him away and back to her boat. No one spoke further of Todd's involvement in the events. Jane Marie cleaned up his rather minor wound, then applied superglue and butterfly bandages.

Harrison Teller was still going through the whole assertion of Ned's Fifth Amendment rights as the EMTs wheeled him past Jane Marie's boat and up the ramp to the waiting ambulance.

"And that goes for you too, little lady." Teller looked at Blossom. "You have no immunity from testifying against him if he talks to you about anything. So I am advising him not to talk. You got that, champ?" He looked down at the young man with seven toes on the gurney who was dreamy on the fentanyl they were pumping through his IV.

"Got it, boss," he said. "Hey, boss?"—he was grinning—"I love you."

"I love you too, kid."

"No . . . no . . . I mean. I love Blossom. Really, I do. I told her I did. I told her and I DO!"

Harrison Teller smiled at the boy with genuine depth of feeling and then at my daughter. "Of course you do, boy. I mean, who doesn't love her?" He held out his hand for her to climb into the ambulance to ride with Ned to the hospital, where her mother would once again pick her up later that night.

14
THE END

When Tommy Thompson was let back into general population, all the inmates had already heard about the death of his man Kenny Walters and his failure to kill young Ned. But Mr. Thompson was not aware that he was already known to be both a child abuser and the killer of the only person who could get an inmate out of jail on an unofficial furlough. Even if most convicts could not afford a furlough or get in the good graces to receive one, everyone liked the idea that the unofficial furlough existed. Suffice it to say that Mr. Thompson was not popular among the prison population. It is an interesting thing that convicts have a rigid morality when it comes to men who hurt children . . . and also men who overstep their privilege.

Mr. Thompson was basically a snob and a whiner who liked to hoard power and control, then lord it over people for sexual gratification. It's tempting to think that prison would be a fun place for someone who gains pleasure from beatings, but for a masochist, the whole trick turns on the knife-edge of control and dominance. Mr. Thompson may have liked trading off roles of control and submission, but it was the strict ritualization that got him off, and that just was not going to happen in jail.

Here, his life became chaotic with random violence, and he found himself at the bottom of the pecking order. Anyone could have him, and did, without consequence. He was utterly alone and had no chance to heal, until he pleaded with authorities for life in protective segregation. Eventually he was found guilty of first-degree assault. Blossom had no memory of the assault once the beating reached a certain point, and the physical evidence of sexual penetration was inconclusive, which is more common than most people think. He was investigated for the contract killing of Ida Paul, but with the death of Kenny Walters, there was not enough proof that Thompson was behind that, even though there was some very murky physical evidence found in the law library closet and the forensic autopsy could have benefited from a closer look. The DA had lots to work with at trial, but in the end Thompson took a deal. When he pled guilty to the murder of T. Rex and Kenny Walters, the Ida Paul murder was dropped, and his rape and assault in the first degree was dropped to misdemeanor assault. He was sentenced to two 99s—two ninety-nine-year sentences, served consecutively. In prison parlance, Thomas Thompson was on the bench for the rest of the game.

Kristy Thompson went and told her story first to Harrison Teller and then to the prosecutors who were bringing the charges against Richard Paul. Shannon Lakeside had somehow gotten a tip from an "unusually well-informed source close to the case" who attended a local high school, and she wrote a very sympathetic story about the Paul family, even going so far as to hint that Mrs. Paul may have been "silenced" in prison, rather than having committed suicide. Though it had to be admitted that the Pauls had raised a child not of their blood, the community began to see that maybe they had saved the girl from a life of danger. The prosecutors did not get any blowback for offering Mr. Paul a time-served misdemeanor deal for child endangerment with five years of probation, which he took in a heartbeat.

I was never charged criminally for anything that happened during my unofficial furlough. Ned was never charged for the shooting of Mr. Thompson, though Thompson threatened to sue Ned, the police and the city, from inside jail. He could not get anyone to take his case, which came as no surprise to me. He was a tremendously unattractive client.

I lost good time in the prison system, for in an audit of T. Rex, they uncovered "suspicious circumstances of graft," meaning they figured out the whole unofficial furlough thing. But the warden and the officials at DOC didn't need that story going public. So they just let the whole "T. Rex was the victim of a madman" thing become the public version of events. I also lost time for being involved in "violent incidents": getting beat up by Mr. Munro as well as others. But I was worried they were going to stack it, because the troopers looking into T. Rex figured out the timing of my work for him and suspected I was in the basement when Thompson got shot. Especially since Thompson wanted to tell everyone he met about it. But in the end, the troopers didn't care.

Fourth Street testified that he had broken ties with me and Shawn Day and had nothing to do with us. He had witnesses to testify that he and I had been in a fight the day before the basement assault. As always, Fourth Street was clear of suspicion. The cops had a hard time putting the whole timetable together, so they just figured I had somehow managed to do the right thing to protect my daughter. They didn't like Street much, and the rumor was they seized the money out of the furlough accounts. So I fell out from Street's official protection, though all of us remained on speaking terms and I felt sure that if it were in his interest, he would still have my back.

A fine professor and writer named Ernestine Hayes came to Lemon Creek to teach a class on the literature of repression, and I got Street and Shawn Day to take it along with me. I'm proud to say that we all got one hundred percent in the class.

I fell in under the protection of Shawn Day, and she takes care of me now. She never hits on me because she still carries the torch a bit for Street and considers herself more and more as "a bit of a lesbian." Of course I know that love and gender are fluid, particularly here in jail. Shawn Day and I are still reading together. One day in the library she came across an old picture of Joan Didion when she was young and living in LA and Shawn developed an instant crush on Joan. So we read *A Book of Common Prayer,* which I think Shawn thought was the most feminine, sad and sexy thing she'd ever read. She said she liked it more than *National Velvet,* and I agreed.

I still meet with Street, but not in his office anymore. I stay on his good side, but I have come to be a bit more suspicious of his advances. Especially after I found out that Kenny Walters had possessed some photographs of Street from a time when Street himself had dabbled in the activities in Thompson's basement club. It appeared that there was a time that Street very much liked the dominant position and handing out the lash. During his short time in LCCC, Kenny had been trying to use his photos to make a move on Street's authority. This was how Kenny found out about the safety-deposit box and the furloughs. Sadly, he trusted Thompson with the information and even if it was foolish and desperate, Thompson clung to it as his escape plan.

Did Street set up any or all of this to kill Walters and Thompson and save his money? It seems unlikely. I mean, how could he have known what would happen? But . . . when the music stopped, Walters was dead, and Street had a chair. He supposedly lost his money in the safety-deposit box, but who really knows that for sure? All I know is that kissing him felt dangerous, in both a good and a bad way.

Todd did in fact move back to Sitka on his own. He lives in our old house and looks after it. We have friends who peek in on him. He takes the ferry over to visit with us when it works out, but that rarely happens because of state budget cuts to the ferry system. We all met recently under the cover of me signing a new will and a new agreement for Jane Marie to be a short-term foster parent to George. Teller had worked it out: as long as I signed my authority and assets into a trust managed by Jane Marie, my felon status would not be a problem. She could be the official foster parent as long as I was in jail, and it looked like it would be a short time anyway, because Kristy Thompson and Richard Paul had the support of everyone, including the tribal authorities, to each have contact with Georgianna, which was all to George's liking.

The institution allowed us all to meet in the contact visitation room. I was certain that everyone was going to have to go through serious searches upon leaving, but it was a lively gathering. Jane, Blossom, Harrison, Otis, Kristy Thompson, Richard Paul, Lilly, George and Ned. Harrison had somehow even arranged to have the prison cater a meal, with a vanilla sheet cake, dry ham-and-cheese sandwiches on soft white bread and warm off-brand sodas.

Ned hobbled around on his crutches, his foot encased in a heavy boot and brace, while Blossom doted on him. I had my arm around Jane Marie's waist. Kristy and Richard stood at opposite ends of the table and didn't speak much. But they had been cooperative in arranging care of the girls together while the overworked social worker kept an eye on them whenever she could pencil them in. Richard was as grateful as he could be for Kristy's help in getting his deal, but still they were a long way from becoming friends—after all, Kristy's husband was responsible for his wife's death. But Kristy had tried to make it up to Richard Paul by agreeing to shared custody and pressuring the DA's office to give him the time-served deal.

Harrison was packing up his office and Otis Betts had already started scoping out cases farther north, but he had been making noises about possibly buying a boat and keeping it out in Hoonah for fishing the outer coast. Otis Betts had also given Ned and Blossom ten hours of lock-picking lessons as well as fine leather cases with the necessary unbreakable tools to open most small locks. Harrison Teller gave them legal advice about where and when to use and store their new tools, as they were illegal to possess without a permit in Alaska. He advised them to start their own locksmithing businesses, or at least to start the application process, which would give them a colorable defense if they were ever caught with the tools.

We drank soda from paper cups as I signed my new will. I also agreed to be a foster parent in absentia, supporting Jane Marie to help George Paul get to know her new family. We signed the papers, and there was a pattering round of applause. The whispering woman from jail admin came in to notarize the documents, but didn't stay for cake. I now officially owned nothing. I hugged Jane Marie and we kissed. I hugged George, which started a whole round of hugs. Mr. Paul and Mrs. Thompson tentatively shook hands, for they still had things to work out. Mr. Paul was not comfortable with George going to the house on the flats, but they were working things out slowly. They would begin by sharing traditional meals, and see what the girls wanted. Ned was a little awkward on his crutches besides just being shy about hugging his girlfriend's jailbird pops, but Blossom cried genuine tears of happiness as she hugged me, holding me high around the neck and tight.

"Oh, Daddy, I'm so glad."

I could feel her wet breath on my cheek. She had, by that time, slept for almost a week straight. She had cried in her mother's arms for hours on end and her mother had stopped herself from giving advice or trying to teach her daughter lessons. No, my wife the professor did what she did best as a scientist—she simply listened and looked at the evidence. She listened and she convinced our daughter to see a good therapist of her own choosing.

"Daddy?" She looked me in the eyes.

"Yes, sweetie."

"What does WOP stand for? It was carved on his door. I could see it every once in a while. What the heck?"

"You mean under the picture of the Earth, down in that basement?"

"Uh huh. I don't know why but it bugs me. What's that about?"

"I think it means 'world of pain,' baby. It's something you shouldn't think about again. You are never, ever going back."

Then she hugged me once more.

Even Otis Betts's eyes were wet when he shook my hand. "Congratulations, Mr. Younger. It's a good day," he said, smiling.

"Younger, you take care of yourself. You need anything . . . well, you understand." Harrison Teller gripped my hand probably too hard to overcome all of the soft emotion in the room.

"Yes," I said, then wiped my eyes.

I hugged Jane Marie one more time and patted everyone's back again as we finished our sandwiches and cleaned up. I smiled and touched them all as they left. I held Janie's hand until the very last minute. Then they buzzed her out the door and it clicked shut behind her.

I was alone with the empty boxes and the refuse from the party. Soon the other heavy door buzzed open and a nameless guard walked in. He looked around, saw me and signaled with his hand, as if he were commanding a dog to come, and I walked back into prison.

AUTHOR'S NOTE

This book is a work of my imagination. I wanted to write a crime story about love, honesty and the power of certain kinds of self-knowledge. When I saw a small notice in the newspaper about a young woman who took a DNA test and learned that the people who had raised her were not her biological parents, I'm not even sure I read the entire article. I just ran with the idea of what those circumstances could have been like for everyone involved. Obviously, my characters are based on no actual human beings, and any similarities to living people can be written off to coincidence.

If some of the characters seem familiar, I did borrow names and a certain tone from the early Nancy Drew mysteries. I did that because I liked the books, and Nancy's influence runs through the thematic pulse of so much crime fiction.

Lemon Creek Correctional Center is a real place in Juneau. I have spent a lot of time in the interview rooms, but very little time inside. This novel was written in the time of COVID. Like most of us, I had no idea how long the pandemic would last, and since I was not allowed in to visit and I figured all the COVID protocols would complicate all of the movement and visitation in the prison that I needed for this story, I let it happen sometime in the pre-COVID era.

I got some information and details about life inside from inmates and guards. Although I detest the wholesale isolation and warehousing of human beings in America as a solution to much of anything, as long as prisons exist, the people who work in them should be well trained and well paid. The guards at LCCC are in reality professional and are usually solicitous of the inmates' health and safety. Funding and overcrowding are their constant challenges, but their professionalism is not questioned by me, at least. If they fall down on the job it is because, in my opinion, that job is impossible.

The entire "unofficial furlough" in *So Far and Good* is a plot device of my own design and to my knowledge has never happened at LCCC.

My thanks go to my editor, Rachel Kowal, for her patience and perseverance, and my agent, Kerry D'Agostino, for her wise counsel, as well as to Finn Straley, Martha Straley, Serena Tang, and Stephen Mack Jones for their sensitive reading of the manuscript. Of course as always thanks to Nita Couchman for her fine eyes and first round of line editing, and to Jan Straley, Finn Straley, Emily Basham, Bonnie and Dot for making my life worth living during this most appalling year.